Under Country

JONATHAN TRIGELL

UNDER COUNTRY

Merdog Books

Merdog Books
The Exchange, Castle Avenue, Buncrana, Co. Donegal, Ireland
Web: merdogbooks.com
Email: info@merdogbooks.com

First published 2022

2 4 6 8 10 9 7 5 3 1

ISBN 978-1-915318-03-9 Paperback
ISBN 978-1-915318-04-6 Ebook

Typeset in Ireland by Merdog Books
Printed and bound in Great Britain by Clays Ltd, Elcograf S.p.A.

Praise for Jonathan Trigell

'Unfolds with a gathering horror that invites as much compassion as revulsion and leaves the reader (this one, anyway) in need of air.'

The New York Times* - on *Boy A

'It is an old saying among science fiction fans that anyone can predict the car, it takes brains to predict gridlock ... No one can fault Trigell's ingenuity.'

The Times Literary Supplement* - on *Genus

'At the other end of the spectrum are those writers who have literary ideals but - almost in an act of defiance against some of their peers - still manage to entertain their readers with a story. For some reason many of the best of these - Emily Brontë, Leo Tolstoy and so on - are long gone. There are contemporary writers, however, following in their footsteps ... Jonathan Trigell is one of these writers.'

The Sydney Morning Herald* - on *Cham

Also by Jonathan Trigell

Boy A
Cham
Genus
The Tongues of Men or Angels

For Eleanor Trigell, Helen Morland and Seren Morland-Trigell, my Geordie girls.

PHASE THE FIRST

so remote from our experience, so invisible, as it were, that we are capable of forgetting it as we forget the blood in our veins … all of us *really* owe the comparative decency of our lives to poor drudges underground, blackened to the eyes, with their throats full of coal dust, driving their shovels forward with arms and belly muscles of steel.

The Road to Wigan Pier – George Orwell

Blackmoor Colliery 1971

Charlie was a miner. Son of a miner. Son of a miner's son. And though there had been others, others who must have lived lives other – given a line that had roamed and reived the North East since Saxon and Viking – those tales were just fables, for no one alive knew of other than mining.

Charlie handed in the safety token with his number stamped on it. The brass disc was then hung from a nail by the banksman in exchange for a cap lamp. Counted in, counted out, for safety and wages both. Practice started after the West Stanley disaster, not so far away, a hundred and sixty-eight killed in a day. Now every pit in the country used brass checks. There was blood on coal, it didn't come for free. Counted in, counted out. Miners arriving, miners leaving. Gagging for a tab as they came out of the pit-head. Smoking before they showered. The smokers said it helped to keep the coal dust down. Hard to say who coughed more. Miners leaving, miner's arriving. The mine never stopped, twenty-four hours a day the winding engines ran. Eight-hour shifts. The only way you came out before eight hours was on a stretcher. If you were middle shift in winter, it was dark when you clocked on and dark when you left. Daylight was a stranger. Was two a.m. when Charlie signed in for his first ever day of work.

Charlie filed on, among the mill of men, into the cage. The signal rang twice, for a meat load descending. The banksman dropped the metal mesh netting of the pit-lift door and the cage dropped in the shaft. Dropped like a rock from a cliff, like it was free-falling, with no thought to landing. Left Charlie's stomach behind the first time. Became common as coal dust before you noticed. Twenty men, crammed tight. Men behind, men in front, each alone. Bone pale. Orange jump-suits. White helmets. Twenty men crammed tight. Bait-boxes, cap-lamps, self-rescue respirators. The bricks of the shaft floated by, wet and red. Then pitch black. Took a while, even fast as it dropped. Twenty men packed in, too close to turn and talk. Cap lamps were off, else they'd blind each other. So they dropped in the dark. Twenty thousand leagues beneath the sea. Or two and a half thousand feet anyway. The pit-lift stopped and the cables screamed. Always sent it through him the noise, sounded like the shriek of steel on the edge of snap. Safe as houses though, cables were checked twice a day. Safe as houses. Three houses had collapsed in Blackmoor the previous month, subsidence, the whole county was riddled with ever-expanding mines, like the last stage of cancer. Was a wonder it didn't all sink in on itself.

One by one the miners left the cage and clambered aboard the man-rider. Painted white and coated black like all machinery underground. They kneeled down on the conveyor that carried them out to the seams they were cutting. Miles out beneath the sea. Too distant to walk to without losing valuable work time. Cap lamps flashing along the rock roof.

They still used pit ponies at the mine where Charlie started. Where Charlie started as a pony driver at fifteen. Charlie had loved that pony like that pony loved mints. Would nuzzle his pockets for a mint. Charlie used to ride out on his pony's back at the end of the shift. Clinging to the leather haulage harness.

Was a drift mine, inland, he worked on back then. The ponies were stabled outside and they couldn't get to fresh air fast enough. Wasn't allowed, to ride them, but all the lads did it. Could scalp yourself on a low girder, but all the lads did it. Second time they caught you, they fined you; third time you'd be sacked. But still the lads did it.

Charlie liked to joke how his pony was a union man, knew his rights. He was allowed to pull two tubs by regulations and he'd not pull three, not even if the last one was empty. He could pull three easily, but he knew his rights. Even if you tried to hide the noise of the third one hitching, he somehow knew and he'd not have it. Not for a mint or a titbit from your bait box.

Now there were man-riding conveyors and boring machines and there was talk of using lasers for precision. Ponies to lasers in barely a wedge of a working life. Charlie's father wasn't alive to see the change. His lungs got him. They got many or most of the older men. No one even saw a dust-mask until the sixties. They'd only just become mandatory by the time Charlie started.

Charlie remembers the health and safety course, back when he began: the deputy took him aside before his first shift and said, 'Now then, lad, it's dangerous down there, so don't do anything daft'. That was the health and safety course …

There was blood on coal and nothing came for free: every time hazard was reduced, whenever working conditions improved, it was because unions and miners had been ready to strike.

Blackmoor Colliery - 1971

Charlie had taken his bait break early. He'd needed a crap. Wanted to eat his food before he went. Nowhere to wash your hands after. You shat just out in the black. Some disused space or pile of rubble. Somewhere folk would likely not walk over it. Covered it as best you could with a shovel. Or else you shit on the shovel itself and slung it away. Hence the expression. You'd best not fling it near a ventilation fan. Hence the expression. Nowhere to wash your hands after though. Charlie wanted to eat first. Some men didn't care. Wasn't right by Charlie though. Charlie had pride. Eat first. Didn't take a minute. Just as well: he only had twenty of them for his bait break.

The eyes watched Charlie as he ate, glowing, evil teardrops, reflecting Charlie's cap lamp. He could never get used to the rats, little bastards they were. Charlie ate with one hand close to his face, the other shielding his bait-box. Otherwise they might filch from in front of him. Some rats were that brave that they would take a leap to steal the bread from your hand. All the miners kept their lunch in steel bait-boxes, anything less and the rats would have it. You could hang it from a wire in mid-air and they'd still have it.

The stotty tasted of coal, everything tasted of coal after a while. Laced and layered with it. The eyes followed Charlie, twitching, watching. He chucked a lump of rock at a clutch of them. They scattered, but came right back. One of them only had one eye; Charlie could tell from the spacing. Turned to look with his cap lamp on it. Nasty looking mess one side of its nasty looking rat face. Been in a fight most likely, rat on rat. Charlie thought of one-eyed Geraldine from school. Poor lass. She'd fallen on a fire grate or something, as a toddler. Couldn't have a glass eye as a child still growing. Couldn't afford one after maybe, or gone past caring about looks. She'd not have been the bonniest of lasses if she'd had both eyes. He'd seen her on the street, the other day. Said hello, asked after her dad. Poor lass.

Charlie finished and pushed the greased paper back into his bait-box. Stop the rats having it. Rats would eat anything, rope, cardboard, cloth. Only metal would stop them. They called bait-boxes *snap-tins* in Sheffield, *piece-boxes* in Scotland, but every miner had one. Charlie made his own bait still, for now, but soon enough he'd have to marry his girl. She was letting him have her for free for now, but soon enough he'd have to marry her, one way or the other. At least he'd not have to make his own bait when he did.

Charlie relieved himself. In a cove behind a pile of spoil. He wasn't the first: the ground was littered with bits of newspaper and other matter in varied stages of disintegration. The rats would get through it all in the end. Leave their own shit in its place. Charlie sometimes found it hard to believe in a God who had made men so damned near to beasts. But still, he did believe. The teachers and parents who taught him how to spell and right from wrong told him there was a God, it was all entwined, must all be true. Charlie looked up, as if to catch a glimpse; but the heavens were hidden by half a mile of rock. There were fossilised trees and ferns hid in it. You often came across them. You were miles out beneath the North Sea, but it must all have been land, once a time.

Rat eyes still watched him.

Charlie was once alone at the seam when he saw eyes as big as shillings staring at him from the dark, big as shillings and about two foot off the floor. Charlie had grabbed a shovel and backed away, scrambled away, but the beast came forwards at him. Charlie had shouted curses, muttered prayers, but the beast came forwards at him. Was about ready to try and brain it with the shovel-blade until the beast barked. Bloody deputy had taken his dog to work, hadn't he. Deputies could. Deputies could do as they pleased. Charlie could see himself as a deputy. It was about as high as a miner's son could aspire. Miner's sons became miners. You either worked for the mine or you left town. Miner's sons became rippers; shifters; drifters; drivers; packers; hewers; stonemen; ropemen; even banksmen, if they got lucky, though such surface work was considered a bit effete. Could a miner's son make deputy? They could, though you needed learning to be a deputy, training. Deputy wasn't just a manager, he was in charge of safety. The deputy went round with his Geordie lamp, start of shift, to check for firedamp – flammable gas. Rest of the world called them Davy lamps, but Geordies sometimes still called them Geordie lamps; for George Stephenson, the original Geordie.

Bent double, Charlie made his way back to the forest of hydraulic jacks. The noise of the cutting machine was deafening, even in the distance. The mine had a solid rock top, so there was space behind the chocks – would be easier to make your way that side – could make you complacent, fatally complacent, had to be careful, never to get back of the jacks. The gob could hold for twenty metres back in good rock. But sooner or later it would break and collapse. At the rear of the chocks, armour plates chained together – like something from a medieval siege engine – gave a bit of protection against the dust and debris when the gob dropped. But the force of air alone could near knock you over, if two hundred meters of gob rock dropped at once. Which it might. Which it did. Made you think the whole planet was crashing down behind you. Which it was. You pulled the last row of props out at the back and set them up at the front, as you cut on through the seam. And the gob at the back would hold for a while; in good rock, could hold for weeks. But still it would fall. Had to fall at the finish. No telling when it would come.

And that's what Charlie thought at first, as the blast tore him from his feet: there was one of those moments when time slows, long enough for Charlie to think: *gob's dropped then.* But after that he was slammed clean through the palisade rows of chocks, winded and choking on grit. The air so thick with dust he couldn't see his own hands. His bump cap was still on. Luckily, because he thought his head must have hit the seam, lucky not to have been wrapped round a jack first. His back hurt, maybe his back took the brunt and his head after, it was hard to know. His lamp still worked, but he could only tell the lamp was on by the brightness of the dust in his eyes, couldn't see anything, that aside. Just thick dust, so thick there could be smoke in it. And he figured there probably was smoke in it. Gob dropping couldn't have done that, so there must have been an explosion. Charlie checked himself. Couldn't see a thing, but checked with his hands, felt that he was in one piece. Back was killing, but not broke. Not broke the bad way anyway. He could use his legs. But he couldn't bend his back. Pain flailed through him when he tried. But he could sort of crawl. Pushing with his legs, on hands and knees. He could sort of do that. He tried to get a sense of where he was. When he could touch the seam with one hand and the chocks with the other, he knew he was heading the right way. Hurt his back to raise his hands like that, but it was the only way to know. Had to keep stopping, to feel the seam, feel the chocks. But it was the only way. Couldn't see a thing. Tried to make his way to where his marras – his work mates – must be. Crawling, one chock at a time. The muck and smoke wasn't getting less, it got worse, the closer he crawled to where his mates must be: Stan and Bobby. Bobby was only eighteen. Charlie and Stan called him Bonny – for bonny lad, for Bonny Bobby Shafto.

Fingers in the rock floor, rock and coal shards, knees cut to ribbons. Feel the chocks, feel the seam. Charlie shouted *Stanley, Bobby, Stan, Bonny Lad*. Nothing came back. Couldn't be far now though. They couldn't have cut much further than this. Every so often Charlie would turn off his cap-lamp. To see if there were lights ahead. Most folk, non-miners, have never seen true dark. After the light behind his eyelids had died, Charlie saw only black. The darkness of night-time in a forest would not even be close. A steel chock didn't glint with it right before his face. He still couldn't see it, when he pressed his nose into the metal. Charlie was a lean man, bore not an ounce that wasn't muscle – prided himself upon it – but even still, he kept bumping the chocks, which sent a shriek of pain through his back. He could move through the tunnel of them easy enough normally, when he could see. But crawling on wet elbows, to feel the seam, feel the chocks, heart plunging against the self-rescue breather dragging at his breast, he couldn't keep from chocking himself.

Charlie wondered if he should put the self-rescuer on. He felt like he could breathe, aside from the dust. He felt like the oxygen was there. But that was the thing with gas, wasn't it? You didn't know. You didn't know if you were being poisoned: whitedamp, afterdamp, blackdamp, chokedamp. And you also didn't know if you might need your self-rescuer more later on. Had enough air for an hour, so they said, if you could breathe calmly. They'd only just brought them in. Charlie didn't know anyone who'd used one for real. Had enough air for an hour, so they said, if you could breathe calmly. Who the fuck could breathe calmly, after they'd decided they needed to put the fucker on? Charlie would have liked to have had a conflab with Stan about it, that's how things got done.

Charlie had never felt lonelier than that moment. When he was probably still not fifty yards from his marras, he had never been more afraid and alone. All the more afraid because alone; all the more alone because afraid.

He had one more shout, *Stanley, Bobby*. Then put the breather on. Had never done it outside of practice. Had never done it in the dark, fingers covered with muck and wet. Spine piercing skin. But he got it on, got the rubber teat in his teeth. Got the nose clips on, squashing his nostrils flat. Had it on right, best as he could figure.

And as he kept edging onward, lizard sliding now on a caked belly – seemed to ease his back to change the movement – he couldn't help thinking of what might come when this was over. If only he could make it out. He needed focus just to keep from screaming. If he could just make it out, he would marry his girl, leave the mine, never complain about anything ever again. He tried to make a deal, there in the darkness, make a bargain with God. About what sort of man he would be, about the things he would do, if only he could get out alive. But no one answered him. There was no sound but his own struggled breathing through the respirator. And Charlie couldn't think of a promise he could make, big enough to merit an answer. He couldn't think of something within his power to enact, sufficient to tempt God into a compact.

What did it mean to offer to marry his girl? It's what she wanted after all. What he even wanted, maybe, eventually. Would happen inevitably anyway, one way or another. God would not do trades on easy choices.

Charlie kept squirming forwards, must be nearly there. Dust was starting to settle a little now at least. Smoke still drifting, but he could see further with his cap-lamp now. The work safety lights were all out. Power most likely cut off.

He came to where they were. Stan and Bobby. Where they were ... Stanley's thermos flask had been shot halfway into the coal seam by the force of the explosion. That's how strong the blast had been this end. The force had been sufficient to send Stanley's steel flask six inches into solid coal. And Stanley had been holding it. Charlie had to take the respirator from out of his mouth to let the vomit go. Spat it, black vomit, full of dust and coal. Stanley was coated in dust as well, the bits of him you could see. Charlie let another urge go. Bile and coal.

He looked for Bobby, couldn't see him. Charlie crawled through his own vomit, towards the cutting machine. Visible through the remaining smoke. Painted white, coated black. Smoke wasn't clearing quick though. Could tell by how it hung static that there was no draw. Made him think ventilators were out or airways compromised. Made him think he was right to put on his respirator. Charlie wondered how much oxygen he'd used. He didn't know. Didn't wear his watch at work. Didn't think he was breathing calmly though.

He found Bobby. Seemed intact. Unconscious, but intact.

Shielded by the cutter somehow. Kind of a miracle. Gave Charlie hope: maybe God had plans for Bobby. Bobby was breathing. Might have been knocked out by the blast. Might have been knocked out by afterdamp gasses. But he was breathing. Charlie slapped him. Shook him. Tried to wake him. Wasn't working. Bobby had a bairn's face. Black with dust and muck but smooth of stubble. Charlie got Bobby's respirator on. They were both going to succumb to carbon monoxide if they stayed here. That much was sure. Could tell by the lingering smoke there was no draw. Charlie figured the roadway might be blocked by roof fall. Charlie wrapped wire round Bobby's belt, ran it under his armpits and then, a couple of yards on, fixed it onto his own belt. Was a shit plan. Was his only plan. Charlie tried it. Crawled his way to the end of the wire. Hauled Bobby back to him after. The wire cut into Charlie's hands. The pain through his back, God only knew. Shit plan. Only plan.

Measured by distance to the roadway, it didn't seem like they'd come far. Measured by respirator air, it had taken a long time. Measured by hope, Charlie was more and more certain that the roadway was blocked anyway. Must have been a roof fall, otherwise someone would have got to them by now. But what else was there, but to go on.

'Let us leave here alive,' Charlie said. Only in his head. Only to himself and to God. 'Please Jesus, bring us out breathing.'

He could not offer God an orphanage, or else he would. They wouldn't take him in a seminary. How would he make a priest when he couldn't even make deputy? 'Tell me what You want,' Charlie thought, 'Just tell me and it's Yours.' But no one spake. Just the heaving of his respirator. So on Charlie crawled. Snaked a short way, then heaved Bobby up to him. Every strain tore through his back, cut into his hands. The wire wasn't doing Bobby's body much good either. He was bleeding by his armpits. But what else was there? Charlie checked Bobby was still alive. Checked he was breathing. There were troughs in the tunnel, shallow pits dug to let the water clear. And in one of them Charlie pissed himself. Letting it flow out in his overalls, in the trough.

Regularly rats scrambled by. Trying to get elsewhere. Had the sense not to stick around. Didn't have the knowledge to be as scared as Charlie was. Didn't know the air was running out. Didn't know about whitedamp, afterdamp, blackdamp, chokedamp. Didn't know they might be slowly suffocating or waiting on another explosion. He did his best to swipe the rats away from Bobby, they might not be shy to take a bite, even as they fled.

'Just tell me, God, speak to me. Tell me what you want and I'll do it.'

God didn't reply.

The mine did: Charlie saw his worst fears realised. The roadway was blocked. The roof had dropped. He could make out a pile of rock and rubble where there should be tunnel. He put a hand on Bobby's shoulder.

'Sleep on, bonny lad,' he said, 'nothing to be gained from waking now.'

And even still, Charlie continued. There was nothing to be gained from stopping either. At least they'd know he tried. If he got to the foot of the fall, they'd know he'd done his best. They'd raise a glass to him. They'd think of him with honour. Charlie's eyes had been watering that long from the smoke and dust, that he didn't realise he was crying at first. Not until his breathing went choked and ragged. But it wouldn't stop, he couldn't get his breathing back. He'd reached the end of his oxygen, as well as the end of the road.

He thought for a moment about taking Bobby's respirator, just for a share of it. But it wouldn't work. Too difficult to switch between them. And the breathers were numbered. Charlie was too proud to be remembered like that.

'Sleep on, bonny lad,' he said.

Charlie pulled the clips from his nose. Pulled the rubber from his mouth. Chucked it all aside. Crawled onward. He'd reach the rubble. Then they'd know he tried.

'Tell me what you want,' he challenged God, shouted it, now his mouth was free; shouted in the black at the walls and the rats; but no one spoke back.

Charlie hauled Bobby to him. The final yard. Wasn't sure he could have gone further anyway. Had nothing left. That might have been the carbon monoxide though. He could feel himself slipping away. Getting sleepy. Wouldn't wake from this one.

'Night night, bonny lad,' he patted Bobby.

Then, as Charlie slumped on the ground, as he prepared to let go, a final thought entered his mind unbidden:

'I'll marry one-eyed-Geraldine,' he whispered to God, 'Save Bobby and I'll marry her. Save me an' all, else I'll not be able to.'

And Charlie heard God say:

DEAL.

At least, DEAL was the sound of the drills in the rubble. DEAL was the noise the air made as it whistled through new gaps. DEAL God said in every bounce of every rock that fell from the pile blocking the roadway. DEAL was the whine of stone cutting discs. DEAL said the muffled voices behind the collapse. And there in the black, blanketed with dust, at the edge of death, trembling with terror and salvation, Charlie's ears rang DEAL DEAL DEAL.

1971

When he was finally released from hospital, Charlie was presented with his award – 'The Order of Industrial Heroism' – at the Miners' Association in Durham city: Red Hills, home of *The Pitman's Parliament*, a crimson-bricked hall, set apart in its own park. Scargill himself was there to give the honour, King Arthur. They said his head was like a dropped toffee under that American style baseball cap, but he'd met presidents, prime ministers and dignitaries and hadn't doffed it to none of them. Charlie liked that. Charlie wasn't a doffer either. He shook Arthur's hand and a photographer from *The Northern Echo* froze the moment in time. And the editor of the *Echo* presented Charlie with a camera of his own, as reward for his bravery. And Charlie told them the story, as best he could. The full inquest was yet to come. The rumours were that a dust blast caused a roof collapse and the roof collapse released explosive gas. The cause of ignition was unconfirmed. The full facts of what went on in the dark were untellable and unknowable. Known hardly by Charlie. Known only to God.

They took him out for a night on the town. Durham town. Underneath a cathedral, beneath a castle, beside the king. A city of bridges and weirs, walled edifices and ancient spires. Steak and chips and peas and pints of beer with Arthur and his knights. And after, Charlie stared at the peach flesh moon and for once didn't struggle to believe that men had actually walked there.

Charlie didn't have a car. Most people didn't. Most people in Blackmoor at least. So heading home from his night in a crisp sheeted bed and breakfast – feeling like a Prince Bishop – Charlie meandered back by bus, half as often heading further away in order to creep a little closer.

Charlie took some photos along the route, to document and test. And he found that squaring off the world through a Nikon lens helped to hold it at a distance.

He hitched the last stretch into Blackmoor Colliery in the back of a planked-out coal truck. Sitting on sacking to save his trouser seat. In the next edition, Charlie would be hailed a hero in the *Northern Echo*. But the newspaper clouds that greeted his return were ink smudged grey and bore bad tidings.

Charlie dropped off the truck's tail with his certificate in the pocket of his blue serge suit and his new camera bandoliered over his shoulder and a quarter left of a quart of brandy in his fist and he marched off to do what he had to do, before he lost his nerve or found his sense.

Geraldine was hanging up washing in the backyard, when Charlie trudged to her father's house. She was pronging sheets with gypsy-whittled pegs. Wouldn't have surprised Charlie if she still used soap wort or lye as well. Next to the coal store and the outside toilet was a rabbit hutch – for eating not petting – with a roof made from a Swan Vesta advertising board. She wore a blouse printed with baskets of fruit and pineapples, which looked like the material would have been better suited to a tablecloth or something.

When she turned around, she had a strip of brown-paper

hanging out of each nostril.

'I got the hay fever,' she said.

The streamers blew with each word. They looked like puffs of smoke, a drawing of a dragon in a story book.

'I've thought on you a lot of late,' Charlie said, and it wasn't a lie.

Her one eye widened and her lips split into a smile, slight as a paper-cut.

Charlie had a fuse too short to safely use for blasting coal – it was well known – so Charlie's friends didn't prod as to why he had dropped his girl and taken up with Geraldine, plain as homemade sin. Charlie just said that all cats look grey in the dark.

Sometimes Charlie woke in the dark, those first weeks. Sat bolt up in the middle of sleep, either screaming or searching, and he didn't know what he was screaming for when he screamed or was searching for when he searched. Both were buried in the smoke and dust of the past. Other times he would wake to find he was crying, but those times he knew why he cried: he cried to be alive.

The mine agent liked the idea of having a hero on his staff. So he gave Charlie a job clerking, away from the black and the maddening crashing of machines. And Charlie performed well enough. For all his failings, Charlie was fairly school-smart, which was not so unusual for those parts. Charlie's mam hadn't been alone in insisting that even miner's sons needed to read books, education was prized, among the denizens of the under country. Though, in point of fact, back when she was alive, Charlie's mam had been prone to occasional bouts of full thrown delusions of grandeur: used to talk about her great-grandpa, who'd been a horse-trader, had a house as big as the post office, so she claimed; though she was vague about where it had been sited.

But, though he now wore sleeve braces, Charlie took on no other airs or graces. He went back to playing football on Sundays, the same teams as always – *no teams* – the same time – *begins when it begins, ends when it's over* – the same special Blackmoor rules: everyone's a centre forward, anyone's in goal, everybody drinks; no one keeps the score, nobody loses, nobody gets in a radge, nobody starts, nobody gets knocked sparko.

The Free Love movement that had swept the rest of the West had never penetrated noticeably into Blackmoor. But enough penetration went on that Charlie and Geraldine got married, not a whole many months after that day that Charlie got back. And the child was called a honeymoon baby, by people quite liberal with maths.

1972

Charlie was there for the birth. Charlie went. Most men in Blackmoor wouldn't; or couldn't get the time off if they wished. But Charlie could. And he did.

They went to the Royal Victoria Infirmary in Newcastle, the RVI, Charlie had heard it was better than the local hospital. Birthing was elective. Charlie knew his rights.

They marvelled at the modernity together, him and Geraldine. At the state-of-the-art equipment inside an ancient building. New wine in an old flask. They drank cups of tea and Geraldine took evening primrose oil, which was said to bring on labour. Divided by curtains into their own little world on the ward. Yet surrounded by other people in exactly the same situation, only with other lives and cares and callers. Nervous and hopeful and anxious for it to be over. Charlie slept on a hard chair next to Geraldine's gurney. He shifted and twisted and barely drifted off all night. His back was still not completely right. Would probably never be good as it once was.

When the midwife was decided, they were moved into the birthing room. Charlie was not well accustomed to having a female in charge of things. But he did his best to hide his pride and be the midwife's infeasible assistant: simultaneously of use but out of the way.

And it was hard not to fall a little bit in love with a woman, when you watched her give birth. It was hard not to; it was so impressive. The vigour, the instinct, the determination. Charlie knew hard men, big men, miners with biceps of iron, that he wasn't sure could have done what Geraldine did. When they made her put down her hands, to feel the head; to touch its head, part out, Geraldine burst into tears. But just for an instant. Then she went back to task. And it was enough to make a man fall just a little bit in love, to see that.

The baby came out, all blue, with a crumpled ear, squashed flat. Looked like a little cobalt monkey when it appeared. Soon started to pinken as the oxygen got into its skin. Charlie cut the umbilical cord and it was tough as shearing through pig gristle. He hoped the bairn would be tough when it grew up too, because the babe was a boy.

They ate toast and butter, Charlie and Geraldine, still in their private room. And it was maybe the best meal that Charlie had ever tasted; was at least on par with the steak and chips he'd had with Arthur Scargill. Geraldine ate one handed, a wrapped creature against her skin. Until the midwife took it to be weighed. 8lbs 8oz. Seemed like a perfect number to Charlie. And he was beginning to come to the conclusion that the baby might be entirely perfect.

By the time they were taken back to ward, Geraldine wheeled there in a chair, Charlie felt sorry for all the other parents. Some of them starting to leave already, with their little swaddled bundles. He found it strange that any of them could look so happy with their babies, when it was so evident that Charlie's was the finest. He supposed that everyone naturally falls in love with their own child, but they must still have been aware, still have been able to see, that objectively, Charlie's was the finest. Just a glance at Charlie's boy, his ear already unfurling to lie flat, must surely have told them that.

Charlie took a turn at holding the bairn, skin yielding and podgy next to Charlie's sandpaper chin. He had felt nothing softer, nothing stranger, nothing more distinct, than the crinkle of his bristle upon his baby's face. It felt like Charlie's stubble could take the shape of it, as if his whiskers were organs of sensation, like those of a cat or a stickleback.

And when their turn came – once the midwife was assured that the babe could latch and suckle; after it had a poo, black as coal, small as a ha'penny; following some papers being signed off – they were discharged. They were sent home, to a home they had hardly lived in long enough to know it as such. To a world changed in every way, but altered only as Charlie supposed it must once-a-time have been to all of his ancestors, in their due turn.

Charlie said it was to honour those ancestors, that he insisted they christen the boy *Bluford*. He claimed the name had distant history in the family – a seller of equines maybe – but it was done mostly, knavishly, because the bairn was born with one eye brown and one eye green and Bluford would be shortened to Blue.

And Blue stared at the priest, while the deed was done, the task of daubing holy water on his brow, but Blue made no sound. He just watched through mismatched eyes, forehead wrinkled, as if he endeavoured to solve some great puzzle. And all of the gathered, agreed he was an angel.

Though he had no comparison, Charlie was certain that Blue was a perfect baby. He barely cried – only when hungry – he wanted nothing more from life than milk and sleep. Needed no coddling or cuddling, was content with his own company. But when he smiled his gummy tortoise smile – which he did, almost the whole time, as soon as he was able – he was able to make Charlie ache. When Blue laughed – which he did, at the slightest provocation, once he'd managed it once – his black-rimmed irises glistened.

The gifts of strangers paid for the animal mobile above Blue's cot. And his eyes followed the twirling menagerie. Tongue out in concentration. Fingers opening and closing with the joy of existence. Arms and legs kicking and flicking in method-less test-firing. Hands so fat that his knuckles were little indents, instead of proud. The gifts of strangers paid for it, because, from the beginning, Blue had them all melting around him. Blue became well accustomed to strangers commenting on *what a canny bonny lad* he was, long before the words made any sense to him. Not just the old ladies – in their see-through hoods with windows in the sides and little plastic throat ties, cooing like a pigeon loft – but whitleather miners. Blue would gurgle and grin, and they all softened. Strangers would give Geraldine a two-shilling coin for the baby. Though two shillings had lately become ten pence, the practice still continued. A lot of folk did that for newborns. It was lucky to give a coin for a newborn. But folk were still doing it for Blue when he was two.

By the time Blue was two, his real hair had come in. And it was as blond as a kid's from a colour TV show, but curled at the bottom, like Shirley Temple's, in black and white. At the front, curious double cowlicks swirled; which gave an appearance almost of horns when it was shorn short; but became a thatch of straw when left longer, a Worzel Gummidge bird's nest of blond, thick as a fairy ring. There was something of the Puck about him, something of the sprite and the forest: with his hair and his eyes, he looked almost other-worldly. Some folk maybe even wondered if the child was indeed a quisling, swapped by the fairies, for he favoured neither parent, and most certainly not his mother.

In Blue's earliest memory, he was about four or five. He was painting. He was painting at home, on the scullery table, with his little flip-top-tin paint set. He had painted a black horse, next to a black tree, under a black cloud. The horse was stood upon black ground and near to it was a black trough. And he remembers his mother asking him:

'You've got lots of nice colours in your paint set, why have you made everything black?'

And Blue said, 'But everything is black.'

'The sun's not black, why don't you paint a bright yellow sun?'

And so Blue did. He added a big splodge of yellow and he was so pleased with it, that he painted another sun too, just below it. And he was about to embark upon a third one, when his mother said, 'Two suns is nice, two suns is enough. I've never seen more than two.' And she kissed the top of his head. And that was Blue's first memory.

PHASE THE SECOND

The only good in life was in not being, or, if one had to be, then to be wood, to be stone, less even: a grain of sand, which cannot bleed beneath passing heels.

Germinal – Emile Zola

1981

It was the Nativity play that started it. Somehow started it. Blue was nine. Blue was cast as Herod's slave and the teacher had him dressed in just a loincloth. In just a loincloth but with his junior Y-Fronts on under it. Blue had pranced about in his scant costume at home. To narrowed eyed glances from his father. Blue had liked how he was like Tarzan. But he had to stay motionless on stage. He had no lines; no role except to hold a big paper palm leaf above the king. Although exactly who was king seemed to be the thing that was causing all the trouble. A subject as confusing as the matter of who Jesus's dad was. Thankfully, such mysteries were not a slave's to worry about. Blue had just to stand there, holding a palm leaf. Bare-chested, bare-legged, barely clothed. Cold in the assembly hall, even though the pipes ran hot in the school from its coal boiler. Even though the room was packed, with parents and children, for the Christmas spectacular. And Blue saw that a boy was staring at him. A boy from the year above. And Blue felt a strange sense of shame at it, at the fact that the boy was staring at him. But when he caught the boy's eye, the boy was even more ashamed. The boy blushed red and looked away. But then looked back again, now angry. And that's what started it.

Blue was a loner. When he was smaller, he used to plod the schoolyard solitary, eyes to the ground, with Mr Cubby, his wonky-nosed bear, zipped inside his parka.

By nine years old, Blue knew that he was too grown for bears, at least in public, but he still didn't play football with the rest of the boys. Not usually anyway, only occasionally. Someone would sometimes be sent to summon him, if an extra man was important.

They knew where he could be found, because he generally passed his playground hours in his own corner, playing a game of his own invention. He called it *Chocks*, because it had elements of Chess and Jacks, but used rocks. Maybe also because chocks was a mining word, that he'd heard around.

And so Blue was alone there, in his usual place, when the boy came over. The boy who had stared at him during the nativity play. The boy gazed at Blue anew, with that strange look in his eye. Blue didn't know what the look was, but it somehow glowed. It wasn't love, Blue knew what love was like, shining from his mam's one eye. But it might have been related to love; related, yet different; related yet wrong. But it wasn't quite its opposite either, it wasn't hate. Was it covetousness then? The word that Blue didn't really understand, but knew to be a sin. A desire to own something that wasn't yours. 'Thou shalt not covet thy neighbour's ass,' the priest had said. Did the boy covet Blue's ass?

Blue smiled, to silently break the strange silence. And at this, the boy flushed red and pulled Blue downward by the ear, then thumped him on the back, to send him to the ground.

'You little poofter,' the boy said, as he walked away, leaving Blue spread-eagled, shaking and shamed.

After this first time, after the seal of decency was broken, such acts became a near daily occurrence. Often the blows themselves would not even be that hard, not really, it was the anticipation and the humiliation that caused Blue such deep felt trauma. The boy would arrive, with a worm of a smile on his mouth, his pupils enlarged with the coming pleasure of Blue's pain. Sometimes he came with friends, but more often alone. It was like a little ritual that the boy needed. And quickly Blue began to need it too. Not because he wanted it, he hated it, he dreaded it; but once it was out of the way, he knew that he was safe for another day. He didn't have to live with the fear that the boy would get him later on, or after school. Not until tomorrow.

Dead legs, dead arms, head locks, Chinese burns, flicked ears, camel bites, knuckle rubs, slaps on the cheeks, raps on the forehead, knees in the stomach, knees in the goolies, pulled back fingers, stamped toes, the boy knew many ways of making pain and even the pain was better than when he would spit or smear bogies. But it was not the acts themselves, so much as the fear of the acts, that became all encompassing; it was not so much the humiliation, as the constant nagging dread of being humiliated.

And worse, as others noticed how the boy was able to treat Blue, seemingly with impunity, other boys, other bullies, started to target him too. Until even that feeling of relief, once the day's torture was over, was denied him.

And the boy encouraged it. The boy encouraged other boys to chase Blue, to pin him down, to laugh at his mismatched eyes and his horns of hair and his stupid name.

One day, as Blue lay there, curled into a ball on his side, finally released, the boy and his gaggle of tormentors temporarily gone away, a kid from Blue's class, Nick Nickelson came up to him and sat beside him. Nick – cross legged, and with the weary burden of wisdom, which was perhaps what one acquired as the oldest in the year – told Blue that he needed to hit the boy back.

'You have to punch him,' Nick said, 'Would be best to punch him on the nose. Would be best to punch him hard on the nose. But any punch, anywhere, would be better than what you're doing now. Even a kick, even anything, would be better than what you're doing now.'

'I could never beat him up,' Blue said, 'He's much bigger than me.'

'You don't need to win, but you need to fight at least.'

'Will you not hit him for me?' Blue said.

'No. You need to do it yourself. But I'll stand with you when you do it. If you want me to. I can be there, but you have to do it for yourself.'

Blue hardly slept that night. Wracked with the weight of decision. The same fear of worse reprisals, which was what prevented him from telling his parents or teacher about his troubles, made him near sure that to fight back would be a mistake. And might not Nick forget or decide against standing with him? He knew he couldn't do it if he was alone. Maybe it was all a trick, maybe Nick would side with the others against him, mock him for being gullible. Nonetheless, in the middle of the night, Blue rose from his bed and tried to practice boxing. He tried to picture how the *A-Team* did it on TV. To imagine himself as B.A. Baracus or Hannibal was a leap too far, but even Face could fight. Blue tried to picture how Face punched. And there, in the dark, on a rag-rug, he repeated the movement over and over and over.

Nick's word was good though. Nick followed Blue out of class, and then stood by him, through first break and lunch break until the boy came. Until Blue saw that same familiar glint of something in the boy's eyes, which always arrived just before a blow. It was like the glint was the trigger. The glint was that feeling. The feeling of coveting, the feeling that the boy was so ashamed of. The glint came and the boy separated the knuckle of his middle finger from the rest, a new invention, a fresh way of creating pain. And Nick looked at Blue and nodded. And Blue roared – a noise came from within him – as he launched himself at the boy. Blue rushed at him and flailed wildly, with both hands, and both feet. His channelling of the Faceman was completely forgotten. Blue swung more like a chimp, or like an octopus, he felt like he was possessed of so many limbs. He thrashed and kicked and thumped with such a multitude of blows that some at least connected. And the boy was initially so stunned that he didn't even react, except to cover his face. When he did respond, he tried to wrestle Blue to the ground, instinctively to use his greater weight. But Blue squirmed free from the grip and continued to flail his rain of blows.

One of the boy's friends tried to grab Blue from behind, to pin his pelting arms. And Nick punched the new assailant in the eye. So neatly, it was almost like a swashbuckling swordsman's strike: a rapier thrust, full of artistic precision. And Nick's target immediately began to cry.

Blue did not cry, though the boy began to get the better of him, though the boy began to land blows of his own. Blue did not cry and he continued his tirade of swings. Eventually, the ever-expanding ring around the combatants, shouting *Scrap-On*, *Scrap-On*, *Scrap-On*, caused the teacher on playground duty to put down his brown mug of grey coffee and break it up. He dragged the pair apart and eyed them over. And, seeming to conclude that each was about as battered as the other, he sent them off, both to stand alone at a separate end of the yard and let that be the end of it.

Blue's bruises had swelled well visible, by the time he went home that day. His dad, Charlie, was in the backyard. He looked Blue north to south. But he made no comment on the injuries or the coming black eye. He took Blue's hands, lifted them and studied them. Saw knuckles skinned and fingers swollen. He dropped them again, with a hint of satisfaction on his face and patted Blue on the back. Blue felt like he was going to burst into tears. But Charlie glanced away, to give Blue the moment to fight it, to bottle it up, to keep it safely stuffed down, buried inside.

'Someone looks like they could eat an ice-cream,' Charlie said.

'It's winter, Dad.'

'Tough men like us don't care about things like that.'

The boy did not come back to find Blue, the following day. But Nick Nickelson did. Nick came to find Blue, in his usual place in the playground.

'Do you know how to play Chocks?' Blue asked Nick, 'I mean, you wouldn't, you couldn't: no one knows how to play except me. But I could teach you.'

'I think I'd like that,' said Nick.

And Blue discovered, to his surprise, that Chocks is a game even better, when played with two.

1983

Over time, by the time that Blue was eleven, Nick Nickelson had become like Jesus – not just as a personal saviour – but like how the teachers told Blue that Jesus was: with him everywhere he went.

Jesus and Nick Nickelson accompanied Blue onto the moors of purple heather and the black shores; goaded guard dogs; climbed spoil heaps, cliffs and fences; played conkers and truant. But Nick Nickelson was more faithful than Jesus: Jesus walked alongside everyone in Blackmoor and – so it was said – the rest of the world too; while Nick Nickelson mostly only hung around with Blue.

Nick Nickelson was a blond bairn. Nearly canny bonny, but with an impish face, stretched at the centre, kind of too pointed, like it was aimed at something in particular, or as if the maker had finger-pulled it outward, as one can with clay. Nick was slight, but wiry not weedy. Always picked before Blue for sides, but then Nick was the oldest in the school year, and Blue was among the youngest. They weren't in any danger of being promising athletes, and they weren't much bothered by that. They would occasionally belt wet leather footballs with the Blackmoor boys, when the urge and opportunity presented, but spent most of their time only with the other: a pair of loners, if there's such a thing as that.

Neither were they great scholars; though Blue had a certain

thirst for story books from the mobile library and for the forms of knowledge to be found in *Amateur Photographer* magazine, which his dad subscribed to.

Nick Nickelson's dad – Nicholas – was reckless and feckless. A cash-in-hand mechanic with a moustache-less beard that sort of wrapped around, like the bandage holding up Jacob Marley's jaw in Blue's heirloom copy of *The Children's Illustrated Dickens*. Nick's dad wore a belt on his dungarees, so he could drop the top when he got hot, which always made Blue wonder why he didn't just wear trousers. Nick's mother was a redhead, with perfume stronger than the smoke of her cigarettes. She was a looker and she knew it. In the summers she wore her shirts knotted to show off an inch or two of waist and unbuttoned to show an inch or two of freckled cleavage. Her hair was as watchable as the flames of a fire you'd lit yourself.

Because of her, Blue liked spending time up at the Nickelson place – she wove smiles among the piles of bald tires – but the friends still mostly hung out at Blue's house, on such occasions as they were to be found indoors at all.

Back then, one shore, one moor and its one mining town was the whole world. And it was so big and so crammed with wonder, that it was all the world required.

In the winter, they sledged Bagman's Mound on sheets of some tough plastic that Nick's dad had filched or salvaged to use as a roof on one of his outbuildings, but never got around to fixing up. It went as quick as anything on the hill, but had no runners, no brakes, no steering. You just pulled the front up over your knees and set off. Spinning as you flew, friction making this weird growling on the ground, laughter drowning out even that sound. And you could trade a ride with any other child there, no matter how fancy their sledge was.

Blackmoor was near enough on the sea, but you couldn't swim in it. The tides were too strong and submerged rocks would skin you to the bone as you tried to get in or out. The beaches, such as they were, were black; smothered with the colliery waste constantly arriving on mechanical aerial buckets. Dumped spoil: broken rock, mud and muck, shale and unsellable coal. Just dust and shards, small enough to blow and scatter. Small enough not to be worth the bother of gather, even by the broke. At high tide, the water came right to the foot of the eroded low cliffs. There were a few wind-stunted tries at trees but the landscape was mostly stripped away to coal-dusty bushes and thistles. The only colour came from occasional dandelions and bulbous buttercups among spiny gorse too sharp even for donkeys. Though goats would eat it, so they said. Blue would have liked to have seen that: you couldn't even pick it, much less chew it.

But there were still places for kids to splash. In the summer, Blue and Nick would swim at The Spot. Their secret spot. Blue can't remember when they started swimming naked. But it seems like it was probably because *The Adventures of Tom Sawyer and Huckleberry Finn* was on TV back then. Huck and Tom were always stripping off and diving into the Mississippi, that was their thing. And it became Blue and Nick's thing too, though they weren't pretending to be Huck and Tom. They were just being them.

The Coal Fair came each *backend*, as the days started to shorten, with brass bands and beer stands, shuggy boats and waltzers, shire horses and pit ponies. And Blue went along to everything, with Jesus and Nick Nickelson. And Nick Nickelson swore – swore on lives and Bibles – that all of them always would.

1983

The horses that pulled the beer carts were the biggest creatures Blue had ever seen up close. Who knew where they lived or what they did for the rest of the year, but every September they came to Blackmoor. Surer than Santa; faithful as Jesus or Nick Nickelson. The fur of the dray horses' lower legs was lengthy and dense as collie pelt, the rest of them velvet smooth, but bulbous with barely contained muscle. They were liveried in fitments of leather and silver, brass and feather, ribbon and silk. And bells that tinkled to the off beats of the clop of metal-shod hoofs as big as your head.

The Coal Fair was the high point of the Blackmoor year. Held since time unremembered. And something about the fair whispered of ages even older: before the mines, before the Prince Bishops, before Christianity itself arrived perhaps. To an Anglo-Germanic past of myth and legend, famine and abandonment, woodsmen and cannibals, Hansel and Gretel. And stalls sold rock walking canes and gingerbread shaped like forest cottages, to play with and prey upon children well versed in such fairy tales.

It was not all sweets though, there were also flame-licked fish, impaled through their mouths on sticks, a long line of them before fire pits, skin burnt to a salty crisp. And there were Cumberland sausages in stotties with onions. *I know someone whose mam likes sausage*, cackled a beer soak, just as Blue and

Nick Nickelson passed by. There were chickens, roasted whole and cleaved into quarters before your eyes. And pigs and sheep skewered on spits. Tatties so thickly buttered they slipped from fingers. An annual orgy of excess, a celebration of the fact that hunger belonged to the past. Old King Coal provided. Mining was hard and dark and dangerous and the dust got into your lungs, but the money was good, thanks to the unions. The National Coal Board paid decent wages, with free heating and cooking coal on top. Many miners had money spare to spend at the end of every week. Miners were the aristocracy of the working class. And they were a guild of brothers, they had a comradeship impossible for others to imagine, outside of times of war; their solidarity was unbeatable, and coal was essential, so who could imagine a way that their world wouldn't continue?

Charlie treated Blue and Nick to a ride on the Speedway. Wooden planks linked with metal pins, bounced them up and down as they span. On a galloping painted horse, they rose and fell over hidden risers, the force almost pulling them off the side. Gently mocked by the surefootedness of the fairground charva who strolled between the riders checking tickets.

And Blue and Nick played on the shuggy boats too, pumping them, one on either end, until it seemed certain they would send the boat over the top of the bar and tumble out. But it never happened, not to them nor anyone else, whether a trick of gravity or design you could never quite make that extra push.

But the highlight was the miners' games. While watching the teams on the two-man saws, Blue and Nick swore that they would prevail together when they were grown, but neither spoke it with much conviction: the men who won were muscled and brawny. Gleaming with sweat, stripped to the waist. Hewing rocks and running with pit props. The men who won were local heroes, their prize: only pride. A moment of glory in a lifetime of spine-rending, perilous work underground.

For the adults, for all that, for all its many flavours, and intricacies, tradition and competition, the fair was a lot about drinking beer. Even the normally abstemious might be found steaming, from vicar to teacher. Flat pats of rainbow vomit would decorate the streets and fields until next rain, as likely to have arrived from the gullet of a mine manager as a teenager.

Many of the Blackmoor young'uns spent their time at the fair collecting up empty bottles, in part for the dreg sips that sent them tipsy, but also so that they could claim the deposits. Raking through bins and under shrubs, always alert for the possibility of another boy's stash, which could be a find as rich as Blackbeard's buried treasure, but ran those same risks of vigilantes and violence as all piracy.

Blue and Nick were hunting the edges of the fair, near to a couple of old ladies on a tartan rug beneath a tree. The ladies sat with their legs straight out in front of them, like they were dolls set down. One of them Blue faintly recognised, a friend of his mam's he thought, which only meant someone his mam swapped greetings with, should they chance to meet in the street. Blue's mam didn't really have friends in the same sense that other people had friends. Much like Blue himself had been, before he found Nick. The old women were looking at Blue and Nick and talking low out of the side of their mouths, in a way that had Blue sure they were talking about him. He reddened with the shame of a sin he couldn't even name, walked on with his clanking coal sack of empty bottles, out of the women's sight, then to double back and sneak behind them. *Eavesdroppers hear no good of themselves*, Blue's teacher used to say, and what Blue heard seemed to prove the truth of it:

'I tell you, there's something of the cuckoo about the bairn, a catch-colt, a breed distinct from the father's stock.'

And so Blue knew he was right: they were talking about him, about his mismatched eyes no doubt.

'Sometimes these things just come out that way: I heard of a bride in Newcastle, must have had some negro in her family line, but a way back, so far gone there hadn't been a trace in generations, had been forgot in the whole family, until she had a baby curly-haired and coffee-skinned.'

'You heard that did you, hinny? I never heard that story. But I've heard of some who'd have a coloured caller when their husband weren't home.'

A bottle clinked in Blue's sack and the old ladies turned on the rug, suddenly aware of him behind. They smiled with their mouths but not their eyes and one of them gave him one of the new twenty pence coins, unasked for, which Blue accepted though he couldn't bring himself to thank her for it.

'You come up on us quiet as an elf, there, didn't you, pet?' crinkled lips said, 'You know why we have such tales of elves? It was times of starving, used to be so common in ages gone, before the unions, when folk round here were nothing but strugglers and tenant farmers. Famished bairns would shelter in barns and silent as they were, the wives would know they were there. Wives would always know. They would speak loud about chores they wanted done and how they would leave a lick of bread and blinked milk for the elves if they found those tasks were done come morning. But they never let them stay for long, they always had them move along. And if the farmer's own children ever caught sight of them, stick thin, dirty, ragged, eyes big in their shrunken faces, their mothers would say, *tsk 'tis an elf, my child, don't speak a word to it, don't go near, or they'll witch you and whisk you away with them when they go*. And sometimes they did.'

1984

King Arthur called the strike, so they thought. He said the miners were behind him. And they were. The North East pitmen made the first Great Stand in 1765, striking was no novelty. But the N.U.M. had led them to walkout in '72 and '74 and got them better terms, blocked the chiselling of conditions. They'd broken the will of the government; they'd forced a three-day week. They'd brought the country to a halt, until it listened to the miners. So the miners listened to Arthur now. Arthur Scargill called for a walkout and the men walked out. They voted to strike, but pit by pit. There was no national ballot; there was no need of one, not as far as the miners thought. Once a time, men would spit on a stone to seal a strike, in dark of night, that was all the ballot needed then.

There was no national ballot, parroted the right wing press, defenders of democracy. But miners had a vote in 1981 – that no pit should be closed except on grounds of exhaustion – carried with an eighty-six percent majority. And now pit after pit had balloted and subsequently voted with their feet. How many votes did they need? For the miners, the first weeks were cheers and singing and hugging strangers. The first weeks they had the naive joy of children, the fraternity of sailors.

But was it King Arthur or the Iron Lady who really called the strike? It was the closure of Cortonwood Colliery that provoked it; just streets away from Scargill's home; a productive pit with millions freshly invested in it. Miners had only recently been transferred there, with nine years guaranteed work. The N.U.M. justifiably feared it was to be the first of a slew of closures, but to start with Cortonwood was a direct challenge. The Lady had dared the King. And he dared. But she chose the moment. Directly after winter, demand at its lowest meant strikers at their weakest. And the government had been stockpiling coal in preparation, reserves had never been so high, not even in wartime. The state was ready for it. Thatcher wanted it.

Charlie came out on strike. Though he now wore office shoes, he was still N.U.M. to his boots. Though he now rented a small isolated cottage, a little out of town with a little front garden, he still walked past the rows of miner's red bricks. And he still passed the time of day with those outside them. Unaccustomed to such leisure and such lack of funds, the miners would sit on dining chairs on the roads behind backyard gates, all proudly painted different colours, and talk or play cards. Listening to the radio for news. The Police – Britain's biggest band for the best part of a decade – had announced they were splitting in March, when the strike started. But Sting was still a Geordie and The Police were still a permanent fixture on the airwaves. The miners had nothing against the other police back then either, not at first. The police were local men, would have been miners were they not police. The police lived in the same streets, had been to the same schools, drank from the same pineapple pint glasses in the same pubs. The police knew who was a truant and who was a wrong 'un. The police would bring your bike back before you knew it was gone.

At school, the teacher talked about George Orwell's *1984*. Blue and Nick and the rest of the class were a bit young for it really, but Mr Hardy couldn't let an opportunity like that pass him by. Not in the middle of a strike. An authoritarian regime. A surveillance society. An oppressed proletariat. Mr Hardy was a local man, would have been a miner if he wasn't a teacher. Mr Hardy ate the same pork pies off the same plates. Mr Hardy was Labour down to his Clarks desert boots. And anyway, it was encouraged: the BBC children's service played extracts from *1984* on the radio for schools to use. Miners' sons would become miners. Miners' sons might as well learn about the rats.

Charlie was a poacher. Son of a poacher. Son of a poacher's son. Charlie started walking the moors at night. He painted the bead on his father's side-by-side hammer-action shotgun with white florescent mine-paint, so he could follow its line in the dark. He used 12-gauge cartridges against the grouse and the rabbits, a hip-flask of whisky against the stars. But getting drunk was not the objective, poaching was. Poaching was and walking was. There was a lot of time to be filled when a man was out of work. Walking filled the night, sleeping filled the day, meat filled the belly and could be sold and given away. Walking was a therapy. Remembering or forgetting or both, but walking. Compulsively walking. Walking alone to avoid the company of others. Walking so far he no longer knew where he was. Walking out. Walking it out. Sometimes wondering whether he would walk right away. Remembering Blue. Deciding he wouldn't. Not today. Today he would sleep. Tonight he would walk the moors. Tomorrow he'd man the picket line. And the week would be half way gone.

'That's another day done, bonny lad,' he'd say to Blue as he tucked him in; as if this life was a thing to be endured, a burden to be ticked off as it lightened.

And then he'd ruffle Blue's hair, and it lightened.

1984

The *new* house, Charlie still called it – though Blue could remember no other – had a small front garden, with a big elm tree in it. It was a little out of the way, set apart, but still not quite so far out as the Nickelson's. It had an indoor toilet, which a handful in Blackmoor still didn't. But the outdoor toilet remained in place, still usable, still used, in summer at least. The brick coal shed built beside was still used as well. Still well stocked from before the strike started. It had wooden slats at the front that could be removed as the level dropped. But it was nearly full. They'd hardly needed a fire lit that spring and early summer. Everyone knew the government would break before winter. Once the power stations and the big industries ran low on coal. Once people started getting cold. The government would break. They always had, they always would.

Charlie had sealed the edges of the coal shed door so it fitted tight. And he discouraged Blue from peeking, lest he let flies in. But still Blue could not resist from time to time. Many folk in Blackmoor used their coal sheds for storing spuds and onions, but Charlie also used the cool, dry, dark for storing and curing game.

Nothing is more dead than a thing hanged, and Blue felt a strange compelling revulsion to look anew, each time he knew his dad had been out poaching. There might be a pheasant suspended from one of the bent nails in the ceiling, wings akimbo, upside down, looking like how they said Saint Peter was crucified. Smaller birds would dangle from the neck like common criminals, legs limp, claws sometimes spread, sometimes clutched tight together like an old lady holding a sewing needle. Rabbits, marble eyed, stopped mid-stride, fore-legs at the gallop, rear legs string tied. There might be ducks too, there might be anything. Charlie took no prisoners and made no exceptions. He kept food on the table and on some other tables too. Would have happily had a swan, had one come along, Queen's property or not. Charlie had no truck with aristocracy, nor monarchy itself.

'God made game and fowl, so they don't belong to anyone,' he told Blue, 'Nor did the moors themselves, once a time. So how did one man come to own, what was no-man's to sell him? That's what I cannot fathom.'

The sitting room was never used, except for sometimes of a Sunday. There were antimacassars on the back of the good sofa. It never struck Blue as odd, that they had a sitting room not for sitting in and seats which were not to be sat upon. The sitting room had a mirror on the wall, glass mottled brown, tilted down, shaped like a shield. And it had a painting on the wall too, or a print of a painting at least – *And When Did You Last See Your Father?* it was called – a small, scared boy, dressed in blue, standing before a panel of grim, drab, ruthless men. Round-heads.

'Out to kill his dad, they were,' Blue's mam said.

Off the scullery – the kitchen – was the pantry. Either the smallest of rooms or the largest of cupboards. Facing North East, the coldest corner of the house. It would have been the refrigerator before there were refrigerators. Now it was where Charlie kept his shotgun, but more importantly, his darkroom. The shotgun was locked away, but the enlarger was on display. And more, Blue was encouraged to watch his dad at work. Since the strike started, Charlie'd had more time for leisure, they'd passed more hours together than ever before.

The chemicals smelt strange. They smelt of wizardry and alchemy. Blue felt privileged to watch Charlie's intricate labours. And he never felt closer to his father than those times when they were so literally confined in the near-dark pantry.

Charlie dunked the paper down, drowned in a plastic dish and a picture emerged. There in the red-light glow, a pristine sheet became a photograph, the image eerily appearing in the liquid, as if some holy rite.

'It's alike to magic, isn't it?' said Blue.

'Maybe better than magic,' Charlie said, 'All photographs are from the past, it's nigh on to time travel.'

'Dogs can see the past,' Blue said.

'How so?'

'Well, not see, but with their noses. When they smell you, they know where you've been, what you've been doing, who you met, so they're smelling the past.'

'I'd say you're right. I'd say that's a canny clever thing to have thought of too.'

Blue squirmed a bit, wrestling with himself, 'Well, I didn't really think of it all, Nick's mam said it too.'

'She said it did she? Yeah, she's a sharp woman. She can probably smell the past on you too. Don't you and Nick ever try and pull the wool over her eyes.'

'She has pretty eyes. She's pretty,' Blue said.

'Yes,' said Charlie, 'Yes, I'd say that she is. She's got Irish blood, bonny lad, that's how come she has such red locks and freckles, she's not a Geordie since the days of yore, like most of us round here.'

Charlie ruffled Blue's corn-husk hair, 'You know, it's taught me a lot about beauty, this camera. There is a lot of beauty in this world, my son. Remember that. Even in bad times, even in days as bleak as these ones, there is invariably some beauty to be found. Even a tramp can share in the sunset. They cannot take that away from him. Always look for beauty and the world will seem less harsh.'

When they left the darkroom that Charlie had built in the pantry, there were flying ants in the scullery. Blue's mam, Geraldine, was stamping on them and swatting them and boiling pans of water to pour on them.

'They're everywhere,' she said, she seemed anxious out of all proportion to the problem, 'I need to get to the market for some spray, some powder. I need to get to the market for something.'

She was scratching, clawing at herself like the ants were on her. She seemed like she was at the end of her tether. The strike was hitting everyone hard, but they at least had meat and a little money coming in, plenty families had it plenty worse. Yet Geraldine seemed like she was losing her grip, losing her mind.

'I need to get to the market,' she scrunched her hands skyward, like she was pleading with the heavens for a thing she knew to be impossible.

18th June 1984

Charlie shared a ride down with Eric, in his baby-shit brown Cortina. It had a peeling racing stripe under the swage line and a second stripe, of rust, beneath that. Was still Eric's pride and joy though.

'Remember that advert on telly,' Eric said, '*People will always need coal.* Couldn't get enough workers a couple of years back. Had to start recruiting on TV. Now they want to close down twenty pits, and that's just the start of it.'

'Made mining look like a close second choice to being a movie star and all,' Allison said.

Everyone used Allison's surname, because it was canny funny – calling him a girl's name – given how he looked rough enough to bite the nose off a bulldog.

'Miners with glamour models draped all over them. Miners on sun-loungers. Miners off skiing and scuba diving,' Allison's voice was muffled, because he was covered with a tartan blanket.

He was lying, hid as best as was possible, in the rear foot well. Another striker was in the boot, to keep the back seats unoccupied. Charlie got shotgun because he looked least like a coal miner and had the best patter.

Police had been setting up roadblocks for the past couple of months. Stopping any cars with miners in them, with working-age men in them, with men in them. The fewer of you were visible, the more chance you'd be waved through.

Nottinghamshire was the worst. Police riddled it like syphilis. Nottinghamshire produced a quarter of the nation's coal and they'd voted against striking. Their pits were the most modern, their workers were the best paid – after production bonuses – because their coal seams were thick and easy to get at. They believed their jobs were safe. But if they could be brought out on strike then everyone would win. And they were persuadable, with solidarity. You could talk them out of crossing the picket line. Man by man; pit by pit. Because they were just miners at the finish. Just men at the finish. Did the same jobs, had the same families and the same fears. You could point out to them that Thatcher's axe-man, Ian MacGregor, now in charge of the mines, had made the exact same promises to Sheffield's steel workers: divided them one against another; told half of them their jobs were safe; then halved that half again afterwards; and again; death by a thousand cuts; and the steel workers all lost their jobs in the end. You could reason with the Nottingham lads and they had been gradually coming over. And the Coal Board could see it. The government knew it. So they swamped the Nottinghamshire borders with eight thousand police officers, called in from all over the country. Might as well have been East Germany, for all the ease of getting into Nottinghamshire after. Behind an iron curtain, it was. Behind a thin blue line. Behind a thin blue line that was suddenly thick as a brick netty; stank like one and all.

They'd arrest you for obstructing a police officer, if you didn't do what they said. If you didn't turn back. Picket's cars got smashed by police too. Picket's tires got slashed. Smash your lights and fine you for driving an un-roadworthy vehicle. Smash your windscreen and fine you for not displaying a tax disc. Impound your vehicle and make you walk home. Leave a sticker on the wreck: *You've met The Met.* When did British law get suspended? Who exactly voted for that?

Chancellor Nigel Lawson had said that increasing police numbers and training against trade union action was like re-arming to face the threat of the Nazis. Lawson was the kind of politician who'd call it *the will of the people* if the plebs happened to agree with him, but *the threat of the Nazis* when they didn't. Lawson wouldn't know a fascist if one looked back at him from his shaving mirror, Charlie reckoned.

But the government knew what they were doing: the police had been given generous pay rises and tidy overtime, tax free, paid in cash, along with new equipment, and crowd control training, and bolstered ranks. Government was trying to leave coppers in no doubt as to which side their bread was buttered. But they'd face cuts too, if the time ever came, once union power was crushed, they just couldn't see it. Sometimes strikers would see police with no insignia or badge numbers, only visored helmets and dark boiler suits. Rumours abounded that these men were military, or military intelligence, or worse: ex-military: just deputised thugs. Even the normal bobbies had started marching like soldiers, marching in platoons, marching in squadrons, marching in armies.

Yet it was the miners who were called *Arthur's Army* in the media. It was more than just a tabloid tag. It was part of the militarization. Part of the othering of the miners. Miners were demonised in the papers. In the Rupert Murdoch press. In the Robert Maxwell press. Both barons keen to break unions for their own reasons. Red Tops told their readers that the miners were greedy, selfish, violent, the foes of the common man.

The government produced a number – a twisted, distorted

figure, out of all relation with reality – of how much the mines were costing: *one thousand, three hundred million pounds a week.* They repeated it, they plastered it, they put it on posters. The press parroted it – *one thousand, three hundred million pounds a week, think of where we could be spending that money* – the number was reiterated until it stuck. They retold a giant lie, a false figure, painted it everywhere, until it sunk into the minds of the public. Politicians knew the number was a lie. Press knew the number was a lie. But more than half the public bought it.

The figure was a wildly over-blown estimate, composed of already sunk costs and the price of closing down the pits, whereas keeping them running required little subsidy at all. But more than half the public bought it.

Then the government played the envy card: magnified what the highest skilled worker in the most productive mine might allegedly earn – if he worked all the hours open eyes would allow for, in a fantasy year of production bonus – and insinuated that wage was what most miners were getting. Millionaire Members of Parliament and media barons, making out that coal miners were avaricious. Trying to turn the nation against them, against itself.

Prime Minister Margaret Thatcher publicly called the strikers 'enemies'. Thatcher called them 'extremists'. Thatcher called them the 'enemies of democracy'. Thatcher said they were trying to 'kill democracy for their own purposes'. Thatcher called them 'the enemy within', as if they were fifth columnists, terrorists.

Charlie didn't recall Thatcher having stood on a manifesto of massed pit closures, yet the miners became the *enemies of the people* for standing in the way of them; turning ordinary workers into their own opponents. But the N.U.M. was the strongest of all the unions. If you wanted to crush the power of collectives, you had to stamp down from the top. That's why unionised miners had to become 'the enemy within'. Not men exercising their legal right to strike, not people using the democratic power of protest, not even impediments to policy: the enemy …

And when a government names a group the enemy, they are green-lighting any action against them. The police were supposed to be impartial in Britain. The police were supposed to uphold the law, not prop up the Tories. But the police took the government at their word. The police took it that the miners were outlaws; in the old sense, the common law sense – *hors-la-loi* – those to whom normal rights no longer apply.

So Kent miners were arbitrarily banned from using the Dartford Tunnel, to stop them going North. Nottinghamshire became a foreign country, a hostile state. Freedom of movement was over, if you happened to be a miner. You could be arrested for trespass, on public footpaths and public highways. Freedom of movement was ended. Ended in your own bloody country.

But there were no roadblocks that day. On that beautiful June day, no one stopped a baby-shit brown Cortina on its way to Orgreave Coking Plant. In fact, there were signposts pointing the way.

Stranger still, Eric was directed into the ASDA car park. The previous time Charlie had picketed Orgreave, he'd had to come in on foot, over spoil heaps, through abandoned outbuildings and across a railway line to avoid the police cordons. But that day, a smiling copper in a high vis jacket flagged Eric in to park in the supermarket, just at the top of the village. There were coaches there and all. Coaches of miners from as far away as South Wales and Scotland.

And the courtesy continued: they were led down to a field next to the coking park, in a pied piper trail, behind a jam-sandwich police car. All the men from sixty odd coaches and a massed hodgepodge of shared cars were escorted down the street that came from ASDA. Past the terraced houses on Highfield Lane: red brick; white stone lintels; grey lace curtains, twitching at the spectacle; glass milk bottles outside, gold tops, spuggies pecking holes in them to get at the cream. A horned, orange space hopper lulled outside one house, a grinning round demon. Charlie took a picture of it, framing its fiendish innocence next to a glowering riot squad copper. There is beauty everywhere, if looked for.

The miners were led on, all taking the same route: a narrow road, across an even narrower bridge; beneath it, the steep valley of a railway line cutting. They arrived into what could be described as a meadow, or a containment zone, or a trap. Everything is a matter of perspective. Charlie was no military tactician, but he had a photographer's eye for his surroundings and a miner's sense for confinement. In front of the picketers, between them and the coking plant, was a line of police ten deep and over a hundred wide. A thousand coppers in one solid phalanx. An entire Roman legion of them, and with full length Perspex shields making an impenetrable wall, like the Romans used to. The Romans were bastards and all.

Over in the field to the miners' left were more police, with dogs. German shepherds, used for their wolfishness: something primal about the way their snarls ripped through you; the way their lips curled back, their white fangs snapping as they barked, straining against quick release leashes. Their handlers were letting them bark, letting the miners know they were there.

In the field on the right were horses. Mounted police. Batons as long as a deputy's yard stick, but not made for measuring, the batons were sprung, to wrap around when they hit, like a steel whip. The horses snorted. The horses pawed at the dirt with muscled forelegs. The horses cavorted with barely restrained force.

And there were more horsemen behind the massed rank of riot police. And there were more Alsatian handlers at the bottom of the railway cutting and all. The miners were completely surrounded. The only safe way out was the way they'd been led in: across the bridge: a solitary single-carriageway escape route, for all those gathered men.

Charlie was no military tactician, but he'd watched *Zulu* and *Spartacus* at the pictures and he'd read a little Shakespeare at school. And the scene reminded him of the buffalo horns pincer movement, used by the Zulu. The coppers looked like the legionaries and cavalry used against the rebellious slaves in *Spartacus*. The German Shepherds sounded like they yearned for someone to give the order: *cry 'havoc' and let slip the dogs of war.*

Most of the miners seemed entirely unconcerned. Some of the Scots had maybe never seen the sun like it, not like it was that day. Few miners had experienced so much time under it. For once they all looked healthy. That hot June was the longest they'd had in the sunshine since they were bairns. Graft marks, scars and tattoos were gradually melding into tans. Many were shirtless that day. There was a feel of holiday. A field, not of battle, but of play.

Charlie saw lads he knew to work at Vane Tempest, Sunny Brow, Black Prince, Seaham Harbour. Men he knew to live at

Burnhope, Killhope, Pity Me, No Place. And also lads he knew only from other pickets, men from right across the country.

Normally it was miners in body-warmers, miners in parkas. Miners in donkey jackets, commando caps, bobble hats. Miners in double denim. Miners in thick rimmed National Health spectacles. Miners in two stripe jogging bottoms. Miners in army surplus shirts, splattered with stickers and badges. Miners in flat caps and nylon leisure wear. Miners with Magnum P.I. moustaches and Kevin Keegan hair.

But that day, the one hundredth day of the strike, they were almost all in shorts and T-shirts, or else stripped to string vests and bare chests. There were some curious forms on view. Men who worked on their knees, men who worked lying down, built muscles in improbable places. Some ended up bulbous in odd ways. There were muscles on display that wouldn't even be found on Daley Thompson, for all the varied events in decathlon.

Charlie took pictures. Even though he could only print in black and white, when Kodachrome colours would have been better for the bright sunshine and yellow green grass. But still Charlie took pictures. Pictures of miners picnicking, sunbathing and playing cards. Pictures of miners kicking a football about. And pictures of a dark army of police, summoned in such numbers that the country might never witness it again.

Police were dressed for battle. Black tunics, thick coveralls. Bobbies in big helmets to make them look taller, halfway to busbies. Halfway to army. Half of them were army, some said. When they put their chinstraps on, you knew it was trouble. They all had their chinstraps on that day. And steel-capped boots, shins pads, cricket boxes, reinforced gloves, arm and body protection. And that was just the normal peelers. Riot squads were in armour, riots squads were helmed and visored. Long shields and short shields, repel and attack. Police were hot, police were sweaty, police were angry.

A chief inspector was striding about – braggardeering and swagger sticking – as plastered with unearned medals as a minor royal. He looked like one from Monty Python: lean, lanky, strutting along behind the lines, like he was from the ministry of never-you-mind. But he barked orders, through a loud hailer. And dogs barked and all, from the left and from behind. Dogs desperate to do what they'd been bred for and trained for. Dogs urgent to get at the action.

The first act of the day was invariably the same. The push always came as the lorries arrived. Their drivers were outside the law too: speed restrictions had been abandoned; no lorries were weighed for overload. They drove in like they were fleeing the police, not being escorted by them. Company names over-painted. Windows grilled. Nearby roads blocked to normal traffic. Sirens screeching. A miner named Joe Green had just been killed – picketing at Ferrybridge power station – hit by a trailer.

Smelting coke from Orgreave should have gone to Sheffield, but American hatchet-man MacGregor had already stripped the steel works from there. Now the coke went to the rump of an industry at Scunthorpe. But Scunthorpe still supplied car plants and much else besides. If you could block the coke going to Scunthorpe then the government would have to start listening. Rail unions had declared their solidarity and refused to carry the coke. But the government had road haulage firms on standby. Well paid, un-unionised. Some of the drivers stuck ten-pound notes to their windscreens, to gloat, as they drove by. Sometimes the police waved their wads of overtime cash and all. They knew the miners were broke. They knew that families were suffering. Sometimes the miners waved wanker signs back.

Much of the coal now came in from South Africa. Mrs Thatcher seemed to be a supporter of South Africa. Where coal could be dug by black men further blackened. Men on slave wages, men without unions, or even the right to gather, men who didn't get to protest. Men who could be shot without the police even filling in paperwork after.

British dockers wouldn't have it. British dockers supported the miners. British dockers opposed apartheid. So South African coal would always be shipped elsewhere first, to be re-loaded onto smaller boats that could dock at tiny non-union ports and river bays in the UK. The government had plans in place. The government always found a way.

So the lorries arrived and the miners rose. Rose from their sandwiches and flasks of tea. They started their habitual chants. *The miners united, will never be defeated. Here we go, here we go, here we go.* They came down the field, towards the shield line, arms swinging with the singing, like they were dancing to *Madness.*

It had been the same every day since May: the miners pushed at the police line, the police kept them back, the lorries got through. And so, the usual ritual began again that eighteenth of June: miners started down the field, to push against the police lines, like they had every day for weeks. Like they always did: miners would push at the police line; police would shout *hold the line*; the line would hold; coking lorries would get in; everyone would resume as they were, kicking footballs, chatting in the sunshine, eating sarnies or earning overtime, picketing and policing both on pause, until the next lot of lorries came by.

But it was the hundredth day of the strike and someone had decided that one hundred days had gone on long enough. As the miners came towards them, the phalanx of riot policemen – the thin blue line a thousand strong – began beating on their shields. Bashing truncheon butts on Perspex. It sounded like thunder. The noise ripped through you, like that scene from *Zulu*, just before the massacre.

The miners coming down the field slowed. There were kids among them and all. Old men there and all. Women there and all. Come to witness. Come to experience. Come to see. A medieval battle on a beautiful day. Something rich and strange.

Without warning police horses came at the canter. Rapidly police horses moved into charge. It felt like earthquake. Felt like the ground was shaking. Charlie could smell them, Charlie could feel them coming, the world changed, with charging wrath. Charlie felt the slice of air as a mounted copper tried to smash him with a swung baton. Charlie dropped from instinct. Eric dropped from a blow to the back of his head. Blood streamed into his mullet. Hooves were all around. Charlie curled foetal. Charlie feared for his life. Miners wet themselves with fear. Big men, hard men, had never felt a horror like that of a horse charging at them. The pickets suddenly knew something of the spit and shiver and piss and terror of ancient peasants facing armed cavalry. Herdsmen against Mongol hordes.

The riders wheeled and rode back towards their own lines. Back through the crowd of pickets. Back through the bewildered and the injured. The police clapped and banged the riders home. Miners picked themselves up. Miners tried to lift maimed colleagues. Miners bunched tee-shirts onto wounds. Charlie lay there, still curled, in shock, while Allison and another man helped Eric.

The second time the horses charged, panic broke out. The picketers knew what was coming now. The young started running. The old tried their best to get out the way. Wide eyed horses, staring through Perspex blinkers, reared and hoofed. Riders wielded night sticks, from atop one-ton animals, nineteen hands high. Bags of buns and pork pies and pop from ASDA, scattered on the ground, trampled into the mud, flecked with blood.

This time, short shield snatch squads ran in behind the horses. Truncheoning into the carnage. Arresting at random. Arresting the floored and the broken. Wearing black boiler suits, no epaulets, no numbers, no way of identifying who had dealt violence, should a photographer catch them. Pairs of them, dragging men back to behind the long shield phalanx. Where blue Leyland police vans, boxy like Tonka toys, sat waiting, incongruous.

Long shields opened the line to let arresting snatch squads back through. But only just enough to let them through. Arrested pickets were bounced off the shields. Arrested pickets ran a gauntlet of punches and truncheons, fists and sticks, before being slammed off vans and slung in.

Charlie saw a young lad, with a broken leg, being frogmarched across the field. Trying to hop. Crying in pain. Charlie saw plenty of heads smashed open. Always at the back, always running away. Trying to get to safety. Charlie didn't see a single picket with a wound to the front of his head.

But some miners did stand their ground then. After the second charge, miners started to throw stones, bottles, anything they could find, at the police lines. Miners chucked stones at that point, to try and stop the charges. But the charges came first.

And more charges came. Coppers came with short shields, half shields, round shields. Coppers came with batons. Coppers came hot and sweaty and angry.

Miners chucked stones. Beat a retreat. Got beaten in retreat. Pounded to the ground. Truncheoned to the ground. Truncheoned on the ground.

Miners were chased up the field. Men poured down the railway embankment. Cheese rolling down the steep hill. Tomahawking to the bottom. War painted with blood. Men clutching their heads. Men clutching their stomachs. Men clutching their knees. Men were sobbing. Men were vomiting.

Dog handlers were waiting. Dogs barking. Dogs snarling. Dogs biting. Miners fled along the railway lines. More afraid of the canines than the trains.

But most picketers ran the way they'd come in. Across the narrow bridge, into the village.

The village was laid in crescents with intersections. Miner's houses were in the crescents. Police wanted to cut the men off from the crescents, from shelter. Police chased in vehicles. Sirens screamed. Police poured out of vans. Pickets ran through gardens. Pickets ran through private dwellings. Pickets were terrified.

Police chased through gardens. Police chased through private dwellings. Pickets were beaten under bay windows. Blood on the backyards. Blood on the patios. Men with split heads, smothered in blood, marched up the street. Bundled into vans. Marched publicly, *pour encourager les autres*. Bounced off lampposts, bounced off bins. Miners hid in garden sheds. Miners hid in bedrooms and hedges.

Iron horseshoes clattered on the tarmac streets. Horses charged between parked cars. Miners were sick from the fear. From the running. From stitches. From the heat. Miners vomited.

Short shields came after the horses. Chasing miners down sloping streets, swinging as they came, running over the fallen, leaving it to the bobbies behind to hand out a proper beating.

Charlie lay flat beneath an ice cream van that had been doing brisk trade, earlier in the day. For once, forgot his pride. Charlie tried to remain motionless. Charlie tried to keep his breathing still. Charlie tried to imagine he had his self-rescue respirator on. Just an hour of air, bonny lad. Be silent. Be calm.

Charlie realised, in the midst of witnessing that rout, that being assaulted by the police is the position of ultimate helplessness and hopeless: because to fight back will only make it worse; yet who can come to rescue you; who can protect you, when you're being beaten-up by the protectors?

It emerged from miners arrested, that the South Yorkshire Serious Crime Squad were already on hand, behind the lines. A place like Orgreave was normally nothing to do with them, should be nothing to do with them. Yet there they were, ready. Ready to dictate statements to other officers, officers who should have been perfectly capable of describing events themselves.

In the charging rooms, plain clothes coppers from South Yorkshire Police fabricated statements, created the scene, told tales, grim tales, dark fairy tales, stories that allowed for a scene of riot.

South Yorkshire Police claimed there'd been a violent attack on them, that they had no choice but to send in the cavalry to regain control.

South Yorkshire Police were fond of doctoring statements. Perverting the course of justice. Collusion. Statements didn't match logbooks. Statements didn't match photos. Statements didn't match videos. Statements were a stitch-up.

South Yorkshire police said that a stream of missiles came first, before the cavalry charges. The miners knew it was the other way around. But the BBC showed it the same as the police said, come the ten o'clock news, that night of the eighteenth of June. The BBC switched the sequence. The BBC must have buckled under government pressure. The BBC cut the film and changed reality. The BBC knowingly altered the truth of events.

And the miners knew they were screwed then. When even the BBC had it in for them. They expected it from *The Sun*: to have the police glorified and the strikers reviled. They expected it from all of the Murdoch press for that matter. And the rest. From all of the tatty tabloids, with their lies and bile and bias. But the BBC ...

One policeman with a cut ear was shown on the night-time news. Sitting cosy in an ambulance with a cut ear. With miners bloody as abattoir floors. Miners dripping on the streets, on the fields. Miners curled motionless being cudgelled. Charlie had seen a girl get batonned in the face by a mounted man. All of it was filmed. All of it was photographed. Yet they showed one policeman with a cut ear. Charlie smashed his teacup on the scullery wall.

Charlie had seen it. Charlie had witnessed it: police caught on camera, beating unarmed men on the ground. Yet not one officer was prosecuted, no one was charged. No copper was even disciplined. Not in Chile, not in El Salvador, not in

South Africa. Not even in Northern Ireland. In Yorkshire. In England. Because miners were the enemy within. Miners were the enemies of democracy. Miners were the enemies of the people.

1984

The Spot was their special spot, just a stream-filled sink hole, and yet they thought it bottomless back then. Though it was also not bottomless, given that one of their favourite games was fetching stones from the bottom. Making piles of the brightest ones on the bank. White cheeks mooning the sun in the moment of duck-diving.

They started swimming naked, but neither could have said who started it. Likely Tom Sawyer and Huckleberry Finn started it, but who suggested it? Was it Blue or Nick, or some kind of mutual consent of a sort that evolves? Someone surely must have first mooted.

They were still kids, at twelve years old, but they were of age enough to think it was a bit strange – to be naked in front of another – a bit wrong maybe. Neither would have swum naked with anyone other than the other. Not even their parents. Probably especially not their parents.

There was always a jag of unease, as they dropped their Lee and Wrangler jeans. But once they were in the water, plashing and laughing, then all was all right again.

Even swinging from their Tarzy.

'Time flies and so do I,' Nick would say.

Near enough every time, Nick would say it, and Blue would mostly laugh. The joke itself long since dead, he would laugh at the fact that Nick always said it. He laughed because Nick was his friend. Nick was his best friend, his one true friend, in this entire tiny world and there was a joy in that worth laughing about.

That day, the last day they would ever go to The Spot, was a day of Indian Summer, but still cool to be wild swimming. It should have been nearing time for the Coal Fair but it had been cancelled because of the strike, no one had money for rides and extravagances. The words of the old ladies from last year still lingered in Blue's mind. Hadn't they called him a catch-colt and a cuckoo? But the water was fresh and piercing. So cleansing that it swept unease away. You could understand, perhaps, how come some Christians get reborn in rivers.

Blue and Nick swam and splashed, swung and dived. Too young yet to have any sense that time would move on, that things could change. That innocence must end. And yet, on one emergence onto the bank, Blue found himself enlarged, engorged. Between legs still summer browned, a shaded part, rigid and pale as a whittled stick. A strange white bone, known and yet unknown.

And Nick besides, looked at it, as if surprised, then wordlessly took it in hand. Wrapped it in fingers. Held it. Then bent, as if to inspect it, or give it a kiss. Or something else, something other. Something learned then surely, or can nature fly so far? Are we just cuckoos, acting through instinct, programmed to be cuckoos, to do as cuckoos do, who never meet a parent?

The instant froze in any case. A click stopped the act. Whatever would have been the act. A camera shutter clack. A shuffle in the undergrowth from a figure clothed made the naked ones dive once more into the pool. The moment forever gone.

Something clicked, not in the kids, but in the woods; something clicked – a broken twig, a camera shutter – something clicked and everything changed, everything was strange and shameful. Blue and Nick spooked like they'd seen a ghost and fled across the pond; it being known that the dead cannot cross water. They dived back into the covering wet and swam to the farther bank and scrambled to pull on their clothes and ran to be away.

When he got home, later that day, stomach twisting like a hooked worm. Blue found his dad in wait. Idling by the backyard gate, anything but idle. Charlie grabbed Blue by the shoulders and shook him.

'I don't want you doing anything like that with Nick ever again,' he said, 'Not ever. I don't want you swimming naked. I don't even want you swimming. You hear?'

And Blue understood that the thing which had felt a little wrong must have been a great wrong. The wrongest wrong. And punishment would surely come.

1984

Geraldine was at the window, staring out, thinking of the little birds, when the men came hammering at the door. She was trying to remember when the birds had arrived. Trying to work out if it was now too late for this year. She could still see where they'd nested, in the big elm in the front garden. She had enjoyed imagining the chicks grow, turning from dandelion fluff to finished creatures. She had enjoyed the brusque rush of the parent birds too, always flashing in and out of the nest, dashing across the section of sky framed by the window. She was just thinking that if she got to the covered market, she could get some seed. Maybe that would bring the birds back. She didn't know what sort of seed they liked, but if they didn't have it at Blackmoor market, they'd not have it anywhere in the world. Then the men came banging and Geraldine's eye drooped, because doubtless she'd not make it to the market after all.

'Quick, let us in, mother,' one of the men said – little more than youths really – through the window, 'They're after us, man.'

The house, out on its own at the edge of town, was one of the first miners might come to, if they were fleeing from a local picket. And Geraldine could tell the truth of the look of terror on the man's face. You couldn't have faked fear like that. She opened the door and four of them poured in.

'Close the door, hide us, they're after us.'

Geraldine just motioned to the stairs and the men thundered up them. Then she returned to thinking about the birds. One of them had flown into the house once, fluttering and battering about – scared as those poor lads – but she had managed to get it out. Some people believed that if a bird got into your house then a family member would die. Geraldine's mother – God rest her soul – wouldn't even have a Christmas card up if it had a robin on it. But Geraldine didn't have much truck with all that. She was more worried that the birds should have returned by now, if they were going to. She had thought of those little birds as her friends. Geraldine didn't have many friends.

She wasn't really lonely though. Loneliness is a public disease. Like its sister, shame, it exists in empathy, through the eyes of others. You have to consent to be lonely. And Geraldine refused to grant that consent. Or maybe it was not so much consent as contrast. Because most of Geraldine's life would have been classed as lonely by common standards. She had never had any friends at school. Not to speak of. Not to speak to. Not to speak to after the boundaries of strict politeness had been crossed anyway. And so it had seemed an event near miraculous, when Charlie had come courting her.

At back end and in winter, last thing at night, Geraldine would put ash over the coals in the fireplace, to quell them and turn them to embers. To look at it, you would think the fire was out entirely. It was just grey, barely warm. And it could stay like that all night, outwardly at some kind of smothered peace, even if the coals were still smouldering beneath. Geraldine tried to live like that herself, she had grown accustomed to carrying on as if nothing was wrong. And so she barely gave a thought to the striking miners now hiding upstairs.

Women had been at the forefront of the strike thus far. It was, ironically, about the only thing Margaret Thatcher had ever done for women's liberation. In Blackmoor, wives who had been brought up to expect nothing more than scullery drudgery, birthing and minding bairns, were following politics, attending rallies, finding their voices and learning to shout at the self-same time. They were going on protests and flying pickets. They were organising soup kitchens. They were chairing and addressing public meetings. Women who had jobs – which had previously brought in only a little bit of pin money – were now the main breadwinners. The DHSS – 'the social' – was used as a tool of government and refused to pay out to miners' dependents, unless they could prove they weren't getting picket pay. Which they couldn't: how could you prove an absence? So the women fund-raised, shared tricks for splitting pennies, supported each other. A few used it as an excuse to get rid of husbands who'd been knackers from the start and took charge of their own lives entirely. But most women stood by their men and stood alongside them at the lines and marches. Even stood in front of them, because if photographers were around, the police were wary of truncheoning ladies. Though they weren't always shy of it when the press pack was absent. And sometimes too, women hid terrified youths, running from running battles …

Geraldine picked up the rag doll she was making for a hardship fund raffle prize. She liked to make rag dolls. She'd made them for Blue, before he had grown to think himself too grown. She sewed them inside out, so that the seams would be concealed at the finish. She left just a hole between the legs and when she was done stitching, the whole doll would be sent inside itself, through the hole, like a bizarre self-birthing, to reappear right way round. Then she would push in the stuffing and sew up that final place. And the thought of that place, so finally closed, unused, nearly made her break. Nearly made her bubble into tears. But she regained herself and she covered those coals with ash.

It had seemed an event near miraculous when Charlie had come courting her. Him so sturdy and handsome and clever. He could have had his choosing of the girls in Blackmoor. Even before the explosion he could have, and he emerged from that a hero. It had seemed the doing of some guardian spirit, that he should pick Geraldine. A fairy tale. In the fairy tales, to learn the truth of a spell is to destroy its magic. And so it was for Geraldine: her prince returned to toad. In the version of the Brothers Grimm, the slimy beast was smashed against the wall – dashed to death – not kissed. Dark and violent bargains abounded in those old stories. Men sealed strange deals upon the fates of virgins. Truthful reflections of the world.

Charlie had been addled with a fever, fighting it with whisky toddies, and whisky neat. He'd drunk whisky like water. Left his glass of water untouched. He'd sweated cold. Clammy damp as winter windows, dew dropping down him. And he sweated out the story. He never realised. He didn't remember, once the sickness broke. For Geraldine, after the sheets were changed, so was everything else. But Charlie himself never knew, that the world was not the same. Neither did Blue, their grasshopper child. Back at that time, still happy to hug a rag doll, too small yet for school.

Geraldine remembers Blue when he was tiny, nipples so

small and so pale that you could barely discern them on the near translucent skin of his chest. Chubby puppy folds on his legs and arms. Staring at his beautiful unpaired irises, through her solitary one. She remembers when he fed non-stop and she could barely stand up for lack of sleep, and had milk blisters on her breasts, but had just sufficient energy left to realise, that it was the happiest she had ever been in her life.

It had seemed an event near miraculous when Charlie had come courting her, she had finally found the friend that she had been yearning for all of her days. Hadn't even known she was yearning for, until she found him, she had buried the feeling so deep. Though she had still worried that Blue would be alone. He had that part of his mother: a loner, not fully aware that he was lonely. Mistaking aloneness for an act of bravery, of self-sufficiency. Not understanding that people needed another. She had worried that Blue would be friendless. Though he had been happy enough, healthy enough, beautiful as a little bird, children would always leave you something to worry about. But now Blue had his friend, he had found his friend. Maybe you only needed one, if that friend was good enough. At first, Geraldine had believed that she had finally found her friend in Charlie …

Because it had seemed an event near miraculous when Charlie had come courting her. But then she learned that her life was a lie: her world a bet with God. She wept hoarse. She wailed and screamed inside for months, for years, forever. She half died. A part of her died. Thenceforth she had lived a half-life, half dead. But Blue was hers, even if Charlie wasn't. She had Blue. She had him. She had that. And so she had learned to go on; the pain burning her constantly inside, but covered with ash, hidden from view. Just so long as no one added a drawing paper or a brazier plate, she could keep the fire from bursting forth and consuming her utterly.

Policemen charged into the garden, jumping the dwarf wall, combat boots through the flower bed. Shields like centurions and visors like knights. They smashed on the door with batons as big as the club of that *Captain Caveman* who Blue liked to watch on the telly. One of them waved his baton at the window, like he would send it through, if she didn't open the door.

Geraldine had known they would come. That someone would be coming after those poor lads upstairs. But she wasn't scared. You have to consent to be terrorised. The police could terrify the miners because they shared the same world. They couldn't scare Geraldine, because she did not.

'What do you want?' she asked the lead policeman, his face was the flush of raw meat beneath the Perspex protection of his riot helmet, his eyes were fired with battle.

'There's nothing for you here,' Geraldine said, 'And anyway, I'm going to the market.'

1984

You could smell coal smoke on the air in Blackmoor. Even in summer. If you'd been out of town it would really hit you. You grew adjusted again when you'd been around it awhile. Coal in Blackmoor was like the sand at Whitley Bay: it got everywhere. Coal dust on the pavements and allotment paths. Coal dust on your clothes. Coal dust carried into sculleries on boots and bags. Coal dust on bodies, in spite of the pit-head baths. Coal dust in hutch and coop. Coal dusted school satchels, gym plimsolls, reading books. Coal dust on the cabbage leaves and rhubarb leaves and dock leaves and stingers. Every bit of scrub and rough ground was scattered with shards of it. The very dirt was black with it. And it heated and fed, provided life and bread, even if sometimes it killed.

Charlie walked on down the street. Past front doors with little slates set next to them – built into the very brickwork – on which men used to chalk their shifts, so the knocker-upper could wake them in dead of night. All the terraces ran perpendicular to the black and spoiled coast; no one got a sea view. The night was chill, the summer days were turning towards back end. When winter came, the government's will would break. Sure as icicles would hang from the iron drainpipes and gutter runs. Sure as washing not taken in would turn crisp and stiff as cardboard on the lines. Sure as frosted windows and cold fingers, the government would give in to the strikers.

A bike was chained up with its back light still on. Charlie walked over to it and switched it off. He didn't pause to wonder if he should be interfering with another person's property, or if the owner might for some reason want it left on. Charlie knew it should be switched off.

Charlie turned to take a shortcut down a backyard road. Canaries wittered in a chicken wire cage. Some families still kept them as pets, by tradition, from habit, as thanks. A few generations back, they were the miner's only protection against black damp.

Charlie noticed a loose brick, held in with a newspaper shim, a dog's job of repair that. And the fence beside it wanted a coat of creosote. Leaves blown into compost piles by the northern wind had bright confectionery wrappers mixed within. Never used to be litter in Blackmoor. Some people had no sense of pride.

It was like walking into a golden-brown syrup, entering the Imperial Hotel, after the black night outside. Smoke tanned walls and amber pints of beer on the varnished bar. Charlie took the only empty spot, asked for a pint. The available space was next to that gadgie Baggot, not unnaturally. His hair was plastered and so was he. He swayed as he said 'now then,' by way of greeting. His face was a rash of red. He had fur collars on his coat and a cardigan with a shirt and tie on underneath. Old dinner medals on the cardie. He was a banksman at the mine, but rolled like he was on-board a ship when he was drunk, which seemed to be most of the time. A lot of miners would try and make a single pint last all night, since the strike, but Baggot never seemed short of funds. Someone had told Charlie he'd had a maiden aunt who'd died.

Charlie picked up a *Northern Echo*, left on the counter. He didn't particularly want to get stuck in conversation with a drunk Baggot. The man was a bore when he was on form. It wouldn't be read as rude, many in the room had a newspaper open. *The Echo*, *The Mirror*, *The Racing Times*, even the odd *Socialist Worker*. No one had *The Sun*. Not after how it had been covering the strike. Not after how it had covered Orgreave. You'd never see *The Sun* in Blackmoor again.

Baggot was muttering something about a money-making scheme. Charlie gave him a smile, but then turned his eyes back to the paper. A man a few down on the other side asked the landlord if he could use the phone, for the strike, the landlord obliged. Lifted a beige Bakelite onto the bar. Dial like a clock face. The man put his hands around it and drew it to him. His hands were blue tinged, like most miners – from coal dust in work cuts – two of his fingers were brown from nicotine, the rest pale from vibration damage: drill finger. He put one scarred digit in the dial and drew it round, clicker, clicker, clicker, clicker, it ran, as it wound back. You only needed three numbers for local calls in Blackmoor. Charlie knew the number. Charlie could tell from the clicks alone that the man was dialling the lodge secretary, the local N.U.M. head. Last number was a one. A single clicker, a quick shudder like a knee trembler.

The Imperial's landlord didn't mind calls for the strike. He allowed miner's wives to use his place as a soup kitchen as well, out of hours. And he'd reduced his beer prices as low as he could manage. Businesses that supported the miners would be remembered. And so would those that didn't …

'Another one's gone back in,' the phone user said, slamming the receiver down, 'I've got the name an' all.'

'It's like finding out that someone's been shagging your wife that, like,' Baggot said to Charlie, 'Knowing that a scab bastard has gone back in,' Baggot had a sly smile on his face.

Men downed their pints. Men went outside. Charlie knew where they were going. Charlie knew the anger, but it still didn't sit right. They were off to gather round a house like a lynch mob. Off to put paint over the walls. Off to put the windows in. Maybe even drag a fellow out if they could get him. A scab was a scab. But a scab would like as not have a wife and bairns; he'd not have gone back to work else. A scab was a scab, but a scab was still a man for all that. Charlie knew the anger. But Charlie would have no part in it.

1984

Charlie had been going to Newcastle almost regularly, of late: to support comrades in court. Miners charged with riot. Many had done nothing more than be picked out of the picket line by police, because someone had to be. Pulled out by their hair, for having long hair. Selected by some helmed and shielded Metropolitan copper – or one from Avon and Somerset, Gloucester, Gwent, Kent – who didn't like their face, from what they could make out of it, through the mist of a visor. A pal of Charlie's had tried to stop a shipped in squaddy – no shoulder number, playacting at being police – from smashing his car windscreen. He was beaten on the scene, for trying to save his own property. Beaten on the bonnet of his own Ford Anglia. Beaten again in the back of a van. Then charged with riot. A common law offence from medieval times. Before Orgreave, no one had been charged with riot for sixty years. After Orgreave, they were all charged with riot; whatever the offence, real or imagined, they were charged with riot. Because riot put terror into a man. Riot carried whatever sentence the judge decided. Most miners only got three to five years. Only. Three to five years in prison was plenty, for picketing for your life and your livelihood, protesting for your comrades and your community. Like as not for something you hadn't even done. Three to five years in prison was sufficient. Three to five years could cost you your family. But a judge could give you six or seven years, if he whimmed it; could give you ten years, if the police statements swayed him; riot entitled the judge to give a life sentence, if he so chose. And Home Secretary Leon Brittan had called on judges to do just that. Home Secretary Leon Brittan had called on judges to pass life sentences on strikers convicted of riot. The charge of riot was used, with malice aforethought, to put terror into the miners. Which made Charlie wonder, what made it much different from terrorism?

So Charlie had been going to Newcastle almost regularly, of late: to support comrades in court. But he hadn't been to the Royal Victoria Infirmary since back when Blue was born. But the letter he received was one of those where, when you get it, you just have to do what it says.

Charlie went to go along to the picket line first thing the next morning, to tell them he'd not be there. You didn't want to just not appear. Tempers were hot. Nerves were frayed. Rumours about scabs started easily. Often ended badly. You needed to let the lads know, if you were going to be gone from the line too long. If you were going to be out of town and not on N.U.M. business. But Charlie bumped into that bletherer Baggot on the way, who was going to the line himself. Charlie asked him to pass on the message to the others, which saved a bit of time. Was a bit of luck that.

Geraldine was off at the covered market for something. Something she'd, like as not, not find. So Charlie made himself a Tudor crisp sandwich for the journey, shook the packet of salt on the bread, on the slices of thin white, on the margarine, not on the crisps. Tasted better that way. He didn't say bye to Blue, the boy by then already gone to school.

'He's been after seeing you since he came back,' Bobby's

brother said at the hospital, 'He'd barely called on us in years. Then he came back to us like this.'

Bobby had come home to die. He was bare-chested, because he couldn't stand even for sheet-cotton to be on him. His skin was waxed paper, veins of worms betokened worms on their way. He was still scarred from the accident, well over a decade after, dappled patches of burns on his arms and cut lines under his armpits, where the wire had bit as he was dragged.

'You ever think about the explosion?' he said to Charlie.

He spoke with a rattle to his voice that Charlie had heard before.

'Only through the dark nights. And in the day.'

The Greeks called it cancer because they found crab shapes formed on the dying. There were no crab shapes on Bobby. Just a man who'd got thinner and thinner until there was nothing left of him at all. Eating had gotten too much. Now even moving had gotten too much.

'Doc says he can't prove it, but it could be down to the gas and the dust. It's in my lungs anyway. I've never smoked a single Rothmans in my life. And I've not been back in a mine. But the doc says it couldn't be proved and it would do me no good now if it could. Maybe I've been dying ever since. You should have left us,' Bobby said, 'Should've let us alone to die. I've been no use for anything after. I've pissed my life away; drifting around, not even holding down shite jobs.'

'What did you do with the compo?'

'I spent most of it on booze and women. But I wasted some too,' Bobby cracked a gallows smile.

Charlie put his hand in Bobby's.

'You think there's anything coming?' Bobby said, 'Anything coming after? You think I'm going anywhere after this?'

'I used to. I used to believe it certain as Sunday school. Now I'm not so sure. But I have some hope there is.'

'I hope there's not,' Bobby said, 'Because if there's places to go to, I don't think I can be going to the good one. I'll not be going to heaven. I must be going to the other place, to the under country. Because if Jesus loved us, he wouldn't have tret us like this. I just hope I get to rest.'

Charlie went to see the place that Bobby was going to rest, Bobby's brother had organised it, back in Blackmoor. A man was still digging it. Without other occupation, Charlie asked to help. Felt like it was right. The digger was suspicious. Work was hard to come by, with so many striking miners looking. Plenty of local labourers were feeling the pinch as well: getting undercut by hungry men. Eventually the digger relented, said Charlie could share the work but not a penny of the piece pay.

The digger declared them done before it looked finished, it wasn't deep enough, only reached the height of Charlie's heart, wasn't nearly six feet.

'The miner's union are paying for your friend's burial,' the digger said, 'Says so on the docket, it will be a decent quality casket, they look after their own. You only need dig the full six when the coffin's cheap. Cheap ones rot and collapse, leave a sink hole. The better the coffin, the shallower you can go.'

'Maybes he'd not want to go too far down anyway,' Charlie said.

The digger let Charlie share his bait pail at least. There was plenty, even though the digger's dog got a portion. It was an Alsatian, like the police used, but with mixed eyes, like Blue.

'I always give it a helping. It's not much, is it, for loyalty like that? Split my fingers for my wife fifteen year and she left me without a note. Left me the bairn and the bills mind. Half thought she might have been murdered, until a pal of mine saw her out carousing in Chestly-street. Half wished she had been after.'

There were toadstools at the edge of the graveyard, red and white, like in fairy tales. But gnawed at the edges, insect riddled. Charlie kicked them and they exploded into fragments.

Charlie had arranged a meeting that he knew was going to be hard. Knew was going to be draining. He had to finish something that was not going to be easy to finish. But it needed stopped. He had a drink at the Imperial Hotel first, to nerve himself. Baggot was in there. On the lash as usual. Half gone. Asked Charlie if he wanted to come in on a scheme, could use a front-man on it – for a share of the reward – a local hero would be perfect.

'Deal?' Baggot said, 'Deal?' he was holding out his hand for a shake, though he hadn't even expanded on what his idea was, 'Deal?'

'If it's such a canny plan, why hasn't someone already done it?' Charlie said, 'Anyway, I've got enough on my plate.'

Baggot seemed affronted, swayed his way off, had that sly smile on his face again as he went.

Charlie went home after his meeting. After he'd stopped what wanted stopped. He felt cleansed; but broken. A weight had been lifted, but he was still exhausted. Geraldine didn't even turn when he came in the door. She was staring through the window. Curtains curled in with lace. Charlie came behind and cuddled her. Wrapped his arms around her comfy waist. She seemed to sense something changed. Maybe it was years since he'd acted like that, Charlie didn't remember. Maybe he never had. She turned around to face him. Took his hands. Looked like she was going to cry.

They sat, finger-linked, in the garden, under the shade of the big elm. A cabbage-white twitched by. Folks said it was unlucky to have an elm tree, because if it grew tall enough to cast a shadow the length of a coffin, then a family member would die. But every tree will cast a shadow the length of a coffin, when the sun's low enough in the sky. And every family member will die, given sufficient time. We're all going to die one day, Charlie thought, but every single other day, we have to live with ourselves.

1984

They came for Charlie in the middle of the night. Blue – a twelve-year-old boy, in ill-fitting underpants – woke to the storm drum. Fists pounded the front door, sounding fierce enough to send it in. Full beam car lights blinded through Blue's bedroom window.

'You need to come here now, Charlie,' a silhouette shouted, black and blurred.

More figures clustered around it, haloed by headlights, merging into their own and each other's long cast shadows. Choristers of forests and dark fairy tales, beasts from under the bed.

'Don't go,' Blue whispered to his dad, to himself, but to his dad, with force he hoped sufficient to press it to wherever his dad was.

But his dad did go. Charlie appeared at the front porch, 'What the Hell's going on?' he said, 'I've not gone back to work.'

'That's what they all say.'

'What are you doing here? You're not even a miner.'

'I've got reasons of my own. This is not just because you're a scab: you're worse than that: I've seen the photographs.'

And the word, that word, *photographs*. And the voice that spoke it was the voice of Nick Nickelson's dad. And so Blue knew that this was his fault.

The shadow men grabbed Blue's dad, held him by arms and shoulders.

'Dark crimes merit dark penalties,' Nickelson said, and he produced a Stanley knife from his pocket, held it at Charlie's cheek, 'You'll have heard of a Glasgow Smile?'

And Blue's mam screamed then. Blue had never heard that noise before. Hadn't even known there could be such a noise. It cut through the night and the walls and the idling engine. She shook as she screamed it; she shook and her arms flapped, boneless. A shadow shape slapped her to stop it. And Charlie struggled, tore a hand loose, punched one of them. They grabbed him again, but it was clumsy, and he swung a second time. Another shadow joined the fray and they had him tight, head in a lock, though still Charlie writhed in their grip.

Blue stared about in the gloom of his room, lit jagged by the headlights. Looked for something; something he could do. Saw nothing, thought of nothing, did nothing. And his underpants hung so wide, from his skinny child's frame, that they remained almost dry, while the piss poured onto the bed.

PHASE THE THIRD

'It opens the lungs, washes the countenance, exercises the eyes, and softens down the temper,' said Mr. Bumble. 'So cry away.'

Oliver Twist – Charles Dickens

1984

The Coroner declared it *Death by Misadventure*. The Crown Prosecution decided, that those who might have paid, had paid sufficient. The Family Proceedings Judge said that in the absence of anyone she could deem fit and willing to look after Blue, he must become a ward of court. And through the bewilderment and shame, grief and guilt – submerged under a world where people wore suits and talked above his head – that word *ward* seemed to offer some shred of hope: it reminded Blue of Batman, or rather Robin, because Robin – played by Burt Ward – was always called Batman's ward. That was the only place that Blue had ever heard the word. So that word *ward* seemed to offer some shred of hope. Which is just how hard any hope at all was to find.

The building they drove Blue to was built of old redbrick, with battlement shapes on its grey-tiled roof. It was so vast it was more like a series of interlinked mansions, any one of which could have homed an eccentric Gotham billionaire. But the building was in Darlington and the sign said *St Peter's Approved School for Boys*. The sky was black. Blue's world was turned to ash. Blue scratched at his legs as the car slowed. They were already bleeding. A doctor had said he had developed stress eczema. She'd been kind. She had given him some cream and told him he must try to stop scratching. He hadn't stopped scratching, but he had tried to use the cream.

They said that Blue had 'after trauma disorder,' or something like that, he couldn't remember the exact name. He missed his family, he missed Nick. The hopelessness and loss yawned within him like a well, like a coalmine, black and bottomless, filled with wet. Worse even, the horror in the pit of his stomach was like a black hole: it sucked in everything: even time itself. Blue somehow instinctively sensed that he had to build a shell. He had to find some hardness and retreat within it. They wouldn't let him contact Nick. They said it wouldn't be right. Not even a letter. Not even to say sorry.

They showed him to his room, whitewashed walls, a cork board, a sink, a metal-legged bed, bolted to the floor. He couldn't help wondering if it was a cell, or if there was any difference – beyond the long name – of this place and a prison. The window wasn't barred, but it was grilled.

'Someone will come and get you for dinner,' said the latest in a succession of faceless adult strangers, as he closed the door. Blue figured the man must have meant *tea*, seeing as how dinner time had already been and gone. Blue sat on the furthest edge of the bed and scratched until he bled.

The lad who came to get him was older than Blue, probably fifteen or something. He wore a grey uniform and a shield shaped badge with 'prefect' on it.

'I'm Blue,' Blue said.

'You will be,' the boy said, though with pity, not with malice.

He motioned Blue to follow him and led him through an ensnaring maze of corridors to a big canteen, brim filled with delinquents. Half of them looked like adults. All of them wore the same uniform. All of them but Blue. Which left him feeling even more marked and excluded. More soft, more spindly. And even though he also felt more lonely, he wished to God he was alone.

Whoever resorts to violence has already lost the argument, read a big sign on the wall. It had the feel of a quotation, but it didn't say who said it.

The prefect saw Blue reading it, 'That sounds like it should be true,' the boy said, 'May even be true, looked at the right way. But you don't feel like a winner, when you're picking up your teeth with broken fingers.'

He showed Blue where to get an aged, brown, melamine tray. The one Blue picked up had a crack running its entire length, but it didn't split in half. Something still held it together, some invisible internal strength. The cutlery was bendable tin. The beakers were plastic.

'Given you'll finish up fighting someone soon enough anyway,' the prefect said, 'Probably better for you to choose when and who, that way you can fight someone near your own size. Smaller would be better, but I don't think you're going to find anyone smaller. Keep your eyes peeled for a winnable fight, then start it, get it out the way, that's my advice.'

And, seeming to think that with the gift of this counsel, he had done more than enough prefecting for the day, the boy left Blue alone in the food queue, sunken and shrunken between two lads made of muscle and stubble.

Blue wondered if to be beaten up wouldn't help, at least for a while, mightn't it draw him away from inside hurt? Maybe fists pounding him would remove that fist permanently pressed up against the recess of his ribcage. Would the strange, angry, painful love of someone like the boy who had once bullied him, be better than no love at all? Bereft of parents, denied

Nick, would any connection be better than none, or was the sole form of protection to be found in isolation?

That evening, those boys with friends played cards and snooker and talked. Blue watched TV. Blue stared at the screen, scared to let his eyes wander from it. Trying his hardest to disappear into an old straight-backed, wooden chair, ill-designed for disappearing. Though his lack of uniform marked him as a new arrival, no one spoke to him. Maybe this was from charity. Because Blue felt certain he would collapse into unstoppable tears if he was shown any kindness beyond being ignored. As soon as he was able, Blue returned to his room, to the safety of solitude.

The following day, Blue was called to see the headmaster. The prefect who led him there was different from the one before.

'You're lucky the headmaster isn't Mr Beirne no more,' the prefect said, 'Boys that got called to see Mr Beirne got touched up, and worse. Much worse.'

Blue didn't find the knowledge of his good fortune as reassuring as the prefect seemed to think it should be. An urge of vomit acid rose into the back of his throat.

The current headmaster had those half spectacles, which helped him to look down at paperwork and then up into Blue's eyes.

'You probably won't be with us for too long,' he said, 'You don't really belong here. You're arguably not even Catholic. But they couldn't find you anywhere else for now. They're trying to get you a foster home. And, against the normal order of things, they're trying to locate one a long way away, where late events will not be known. So this will be a temporary sojourn for you. Though it will be temporary for all of us now, as it happens, myself included. This school is to close. Perhaps not before time. The past is past and some things are best kept well buried. There might be a lesson for you in that, lad.'

1985

Blue was now thirteen – a teenager – an age that had once seemed impossibly far off, almost adult. But he didn't feel like a grown man. He felt more like a squishable, shell-less mollusc. Or like a hermit crab, always edible, but most vulnerable in the moment of transferring from one hard-spined home to another. He wasn't sure if the driver who dropped him off was from the approved school, or part of the court system, or just a taxi. Though the journey down to Margate had taken hours, the man had barely spoken. But he muttered 'fucking fairy' when he saw Blue's new foster-carer walking between the pot plants to meet them. And in time, Blue came to realise that he was right.

Blue's foster-carer smelt of Polo mints and brandy. His hair was as fine as cut grass goes after it dries, and he swept it around in such a fashion as if to create the impression that he wasn't bald. It was not a very accomplished impression. Maybe he believed that if he practiced it every day, eventually it would be. Blue's foster-carer had a nose that might have been flattened in a scrap but probably had just come flat, because he didn't look much like a scrapper. Blue's foster-carer wore a shiny black shirt, seemingly singularly designed for highlighting dandruff. His skin all over was very dry and very thin. He had cuts on his neck and his hands, like how the ground can crack in summer, turned so arid it becomes brittle. And he had little white links of spittle at the edges of his mouth, which expanded and contracted when he spoke. Blue's foster-carer had very small eyes, his pupils were like woodworm holes, one of the first things he did was to put drops in them. Blue's foster-carer wore dainty shoes that looked like slippers and he shuffled when he walked, as if it was hard for him to raise his knees.

The driver followed the foster-carer and Blue up to the flat. Carrying the small faux leather suitcase, which had been Blue's mother's and contained Blue's life. There was little left in it of sentimental value. Blue had tried his best to divest himself of anything that might cause weakness. Through force of will and fought back guilt, he had even managed to stuff Mr Cubby – his wonky-nosed bear, his last friend – into a bin.

The driver seemed to sneer at the surroundings, once in the flat. He took a good look around and then lowered one side of his mouth quite visibly.

'Best of luck then,' he said to Blue, 'You're going to need it.'

The foster-carer showed Blue his bedroom, a little box room on the top floor. On shaking legs, as if on a gangplank, Blue entered. With the two of them in the small space, it immediately felt choking and confined. Though it was mostly empty, save for a single bed, and a glass cabinet filled with things that Blue found eerie: carved animals and china heads, miniature clay masks and foreign figurines, a brass Lincoln Imp stood in the centre, hands behind its head, laughing, eyeless. None of the objects might have been individually unnerving, but the effect of them all gathered and displayed together most definitely was.

Nonetheless, Blue asked to go to bed early that night; after an awkward tea of egg and chips, that he had tried to eat, even though he felt sick. He was not so much tired, as utterly overwhelmed. He wanted time in his own head. Space to work through his new world. A place to be alone.

But Blue had not long gone up, when his foster-carer came in, and sat on the end of the bed.

'Do you want the door left open to the light from the corridor?' he asked, 'I used to be scared of the dark when I was a boy. A little of that fear even still lingered, once I became pubescent, like you. Would it help if you knew that I was near, dear boy?'

Blue pulled the duvet up to his chin, both hands upon its rim and shook his head, eyes wide in alarm. The foster-carer patted Blue's leg. A movement that seemed somehow stilted, unnatural.

'Well, I'll leave you to it then shall I, for tonight …'

Blue barely slept. The eyeless eyes of the Lincoln Imp, stared at him, grinning, revelling in Blue's predicament. He felt more trapped here than he had even at the approved school. At least there he had learned a form of reclusive camouflage, which had enabled him to go unsociably unnoticed. In this flat, he felt exposed, defenceless. The bedroom door was behind his head and yet too close. Both out of sight and all too much in mind. He wondered if he should run away. Though the approved school had reinforced the dangers of that – told stories of what might befall boys who tried to live on the streets – those cautionary tales had simultaneously highlighted the possibilities: it had almost seemed like, if you were lucky – and stayed off drugs and glue-sniffing – it might not be so bad. At least you could be on your own. There might be worse things.

Blue stayed in bed in the morning. Afraid to leave the relative safety of his duvet and his room. When he finally gathered the strength to make his way down the stairs, he crept, as silently as he could, though he did not really know why he crept, since surely his foster-carer would be up and Blue had not carried down his coat and case, to run away with.

Blue's foster-carer was sitting in the kitchen. Wearing a striped apron of a sort that Blue had only seen before on butchers.

'I think I've gone about this all wrong, haven't I?' the foster-carer said, 'You're my first charge, you see. Aside from a short residential course, I know no more about all this than you, dear boy. And I suspect that I may have grown a little eccentric; my interpersonal skills are imperfect. But I do know that when people of good will work together, then anything is possible. So I have decided that we shall have profiteroles for breakfast. Now, I have never had profiteroles for breakfast before. And I imagine that you have never had them at all. So I think that it will help. I think it will help both of our brains to decipher that this is a new chapter.'

And Blue discovered that profiteroles were puff-balls of pastry, filled with cream and covered with poured chocolate. Liquid chocolate. They were sweet and sticky and rich and delicious and entirely unsuitable for breakfast. And Blue thought that maybe they did help.

In the afternoon they went to the cinema. The cinema was a building that clearly had once-a-time been grand but was now falling to decay; which, from what Blue had witnessed on the way, seemed to be something of a Margate theme. The film they watched was *E.T. the Extra-Terrestrial*, it was a couple of years old, but Blue hadn't seen it. Blackmoor's picture house had closed down. Blue had only rarely been to the cinema at all. He had only seen *The Jungle Book* and *The Dark Crystal* and *Return of the Jedi*. And he supposed that *E.T. the Extra-Terrestrial* must just have been what was on. He supposed that his foster-carer could not have dictated what the cinema played. Nonetheless, the film seemed to help as well. It was about a boy and an alien – two unrelated creatures, not even from the same planet – but who needed to somehow get along.

So Blue did not run away, that second day. Nor did he the next. And when he still hadn't run away by the end of the week, he had begun to think that he might not. With each passing day, Blue's foster-carer seemed less strange. Or rather, his strangeness grew a little less intimidating, a little more likeable.

When Blue asked about the glass cabinet of objects in his room, his foster-carer said, 'I got them for you. I've been collecting things that I thought a boy might like. Things that I thought that I might have liked as a boy. Do you not like them?'

And Blue said that he liked them all, he liked them a lot. And that he liked the grinning brass devil most especially. In fact, he liked it so much, that he wondered whether it might be better down here, on the mantlepiece. Or even, whether it was so precious that it oughtn't to be kept somewhere safe, locked away.

And Blue's foster-care said that he thought that was an eminently sensible idea. And he put the Lincoln Imp in a drawer, which, though it had no lock, he explained was the last place that any burglar would look.

Blue took to walking the Margate front with his foster-carer, on his 'daily constitutional' and, eventually, the man's shuffling gait became as comforting as the soothing monotony of the waves.

'It might be the womb,' Blue's foster-carer said one time, sensing Blue's calm down by the sea's edge, 'Why we find waves so relaxing: they take us back to whence we never wished to leave, dear boy. Though there is also a theory that we evolved from aquatic apes. See how the waders in the chill water almost brachiate: it is said that the sea's support helped us become bipedal; that nutritious shellfish catalysed larger brains; that babes instinctively hold their breath and that even now we have a layer of blubber, closer to that of sea mammals than our hairy kin among the simians.'

Blue quite often didn't understand all that his foster-carer said. The man made no condescension to the fact that he was talking to a child. But Blue liked that. He liked the fact that he was spoken to as if he was an equal; even if he missed specifics, he generally got the gist. Like with Radio 4, which was the only radio station his foster-carer could abide. Or abide some of, at least: the fastest Blue would ever see him move was towards the off-switch at the blast that marked the start of *The Archer's* theme.

They never watched the football. Blue's foster-carer had a loathing for football above all sports and he had, at best, a disdainful ambivalence towards the rest. And yet he had an encyclopaedic knowledge of them. If he chose to, he could tell Blue all of the goal scorers of every England game since, and of course including, 1966. He could equally list the direct line of heavyweight champions of the world – 'Sullivan beaten by Corbett, Corbett beaten by Fitzsimmons, Fitzsimmons beaten by Jeffries …' all the way down to Thomas Pinklon, the current champion. He could reel them off like a royal succession. And he could do the same with royal succession …

Yet he was never above indulging Blue's kid's questions; should Blue wonder which beach hut he preferred, for example – invariably a sensible plain wood, as opposed to Blue's preference for huts garish and striped – or why the lady singing karaoke hadn't picked a song she knew, 'Because I don't believe she knows any songs, dear boy, this is her virginal interaction with the world of verse.'

While his foster-carer shuffled along in his suede slip-ons, Blue would walk atop the wall, astride the concrete line between boulevard and beach, arms wide into the wind, gulping the salt air. Watching the world of the front: the cartoonish hurry of the little dicky wader birds and the coal-oil cormorants, which sat the breaker rocks of the surf line, silhouettes like closed umbrellas; the ghosts of distant ferries and tankers almost invisible against the sky; the scratchings on the sand in the arcane language of toddlers as yet strangers to school, among gossamer films of jellyfish and ocean-weary plastic bags. Blue and his foster-carer patrolled the shore line together, a platoon of two, as unlikely and diligent and hapless as *Dad's Army*.

And Blue's foster-carer was called Huxley. And Huxley saved Blue's life.

Huxley lived on the top two floors of a thin Georgian townhouse – built in the heyday of Margate's ever since descending splendour – now ex-guest-house, subdivided into flats. There were only four floors. On the bottom, lived a Chinese couple who kept to themselves, aside from the smells of cooking, which permeated the hall, lingering with the damp junk mail and the bike of the man from the middle floor; who Huxley said was 'not all there', but was no bother and seemed pleasant, if you passed him on the stairs.

From the outside, one vertical line of windows over the entrance door had been bricked up. There was a tangled mess of piping and wiring across the frontage, like plumbing and electricity had been an afterthought. The paint was peeling and Huxley said that the building's owner wasn't willing to pay to have it redone, so it was destined to degrade further. The bottom two flats each had a bay window, like the fancier terraces in Blackmoor, only stacked. But Huxley's place was the biggest and must have had the best views. From the top-floor front-room – the drawing room, Huxley called it – you could look right out onto the sea and the beach and such wide skies as can only be found by the seaside. The beach was tan and sandy, like a beach from a story book, not a trace of colliery waste. When the tide was out, the flatness of the beach and the sea ran into a child's pencil line horizon, broken only by the stranded boats at the harbour arm.

The first thing that struck Blue, every time he went up the communal stairs and into Huxley's flat, was the books. The hall behind the front door was floor-to-ceiling book shelves and even they could not contain the volumes, because books were piled in front and at the edges of the doors, which led to rooms similarly filled with tomes. And the books were not only stuffed with the same kinds of dry facts as were inside Huxley himself: in Huxley's domain of dusty chronicles, there were also hobbits and borribles, castles and cannibal kings, piglets and donkeys and heroes of Norse and Thrace. And books became a sanctuary, words a rosary. The smell of paper became the smell of safety. As did the smell of Polo mints with brandy.

And so, though it took time, Blue came to realise that the driver had been right: maybe Huxley was some sort of fairy: because he was kind and he was bright and he knew how to weave protection spells.

1987

Every weekend, they would leave Margate – Blue and Huxley – invariably for another seaside town. They let the train take the strain – like the adverts said – leaving Huxley's funny little car. The ride to London was free. At least the way they used the service it was: first departure of a Saturday, via the rear platform gate. And from that hub they could travel anywhere.

Brighton was Huxley's favourite, though he was careful not to go there too regularly.

'I hunt as the Apache did, dear boy,' he would say, 'Choosing a different trail each day, so as not to exhaust my prey.'

By the time he was fifteen, Brighton had become Blue's favourite too. With the crowds and the cosmopolitan shops and the Indian elegance of the Royal Pavilion. And the sweet stench of marijuana in the pavilion gardens, drifting from the lips and fingers of older teenagers; impossibly, untouchably cool; just to sit nearly near them would have been sufficient for Blue, even if none of them were Nick.

The scent of money wafted on the wind in Brighton too. It could almost have been Margate's sibling, but so thoroughly estranged as to be a stranger. Separated at birth, brought up in a higher class, like the twins in that show *Blood Brothers* that Huxley had taken him to.

And the pier, it seemed like every seaside town they visited had a pier, even Margate had its harbour arm promontory.

But Brighton's Palace Pier was the pier for all piers to be graded against, and all would be found wanting, but need not be blamed for that. Because the Brighton pier was a ride into the sky, so high up that you feared to stare too long through the gaps in the slats. The size of a football pitch, built on oil rig stilts, it ended by opening out onto a funfair of rides – dodgems and helter-skelter and a carousel with gaudy horses. And from there, where the pier widened out into a bulb, you could look back through wrought iron railings – past the tarot readings and tattoos and the seagulls thick as flies – at the guest houses and the town houses which were also looking back at you.

A sign on the dodgems read *No deliberate bumping*, which struck Blue as extraordinary, given that was a dodgem's very reason for existing.

'Maybe it's a metaphor, dear boy,' Huxley said, 'Or a rule of conduct for life: drive fast, be happy, but do try and bash others as little as you can.'

Normally Huxley left Blue to his own devices, once they had arrived in Brighton; or wherever else their day trip happened to be. They would arrange a time and a place to meet, with a sensible second time, in case of unforeseeable circumstances, which had never been needed, and then Huxley would disappear to what he called, his 'day job'. It was an appropriate term, since he worked only the one day each week. In Blue's eyes, Huxley's day job was as a member of royalty. He might merit such a rank in any event – clever as Solomon, kind like Princess Di – but Huxley was also the undisputed, undefeated, unacknowledged, King of quiz machines.

Huxley's measureless memory extended to every pub and bar and hotel that possessed a pay-out quiz machine, in every

English seaside resort. And he knew just how often to clean out a town, without getting mugged, banned or beaten up. He would day trip with a sturdy Millets rucksack, to be gradually filled with gold nuggets and fifty pence pieces, and his TSB paying-in-book, with which to periodically dispose of his hoard. Huxley was not a greedy man, one day's work a week, along with whatever he got for fostering Blue, seemed to suffice, to live a full life, not too frugally. To take Blue to McDonald's and museums and the odd matinee musical. Saturdays at the seaside were invariably so busy that the machines would be bursting and the landlords distracted, and Huxley could vanish easily into the crowds.

Occasionally, Huxley would let Blue watch him, which was a sight to behold: Huxley hitting right answers almost faster than the questions appeared; he might have been playing by sense of smell, like that deaf, dumb and blind kid on the pinball. But generally, Huxley preferred to work alone, which was okay by Blue, who would spend those days becoming increasingly familiar with strange towns and their arcades. Growing old enough, by then, to feel the painful beauty of the clutches of young European tourists. Dressed differently and the same.

Huxley would give Blue spending money at the start of each Saturday. Enough. But not enough to get in trouble. Blue would change most of it for two pence pieces and play the coin shoves. Passing time by eying every machine first. Trying to work out, while others played, just how close each edge clump of coins was to the drop. Wondering if he could one day become good enough to work alongside Huxley, to start filling his own backpack with coins, but invariably, despite many wins, his tuppences would ultimately dwindle then disappear. The last one lingering upon a precipice which should not bear its weight; yet did.

The arcades would scatter a smatter of more expensive trinkets over the two pences behind the glass screens. Things to add a bit of colour and a bit of allure, getting gradually pushed towards the drop zone by the coins arriving behind. Probably they were reset to the back each morning. But Blue had, in any event, already worked out that the heavier the goods, the more holding pressure they exerted on the coins. A boxed Sony Walkman might be enticing, but you would never win it, so it was better to go for something light, even if it wasn't really what you wanted. Huxley said that was a metaphor for life too – Huxley said everything was a metaphor for life – *Don't let the perfect be the enemy of the good*, he said. Huxley was not exactly an ambitious man. Sometimes Blue thought of himself as orphaned Mowgli and Huxley as Baloo, the two of them, alone together, against the world, extracting just the bare necessities from life.

One time, on Brighton pier, a tarot reader stopped Blue as he walked by.

'I'll read you for free,' she said, 'You've a strange aura. I've never seen the like. It's as if you're two people. As if you're carrying a close relative – a sibling or a parent – on your shoulders.'

But Blue was too scared to. Too scared to go into her cloth-draped shed, made to look like a gypsy trailer, too scared to hear what she would have said. He tried to pull his arm away, from where her hand was upon it, filled with rings and wristlets and wrinkled, more wrinkled than her face, like they belonged to different souls.

'I'm late,' Blue said, 'I have to be off,' and in truth, his meet with Huxley was soon.

'What you have, the thing you're struggling under, it's too heavy for a boy like you, the size of you. You need to cast it away before it drags you down beneath. Take this, take this,' she spoke urgently, and she made him grasp a little dark cloth bag, which felt like it held pebbles, 'Throw it from the pier,' she said, 'Think of the burden you need to lose, push it in with your mind, then cast it into the sea and try never to think of it again.'

Blue took the bag and passed through the crowds and the rubber thumps of whack-a-moles to the other side of the pier. He tried to think of all the things he longed never to think of again, he tried to force them into a little velvet sack. And when he thought he had stuffed in all that such a small bag could swallow, he threw it away from him, as far as he could. A seagull lunged for the sack, but missed, and it dropped inaudibly into the sea, near to a glove floating upright, like it was reaching up from the depths, and a BHS bag.

Huxley found him there, still staring out at a sea ruddy beneath clouds, colour of an old wound healed.

'See, Homer was not so mad,' Huxley said, gesturing.

'Mad for what?'

'For saying that the sea could be *wine dark*. Some thought him quite mad for it, dear boy. But I should say that seas occasionally are vinaceous. Then again, they had no word for blue, the ancient Greeks, did you know that? A peculiar people, to have no word for you.'

And Huxley put his arm around Blue, which was hard for Huxley; Blue knew that he did not find such actions easy, which made them all the more rare and special. Blue wanted Huxley to hold him, to hug him, to tell him it was all going to be all right. But he knew the arm would have to do.

'The Greek philosophers thought that women were strange leaky creatures,' Huxley said, 'Not quite the like of men. Not the real equal of men. And Aristotle believed the brain's purpose was for cooling the blood. The ancient Greeks were so often wrong. Right about so much, but still so often wrong. Rather like Freud, I suppose, it is surprising, marvellous even, given the fragile evidential base they had to work upon – not that they were so often wrong – but that they were ever right at all.'

And Huxley pulled from his pocket, condoms, in a cardboard packet, the size of candy cigarettes. Blue knew what they were, from the government information leaflet that Huxley had deliberately left to linger in the bathroom, for so many months that it had become moisture bloated.

'I think, henceforth, you should carry one of these with you, dear boy. I'll leave more at the flat, I won't count them. You are almost preternaturally attractive. Or at least you are going to be, when you fully bloom. Sadly, I'm afraid, you are going to come of age in a time of plague. The rules have changed. You must be careful. With great power comes great responsibility. Use it wisely. But do use it, God knows it will fade soon enough.'

'You told me God was dead,' Blue said.

'Yes, He's dead. Him and half my other friends besides, dear boy, we are living through act two of a tragedy.

1988

A few times each year they would go and see Blue's mother. Blue longed for and loathed the visits. They were hard on him before and after. Though there had been kindness and a period of counselling, people who had tried to help, Blue had never managed to process all that had occurred. He hadn't even been able to let the words emerge. It was like they were interred. Going to see his mother brought back a dead world. And it was hard.

The visits were not so difficult for Blue's mother. Because she no longer recognised her son. She barely knew that a person was present at all. She wasn't really there, inside the form that was still her. She was a Geraldine-shaped creature, but not Geraldine.

The doctors called it 'early onset dementia', but Blue knew what had brought its onset. Blue knew what had called it forth. Blue knew that he had called it forth. And so confronting it was hard.

They would travel there in Huxley's car. Huxley drove a three-wheeler, a little Trojan 200 bubble car. You got in from the front, which felt like you were clambering into an egg. It was a pleasurable confinement on short trips. Blue liked to be snug in there, side by side with Huxley on the tartan seats. But it was a long journey to visit his mother.

Lorries would overtake them on the motorway, the slipstream leaving Huxley wrestling to keep the Trojan in a straight line. Wind whistled through gaps, where the seals had gone in places that normal cars wouldn't even have places. They never made good time. And still, when they neared their destination, Blue willed the journey not to be over.

It was mostly very old ladies in the home, Geraldine was by far the youngest. Some were almost a hundred. Huxley would talk to the others, while Blue was taken by a carer to a private room to be with his mother. And on the ride home, Huxley would try to distract Blue with tales gleaned from the staff and patients. Huxley was not a natural at distraction.

'Did you know that Mavis was only put in a home in the first place because she had a child out of wedlock, imagine it. When she was probably just a girl, sent to a mental hospital because of that. Confined by her own family. What ghastly times. Inevitably she was driven mad by the experience, until, eventually, I suppose, she actually belonged there. A self-fulfilling prophecy.'

The home that Blue's mother had been put in was just one building of a large estate. Which had tennis courts and football fields – utterly unused – and a canteen that Huxley could not bear to eat in. Some of the abler patients helped out with the cooking and serving. And Huxley said that while that was all very admirable and socially useful, you might just as well lick the flush-handle of a public toilet as eat there and expect not to come away without some kind of communicable disease. After their first visit, Huxley ensured they brought with them sufficient stocks of sandwiches for lunch and tea, as well as plenty of pennies for the patients who cadged for cigarettes, and small change, to spend on cigarettes. Cigarettes were sold singly, at fifteen pence a pop, which was more expensive than at the newsagents next to Blue's school; but then, the mental health facility had a captive market, while the newsagent was investing in the future.

Though he still missed Nick, Blue had friends of a sort at school. But because he joined late and wasn't from the area, the strongest alliances had already been formed. Because he was a loner, he was often alone. Because he had difficulties with closeness, they weren't close friends. Though Blue had tried his hardest to lose his accent, it was still a little quaint and, in truth, his friends were more like acquaintances.

Blue was an awkward teenager. Many or most teenagers are awkward to a degree, but some are more awkward than others, and Blue was more awkward than them. Though undeniably handsome – or more probably 'pretty' – even by sixteen, he was skinny and self-conscious. He struggled to take part in the coming-of-age rituals. And because he spent every weekend roaming seaside towns with Huxley, he was absent for most of them anyway.

Events such as Rich Dugdale's party, word of which had soared like the gulls until hundreds turned up to the suburban semi that Rich's parents had unwisely left him in charge of while they went to Malaga for the week; where a frightened Rich Dugdale was finally forced to shelter with a neighbour and call the police on himself, but which everyone else claimed was the best night ever.

Though Blue daily missed his dad, missed his mam – missed his mam how she once was – missed Nick, Blue found some form of contentment with Huxley, just the two of them; Blue didn't need anyone else, not in Margate. And so Blue had never become part of a tribe. He had never found a niche with the skaters, ravers, casuals or hippies, not even with the *Dungeons & Dragons* geeks. He never knew what music he was into, what style to adopt. In truth, he barely listened to music at all, in part because Huxley didn't. The only music they heard was the odd theatre production and the *Desert Island Discs* show on the radio. Though Huxley often bought The N.M.E. that was purely for revision and ammunition. But more than this, Blue had a sense almost that music was his enemy. Music made him feel too deeply. It was harder for him to remain restrained, within himself, when music was without. And so he instinctively avoided it. Blue didn't really know whether he preferred George Michael or Vanessa Paradis. But he knew he didn't like Morrissey: he'd had enough misery already. Blue's main role model was Huxley, and so Blue fashioned his own, marginally more modern version, of a quintessentially English, buttoned-up, emotional repression. A stiff upper lip, with which to splint a lower one that might otherwise be in frequent tremble.

Patients in the block that Geraldine was in were either not allowed or not able, to roam the larger site. The ladies spent their days, wilting like the flowers, in an amphitheatre arc around a large television, which no more than a quarter of them ever seemed to be watching. Some were in wheelchairs or on gurneys, but mostly they sat on the same kind of chairs as staff and visitors: wooden with wipeable vinyl cushions. The room smelt of urine and disinfectant. The nurses tried to get the residents up from time to time, to avoid sores. Even when held at either side, they teetered on their tiny feet, backs arched like scared cats.

The one visit when Blue's mam had a moment of lucidity, she appeared to be talking about the dog she'd had as a child. It seemed a strange thing for her to have retained, when all else had gone.

'He strayed, but he came back at the finish,' she said, 'He'd strayed, but he came home to me. And I thought then that it would all be all right. I didn't know he'd only come back for to die.'

When he learned, later that year, that his mother had died, Blue discovered that he was relieved. He was relieved that chapter of his life was finally finished. He was relieved he would never need to go back to the nursing home again. He was relieved that he would no more have to see his mother in such a degraded, atrophied state of being. And he hated himself for feeling relieved. He despised himself. But it was nonetheless a relief.

Blue had never managed to process all that had occurred. He hadn't even been able to let the words emerge. It was as if they were interred. Likewise, it was a fight for him to release to Huxley his greatest fear.

'I'm sixteen now,' he eventually said, one day, upon the Margate front, whispering it into the same wind that kept his eyes dry, 'Soon they're going to stop paying you to look after me. What am I going to do? Where am I going to go?'

'They already have stopped paying, dear boy, not long after your birthday, they haven't been paying for months. As for where you're going to go and what you're going to do: you will stay in our home for as long as you wish and I'll help you to do in life whatever you desire.'

'You mean you'll be there for me forever?' Blue's voice broke and croaked.

'I can't promise forever,' Huxley said, 'How about, I'll be there for just as long as you need me?'

Blue hugged Huxley, which made Huxley visibly uncomfortable, which made Blue hug him all the harder.

And Blue said, 'Deal.'

1989

Blue should have been in the first school year to take the new GCSE exams that replaced O-Levels, but with everything that had happened and the move to Margate, he had been kept back in his new school, so he took them the year after, when he was seventeen. It didn't seem to help a whole lot. Thanks perhaps to all his reading, he did well in both the Englishes, but his grades descended rapidly after history and geography. Huxley suggested he hold off on doing A-Levels until he was ready. As an autodidact, Huxley was not best impressed by exam systems anyway.

Huxley got Blue a job in a sweet shop on the front, The Fudge Factory. It belonged to one of Huxley's friends. There were two plaster cherubs outside – one either edge of the entrance – baring it all, butt naked, and looking very pleased with themselves about it. Above one cherub, a sign read: 'Watch Your Step'. While above his neighbour, in similar print, was: 'Only seven children allowed inside at one time'. That rule was almost never enforced though. The owner said to let it ride. If you wanted to compete with the Woolworth's pick-and-mix then a small amount of penny sweet theft had to be accepted as a business expense. The owner was of a similar age to Huxley, and always sported a cravat, which reminded Blue of how the old retired miners used to wear white silk scarves on Sundays. It was like a uniform for them, a way of recognising their fellows. Though they all knew who each other were anyway.

Huxley's friends were more of an assortment, or a selection box perhaps. As Blue had grown older, Huxley had started taking him along to occasional gatherings and parties. A few times over the years, Huxley had even hosted soirees of his own, at the flat. He didn't serve red wine, though his beige sofas were both ancient and scotch-guarded and the evenings were hardly raucous affairs. The men who came – and they were almost invariably, exclusively men – were from every walk of life: plumbers and professors, postmen and property tycoons. They only really had the one thing in common, yet they all seemed to rub along. It was a breaking of divides that Blue hadn't witnessed anywhere else.

Margaret Thatcher, coal mine closer, a decade in and still Prime Minister, had said that there was no such thing as society. And Margate was a nest of competitive patriotism and petty one-upmanship: shared semi-detached walls, precision half-painted; Union Jack flags; washed wheelie bins; Round Table stickers and Royal Doulton figures. Yet among Huxley's friends, camaraderie and equality thrived.

When Huxley accidentally discovered Blue's stash of *Razzles,* Blue felt embarrassed. It was not so much because of the ferine nudity and the intrusiveness of the reader's wives, but because he felt like Huxley might have preferred it had he preferred pictures of men.

But Huxley said it was good, 'The world is kinder to your kind,' he said, 'If that's what kind you are. There are many ways of being. It need not be binary. It was all-conquering Christianity that made it thus. Persecution forces people to pick a side. I should say that sexuality is most likely a spectrum, with barbell clusters at either end, no doubt, but with a variety near infinite; individual idiosyncrasies as numberless as the stars. That mystical misogynist Saint Paul has a lot to answer for … The Greeks,' Huxley said, 'The ancient Greeks, were wrong about so much, but still so often right. They knew no such thing as sin, and everything had its place, in their sight.'

Working in the sweetshop was mind numbingly dull over quiet periods, like staring at a TV screen waiting for *Ceefax* to refresh. But it had its perks: Blue got to take home any chocolate that had passed its sell-by date. When he did, Blue tried to get Huxley to eat it. Because Blue had an uneasy sense that Huxley was rapidly losing weight.

Sometimes Huxley would meet Blue on his lunch break. They would sit, eating sandwiches that Huxley had made, on the boulder sea-break walls – cockled and polypped and mollusked – watching orca fin yacht sails on the horizon line; watching bath sponge lumps of salt spume tumbleweed along the beach; watching barefoot children cross the hobble zone of pebble, before the heel yield of sand. Sometimes Huxley and Blue would talk, but often they would not talk, in the way that two people entirely comfortable in each other's company can be silent and still at ease.

But one time, while Blue was staring at the fleshless, dried husk of a crab, an exoskeleton, like a suit of Star Wars armour, abandoned after battle, Huxley said to him:

'Do you remember when Princess Diana held that man's hand?'

It was Huxley's way of commencing a hard conversation.

And afterwards, Blue was given the afternoon off, because he was incapable of working.

One day that summer, the Girl Guides came to the door. And Huxley bought all of their cakes, over a hundred pounds worth. But he only took a couple each for himself and Blue. He told the girls to gift the rest away. He told them to walk around Margate and hand them to people who looked old and people who looked sad and people who looked lonely. But to tell those people that the buyer had said to give them to the beautiful and the happy.

When the Jehovah's Witnesses called, Huxley sat them down and made them cups of tea and heard them out. Only when they were entirely done, did he gently, politely, explain why he did not believe in God or in life after death. But he shook their hands and wished them the very best.

When Laurence Olivier died, that July, Huxley took it badly, as if he'd lost a close friend or a relative. Huxley was inconsolable. He watched the video of Olivier's *King Lear* over and over and over. In the drawing room. During the day. With the curtains closed. Crying into his brandy. Shouting 'Stupid old man,' at the TV screen, periodically.

'You should have stayed in control,' he sobbed, 'You should have stayed in control. You asked them what love was worth: nothing, love is worth nothing. Nothing but pain.'

Vomiting and sweating.

Glossy faced, ghost pale, milk pale, milk thin liquid on the floor.

Vomiting and sweating.

Blue mopping. Blue mopping brows. Blue mopping floors.

Vomiting and sweating.

Blue stripping beds. Blue washing sheets.

Vomiting and sweating.

Scared and not scared.

Vomiting and sweating.

Contamination under his finger nails.

Vomiting and sweating.

He knew this sickness could not harm him.

Vomiting and sweating.

Knew it but still was timid before it.

Vomiting and sweating.

Felt the dread primitive fear of it.

Vomiting and sweating.

A flesh-crept sense of infection that lingered beneath fact. Beneath anguish. Beneath duty.

Vomiting and sweating.

Beneath even love.

Vomiting and sweating.

A primordial horror of spread that knowledge could not wholly eradicate.

Vomiting and sweating.

Blue worked through those irrational fears.

Vomiting and sweating.

Blue knew they were not true

Vomiting and sweating.

Blue held them under, until they drowned.

Vomiting and sweating.

Dungeoned them down in Davy Jones' Locker.

Vomiting and sweating.

With the rest.

When Huxley finally had to go into hospital, they wouldn't let Blue see him.

'I'm sorry, but it's strictly direct family, those are the rules.'

'I am family.'

'Not on paper you're not.'

'He's the only family I've got.'

'I'm very sorry, but there's nothing I can do.'

'They let Diana in though, didn't they? I bet you'd let her in and all.'

Blue could barely suppress his fury. Rage slashed at his stomach. But he needed to keep the nurse onside, so Blue had to suck it in, suck it up, tasting the anger that afflicts foreigners and speechless simpletons: people trapped away from what they want to say; for whom words are inaccessible. Blue could only stiffen his muscles in tremble and walk away while he still had some custody of himself. He snapped and then stamped into shards, his newly bought sunglasses. He groaned from a deep he didn't know could make sound, while he pounded a tree in the grounds. He punched until his fists dripped blood on the grass.

One of Huxley's friends worked at the special unit and pulled some strings, Blue was eventually allowed in. By then his hands were healing. But the lumps and bumps on Huxley's face had got worse. And he had grown so pale, without his daily walk along the sea front. They had shaved his wisps of hair off, which made him look even thinner than he was. And he was already so thin that it tore at Blue's heart.

'Don't be afraid,' Huxley said, 'I'm not. I've made my peace.

I'm full of sorrow to be leaving you, but I'm not afraid. Near enough everyone is dead. We, the living, are just a momentary statistical anomaly.'

Blue held Huxley's hand, but didn't cry; he had nothing left, like Lady Di.

1990

Blue was still wearing his black bomber jacket, black Converse All Stars and black 501s. They were probably more suitable now – for what he had to do – than they had been at the funeral. But Blue had no suit and he knew Huxley would not have minded his attire. Huxley would not have minded that.

Blue walked at a half-sunk slouch; fists buried in his bomber pockets; right-hand rolling tight the order of service. He passed a guesthouse with a sign that read *Now taking bookings for Christmas*. The sign was screwed in place. It never came down. Presumably the guesthouse was no longer ever full at Christmas. On a wall next to it, someone had spray-painted: *I love you because we hate the same things*.

The phone-box outside Dreamland had the number for the Samaritans up in it. But it also had its handset ripped off. It was lying on the floor among the tinsel crystals of glass from its smashed-out panels. But it was too late for that anyway. Blue didn't want to talk to the Samaritans. Blue didn't want to talk to anyone ever again.

Dreamland had only just been re-christened; it had always been the *Bembom Brothers White Knuckle Theme Park*, since Blue had known it. Aside from the name, not much else had changed: the park was never busy now, outside of big weekends. Families didn't come to Margate for weeklong holidays anymore, only for occasional daytrips. With less money being spent, the town became ever more rundown; the more rundown the town grew, the less money got spent. The place was dying on its feet, appropriately enough.

Blue slunk around to the back of the Dreamland site. It was closed, lights off, dreams on hold. No screeches of kids, not even of seagulls. There was just enough light left in the sky to make out the brown bricks of the Dreamland buildings and the jagged, grey, brutalist tower block behind it.

Blue made his approach part concealed, tight beside the rear of Beacon Bingo. Ducts blew out a flow of sweated, fetid air from inside. He found a section of Dreamland fencing, more in shadow even than the rest. He would not be seen, dressed all in black, the colour of coal and funerals and trespass. The fence was woven diamonds of wire. It bit into Blue's fingers and had enough sway in it that it leant outwards under his weight, making it even harder to climb, but at least the toes of his All Stars were narrow enough to just about squeeze into the gaps.

He paused a moment astride the top, hands folding over the edge of wire, looking out over the silent, static rides, as if he was choosing which one he would take. Though his mind was already made up on that. His jacket ripped, as he dropped down; caught on one of the finishing ends of wire. A sheep's wool strand of polyester insulation still dangled there. But it was just a tear in the sleeve and Blue wasn't going to need the jacket anymore anyway.

Blue hunkered down in the darkness at the bottom of the fence. He was aware that there must be security guards, watchful against the possibility of drunks breaking in. Can you be drunk on grief? Blue no longer felt like that anyway. He felt clear headed. He was taking back control.

Blue crept in crouched, commando bursts, from one patch of gloom to the next. Pausing a few moments, before moving on again. The bright paint of the rides was grey and black. Clown faces, animal faces, were all dark masks. Once or twice, Blue's own mask slipped, his face crumpled, as if he was about to let emotion overcome him, but he set his jaw straight and regained composure. *As flies to wanton boys, are we to the gods*. That's what Huxley's beloved King Lear said. Well fuck them, fuck the gods, fuck the world. Blue was going to take back control.

Blue reached the bottom of the big wheel. The passenger seats were housed in round cups. He knew they were really red, but they looked brown in the darkness. They looked like the wicker shopping basket that his mam used to take to the covered market. They rose into the air, suspended, motionless on the Ferris wheel. A hundred feet, a hundred and fifty, two hundred, it was hard to judge. But Blue judged it high enough.

The barrier that surrounded the ride was barely waist height. Blue vaulted it in one and then ducked down into dimness again. He could see that there were ladders built on to two of the four steep-sloped supports, which ran like the upturned forks of a bike all the way to the central hub of the big wheel. That part would be easy; easy enough, anyway. But the ladders didn't begin for fifteen feet or so from the ground. A deliberate gap to prevent the park clientele scrambling on them. The maintenance staff must have had portable ladders to bridge the space, but Blue had no such luxury. He flattened himself onto the wide metal of the fork. With his fingers and the arches of his feet pressed onto the squared corners, he could just about keep enough friction not to slide down. But moving up was a different matter. Several times he slipped to the bottom again. Even when he had perfected his technique, it was inch by inch, sliding one limb only, each in their turn, just barely above where it had been. He was sweating in his bomber jacket by the time he was within striking distance of the bottom rung of the ladder. But still he went on, edged just a little closer, aware that the act of sending out a hand to grab would most certainly be enough to undo the precarious grip of the rest of his body. He would only have one chance, so he waited until his fingers were almost upon that bottom rung and even then, he paused, to run through what he would do, to visualise precisely what his action needed to be, to get this done.

Progress was faster once he was on the salt-scabbed steel rungs. The ladder was not even as steep as the angle that the window cleaner used to set his one at, to do Huxley's top floor flat; though higher and more exposed. Blue was not afraid of falling anyway. Falling was rather the point. But he didn't want to fall too soon. He didn't want to break a leg and be found by security staff, to be at the mercy of policies and prosecutions and hospitals. To be once more under the domination of a world beyond his understanding. He didn't want to be pitied, he didn't want to be imprisoned in a system or institutionalised. He just wanted it all to end. He wanted to get this done. He wanted to take back control.

His arms were aching, by the time he reached the Ferris wheel's hub. But there was a gantry there, where he could rest. Blue looked out over Margate. He could see the front, where Huxley and him had walked together a thousand times. Waves swept either edge of the liminal concrete: the sea on one side and wind-shifting long grass on the other. Blue could see his past, out there. But he could see no future. Near the Beacon Bingo, was a pigeon fancier's roof garden; dilapidated DIY aviaries, lit up with rows of suspended bulbs. And Blue could just make out white birds, perched on the railings, eager to be back into their home. Blue had no home. Blue had no one. Huxley had promised to be there for him, for as long as he needed. But Huxley was a liar. Huxley had let him down. For what? From what? For lust. For a few enjoining moments of enjoyment. Huxley had been a fool. And now everything was ruined. Blue's life was in tatters of agony.

Even on the gantry, at the wheel's hub, Blue was not sure the drop would kill him. It looked to be maybe sixty feet, eighty feet at most. He didn't know how high you had to be, to be sure, but it didn't look high enough. He imagined being in a hospital, fed through a straw, breathing through a tube, trapped in with his thoughts for the rest of his days; worse even than his mother had been: at least she'd had the kindness of madness. Maybe she had the right idea: that was the best way to live: to separate yourself so thoroughly from the world that its anguish couldn't reach you. But no, Blue thought, better still not to live at all.

So he continued climbing. First, he had to clamber up from one spoke to the next, near the hub, where they were close together. Until he reached that spoke, which he judged to be as steep as he could ascend on. Then he pulled himself along it. The spoke poles were in matched pairs, with frequent cross bars of support between the two, so he was able to place one arm and one leg on the bars, to provide momentum and to prevent himself from toppling upside down. He couldn't help a feeling of grim pride, in fact, at all he had achieved in getting this far. It was not everyone who would have had the guts and ingenuity for this, he thought. Perhaps there would be a grudging respect from kids he had once known at the Margate school. All of them were eighteen or more now, half of them had moved on. He doubted anyone would cry for him. Maybe a girl or two would squeeze out a tear at the funeral; as long as someone publicised it, so they knew it was happening. But who would even organise it? He imagined himself with a pauper's funeral, paid for by the state, like something out of Dickens. It was like this: not in a passionate way, but in a cold, despairing way, that he had first begun to dwell upon suicide. It was not that Huxley's funeral had sent Blue over the edge; it was that he had thought it proper to wait until after the funeral. And now, with every slide, with every push from a cross bar, he was finally approaching the terminus.

At the end of the spoke pole, a carriage for passengers to ride in was suspended. And if he stood on the bar from which it hung, Blue could just reach the rim of the basket above. It was a risky manoeuvre, because his muscle strength was expiring. But he had nothing to lose, and he wanted the feeling of satisfaction from being at the very top to be the final thing he ever felt. With his Converses scraping and squeaking against the metal for a purchase that wasn't there, panting, aching, he was just barely able to haul himself inside. He rested there, to get some energy back, on the bench within. He would have to repeat this, five more times, to be at the zenith.

Each time was harder than the last. Not only because Blue was increasingly exhausted, but because the carriages swung outwards from one another as they neared the top, so they were further and further from the suspension bar that he had to climb from. When he was at the penultimate basket, Blue was almost at the summit anyway, the carriage he was in and the next were not far off parallel. But something inside him knew that it would not do. He had to make it to the very top.

He would have to jump the space between the two.

Once he had clambered onto the suspension bar, he was actually higher than the basket of the final carriage. But still, it would not do, it was not the true summit. So he stood up on the bar, with nothing to hold on to now. No carriage above him. Balanced against the black sky gusts, Blue lowered and widened his arms like a goalkeeper. He pressed his toes down onto the metal, as if in test. He bent at the knees and tried to feel what force was still left in his thighs.

And then he leapt.

A hundred and some feet from the concrete ground. A scaffolding mess of bars and joists to mangle from on the fall down. Against the dark and death. Blue leapt.

The thud into the side of the basket instantly winded him. Smashed all the air from him. But he had one elbow over the safety bars. It held him long enough for his other hand to grab hold. He hauled himself over with his final embers of energy, with no breath left. But adrenaline coursed through him, of a sort and a force that he had never known. And as oxygen returned to his lungs, he shouted, *Blue*, *Blue*, *Blue*, into the night, creating his own echo, *Fuck You*, *Fuck You*, *Fuck You*. And he stared down at the depth he had intended to fling himself to, but he felt suddenly too alive for that. He had never felt so alive in his life. He sat down on the seat and began to laugh. He was not going to kill himself, fuck that.

But he still had to get down. The top of the mountain is merely the halfway point. Only Blue didn't have the strength left to climb back. He knew he didn't have the strength left for that. He had no strength left at all. But he realised, with a smile, that he could just sit it out. Wait for morning. When his carriage came down, he would get out and walk off, not say a word. And if they protested, he would say he'd been trapped up there all night, from the day before, and threaten litigation. He actually laughed to himself at the thought of how he would show them. Fuck them. Fuck them all. Fuck the gods. Fuck the world. For now, he curled into himself, against the cold. He drew his knees up to his chest and wrapped his ripped black bomber around them. He created his own shell, inside the hard metal carapace of the ride's basket. He stared out, across the Margate night, but no one could see in. No one could see him. And he thought that maybe he could live like that. He could make himself impregnable. The pain of losing Huxley, of trusting Huxley, would never be repeated. It never would have happened, if he hadn't allowed himself to be vulnerable to it. And he would ensure that he never made that mistake again.

1990

Blue packed the best of his own clothes and Huxley's favourite shirt – still flecked with teardrops of dandruff – into Huxley's backpack. In its top pocket, he placed the Lincoln Imp, wrapped in a dishcloth. He looked admiringly at its cold, brass, insouciance, before he folded it away. Familiar, thanks to Huxley, with *Desert Island Discs*, Blue also packed *The Complete Works of Shakespeare*, but chose *Paradise Lost* instead of the Bible. As his luxury item, he took Huxley's cash-point card, he knew the pin, Huxley had told him it. He'd also told Blue what was in the account wouldn't last long.

Blue jumped the train from Margate to London. Got himself to the National Express coach station at Victoria. Bought a ticket to Durham city. From there he would take himself to Blackmoor. Though he was not entirely sure why, he knew that he needed to go back there. The thought of return flashed with fear and with shame, but the call was even more powerful. He felt somehow like a de-mobbed soldier – irreparably altered; damaged by events – wending his return. A survivor going home. Knowing that home itself might not have survived. Not survived how it was, anyhow. But in search of something. Something he could only find in Blackmoor. Something he couldn't define. It wasn't connection or redemption, because Blue had no use for feelings like that. Blue had no use for feelings at all. So he didn't know why he had such a powerful urge to return. And he had no real plan beyond the ride. Perhaps the journey would be its own end.

Blue's coach was not for over two hours. So he sat reading in the grey waiting area. The chairs were hard cast plastic, spindly creased to look like leather. They did not look like leather, but perhaps they did look less like plastic.

A girl sat down next to him. She was a woman to Blue, probably twenty-three or four, but she was girl enough, alluringly lovely, to Blue's arid eyes. There were a lot of spare seats, banks and rows of them, so her dropping next to Blue could have been nothing but volition.

'If you don't have a car then you spend a lot of your life waiting for things. You waste a lot of your allocated hours on earth tapping your toes,' she said.

She smelt of that hippy oil and she had plaits on her head with daisy hair-clips and a smile on her face. She wore trainers, which contrasted with a light cloth skirt – Indian or Eastern or some kind of ethnic – and she jingled and sparkled with bracelets and anklets and rings. Her ears were really pale inside. Maybe everyone's ears were. Only Blue had never noticed it as a thing before, but anyway, hers were, like they were inlaid with mother of pearl.

Blue stared through the windows onto the interior court, filled with parked buses issuing periodic pneumatic hisses when their drivers got on and off. He tried to think of something clever to say.

'Do you like the art?' he finally embarked with, pointing at a poster of horses tearing across a polo field; he had been admiring them earlier; the beasts looked sleek, captured in the moment of cornering.

A pigeon hobbled by on stumps, toes rotted off.

'That isn't art,' she said, 'It's advertising. Art should take you somewhere, make you travel someplace else, not try and sell you aftershave.'

Though they had just met, not even exchanged names, she asked Blue to guard her rucksack while she cleaned up. He watched from a distance, as she walked through an automatic door marked *Wait Inside Terminal.* But she stopped sufficiently close to the other side that the door whoomped open and shut as she moved. She stripped down to her bra and washed herself with baby-wipes, careless of starers who looked askance. Mostly men, wearing masks of disapproval, in order to look at her a little closer and a little longer than proper.

'That's better,' she said, back in the seat, skin shiny, 'I'm Judith.'

She produced a flask of coffee and shared it with Blue as they chatted. The flask was dented metal, looked like it had been on more travels than some of the buses.

She asked where he was headed. And then said 'Never heard of it', when he replied 'Blackmoor'. She said it in such an authoritative way that it sounded almost like she meant it couldn't be a real place, if she'd never heard of it.

After a while, she asked him to mind her bag again, while she went to the toilet, 'Coffee goes straight through me.'

Blue knew what she meant; he could have done with going himself. When she came back, he asked her to return the favour and guard his backpack.

He returned to the seat, still wiping his hands on a paper towel, half in order to show her that he was the kind of guy who washed his hands after peeing. Though he more than half suspected she was the kind of girl who wouldn't care less. Only she wasn't there at all, neither were the bags. Blue looked about him, rapidly triangulating to certainty that this was where they had been mere moments before. Lurching to the reality that he had been scammed. His whole life, such as it was, was in the backpack and he'd lost it to the first person who came along.

'She went that way, your girlfriend,' an elderly black lady said, motioning towards one of the exits with her bright-scarfed head, 'Seemed in some awful hurry.'

Blue set off at a run, jumping over luggage, dodging between tramps and pasty eaters. He caught sight of Judith for an instant, as she disappeared into an underpass. Took the steps himself, three at a time. Through the spray-paint shadow of the tunnel, he saw her mount the stairs at the far end. She was at a half jog, laden with two backpacks, probably thought herself already escaped. She didn't look back. Blue pelted, head down, fists pistoning.

He caught up with her in a side street, about to unlock a van. He wrenched his sack from her shoulder. Hers, already on the ground, he kicked in anger. It shot into the air, light as bubble wrap, hollow as a Trojan Horse.

She looked neither scared nor shamed, to have been caught in daylight theft.

'I liked you,' she said, 'That's why I waited too long, I hesitated, I was torn.'

'I'm a fast pisser,' Blue said, 'Always have been. People comment on it. Strikes me that I just piss faster than you run.'

'So you caught me, so now what?'

'I get my bag back and head for Blackmoor, you move on to the next poor mug, I guess.'

'I'm leaving London,' she said, 'Was just trying to hustle some extra petrol money. You want to come along?'

'Where are you going? And why on earth would I want to go with you?'

She pointed to the sky, to a loose bracket of birds up high.

'Same destination as them: someplace else. I don't think your current plan is any better.'

She opened up the van and Blue saw that its interior was like a little den: a mattress covered in rugs and bedding, pots and tin cups suspended from hooks – handles tied with twine – a couple of wooden chests to serve as seats and storage.

And Blue saw that it might be a place of strange safety in there: a home for runaways that could itself runaway. And Blue imagined it to be just the kind of snug nest, where a person's virginity might get lost.

'If you're still here after I've had my coach ticket refunded, then maybe I'll ride with you for a bit,' Blue said, 'As long as we can go to the seaside. I don't care where, but I need to be by the sea.'

'How do I know you won't bring the rozzers back with you?'

'You don't.'

She had just the faintest sooty smudge of moustache above her top lip, more visible when she broke into an asymmetrical white smile.

'Fair enough. I'll wait and see.'

They drove to Grimsby, stopped at the beach at Cleethorpes, beside the muddy brown waters of the north. The sky was faded and stained by the sea's reflection. Salt waves struck stern and endless, smashing and cleansing by turn. Lumps of driftwood tumbled in the surf; sometimes looking like they might make land, as if they had agency over their destination, only to be sucked back into the breakwater.

They stayed there a few weeks, parked on the front between the flat-roof pubs and the cocoa sands. Low Lincolnshire lands behind, skyline stunted at house height. She showed Blue how to wedge a small cup – liberated from the top of supermarket washing softeners – well-hidden, into the coin return slot of phone boxes. They would patrol between the phones, the length of the promenade. Melody of the sea on one side, competitive lasers and electric tunes of a thousand arcade machines on the other. They could make twenty or thirty quid on a good day. Enough to live a life of luxury, eating fish and chips from Papa's, perched on its chicken legs out over the sea like Baba Yaga's hut. There was a place that did hot pork baps, reminded Blue of the butcher's on Blackmoor high street, but not in stottie and without the peas-pudding. They would sit with tin cups of wine – handles tied with twine – on the back step of her van at sundown – doors all open to let the inside cool and air – facing out to a view better than any hotel in town could sell you. *Even a tramp can share in the sunset*, Blue's dad once said, *They cannot take that away from him. Look for beauty and the world will seem less harsh.* And Blue discovered that it was true.

She would strum her guitar and whisper the words of Simon & Garfunkel and Tracy Chapman; she sang softly, like she was shy, though she wasn't, and she had a good voice.

'Always leave before you're caught,' she said to Blue, once she got a sense that the police were keeping an eye on them. But by that time, she'd anyway made local contacts for harvesting work.

Judith wasn't her real name. She told Blue her real name was Willow. He had lingering suspicions, but called her Willow anyway. Her fingers were toughened from picking guitar strings and picking fruit. They lived together all summer and into the autumn, grafting on farms. They would use the shared sanitations, but slept in her van. Or sometimes under an awning strung from it, if it was warm and they were sleeping during the day; which they often did, rising at three, to pick before dawn. Blue grew lean and muscled from manual labour and so dark-skinned he could have been one of the foreigners aside from his blonding hair and that green eye. Willow was a drifter, offspring of a hippy and a grifter, she knew how to live from the land and how to love. Liked nothing more than to lounge in the sun but could labour like a lumberjack. She taught Blue how to hot-wire and how to hot-knife and how to hustle. She had pointy cow-horn breasts and tan lines on her lower half only. Concentric triangles: first the zone of masked white, then tight black wiry curls, then the slick slit of her, which tasted sweet yet metallic – like the Mad Dog 20-20 they drank – and was open to anything he might introduce: chocolate bars; candles; torches. But Blue himself couldn't let even emotion in. He struggled just to hold her afterwards. He barely released enough of himself for her to cling to, on the narrow pallet of their bed.

They followed the work. Work such as strangers can find. Work among other strangers. Hard work. Picking and cutting and loading and stacking. Often in the dark. Work disdained by those who equally disdained the interlopers, itinerants and immigrants willing to do it. Blue and Willow had moved, farm by farm, nearly to Skegness, by the time the days were growing cool and the nights long, and they had their first real argument: one of sorrow.

'You've never told me a thing about yourself,' she said, 'Do you know that, Blue? You've told me stories, if I've pushed, under duress. But you've never told me a thing about yourself, not really. Tell me something, just one time, about something that makes you you.'

'I can't talk about things like that,' he said, 'I need to stay near the surface.'

'Then how do you think we can move forwards together?'

'Why do we have to move forwards? What's wrong with where we are?'

'You're broken inside, Blue. You don't understand intimacy or emotion. You've become great at making friends. I've seen you learn how, these past months. You're so stupidly cute that people actively want to be your friend. And anyone can think they are your friend within thirty minutes. But they'll know you about as well at the end of that half hour as they are ever going to know you. Because the truth is, you don't really want friends: you would rather be lonely and safe than take that insignificantly tiny risk of opening up.'

'Don't you think there might be a reason why I'm like that?'

'Yes, I'm sure there's a reason. I just don't think you're ever going to tell me about it.'

'Everyone I depend on dies. Isn't that enough?'

'Do you know why so many people love America?' she said, 'It's because of their national mythology of self-reliance. They all act like they don't need help. And we admire that fierce independence. It's noble up to a point. But sometimes people do need help, Blue, that's why it's a myth. Sometimes people need other people. And first they have to let them in.'

Van living is tough in winter. They found a car park in Skegness, where fractured lives gathered at dusk. Some in saloon cars. Some with kids. Some still clinging on to jobs. Taking off their work clothes and trying to keep them clean. Barely sleeping, but still going in early, to wash themselves before their colleagues arrived. Engines would be started, throughout the night, by people who had to run their heating. Blue and Willow were permanently cold and tired. They fought like cats. Fucked like dogs. Drank like fish.

She told him that she knew a scam, to get them out of this. They could use their money to rent an apartment, for just a week, and then get dupes to leave deposits on it. Blue told her they couldn't. Blue told her the idea was too far, too sick. Blue said he'd never do it. Blue and Willow argued.

They tried to continue. They staggered along a few weeks more. Until maybe both of them felt like they were chest-compressing a corpse. For Blue, it was not that they were different, it was that she had eroded his belief in them. Because she was right: he never would allow her beyond his wall. And somehow that meant he could no longer hold onto the idea of them. The necessary faith that they were entwined vines, the idea that they were twin strands of a single story had dissolved. A relationship is a religion which its participants must earnestly believe in, if they are to honestly partake of the sacraments. To simply tread along in the trappings is a betrayal, as surely as to worship at a rival temple. One needn't copulate with strangers at the graven feet of Baal to be in apostasy, it is sufficient to allow in doubt.

Blue came back from the swimming baths one afternoon – where he went to get clean – to find the van was packed, and so was his rucksack. Willow gave him a hug and his bag.

'It's better this way, Blue,' she said, 'I've been here before. You'll thank me for it, at the finish. I can't sign on the dole, not without them finding me for other stuff. But you can. There's half of our food in there and more than half the money. And you still have some in that account. I've reserved you a hostel place for tonight. They'll tell you where to get signed on. Get somewhere to live. Get a job. You've got your whole life ahead of you. Since you bloody well refuse to look back, you might as well move on.'

Blue looked down at the ground. Blue looked at the drizzling skies. Blue couldn't look in her eyes.

As she drove away, as the rust-flecked rear-doors disappeared down the street, Blue started to run after her, but it was too late. He tore along the road edge to avoid the plodding pavement-hoggers and mobility scooters. Motor horns blasted at him; people stuck their fingers up at him. But it was still too late. If Willow saw him at all, she didn't stop. She was gone. He slumped in the gutter. Hunched against the puddle-spray of passing cars. He had been right all along: the only way to protect yourself, is to be alone.

Blue found work quickly, cleaning at a Skegness casino. The manager said a kid with Blue's looks should be trained up for the tables. The casino was redbrick, could have been a leisure centre or student halls, save for the sign on the wall, at best a motorway hotel. Staff accommodation was an ex-boarding house bedsit, wallpaper from the war, shared bathroom, one-bar electric heaters, condensation. When Blue started as a croupier, it was dark when he went to work and dark when he clocked off.

PHASE THE FOURTH

We live as we dream: alone.

Heart of Darkness – Joseph Conrad

1998

The Skegness beach couldn't have been less like Blackmoor's scourged coast: it was as wide as something that Blue always thought you might see in Australia or California, though obviously not under the same sun.

From the pier, monoped cyclops telescopes watched over the bay and the beach and the sea; cast metal, vandal proof, aloof. Blue knew that there was a certain sense of wonder to be had by staring through them. He had used them in the past, with a photographer's gaze. Though Blue had no camera, he was still his father's son, and he had found that he too could see the beauty in the world. The big wheel in the background was always slowly turning, empty or not. Soldiering on, whatever the weather, like Skegness itself, like Blue himself. Music blared out and people ate ice-cream, even when it rained, because the British were a hardy race, nothing could bring down the British. Nothing could break Blue.

The day was warm for June, almost clammy. But few were plodging or paddling, fewer still swimming, that wasn't what Skeggy's beaches were for. People wrestled wind-breaks and recliners. People chased balls and discs. People dug moats and patted buckets. Sporting shorts and Speedos, sporting jeans and saris, sporting football scarves and head-scarves, sporting pork-pie hats and sun-hats and baseball caps and flat caps and turbans and tattoos, every white male sporting tattoos. Every white male but Blue.

There was a small tribe of little kids on donkeys, plodding a coned-off path. The donkey man behind didn't wear a donkey jacket. Everyone wore donkey jackets in Blackmoor, back in Blue's childhood, yet the one man you'd expect to have one did not. The donkeys looked melancholy. Eeyore was based on a true story. They had a look of sad forbearance about them. Pained patience. They trod on with child monarchs atop, something unavoidably Biblical about it all. The harnesses were blue and red; the donkeys were coral and rock and sand. One donkey, rider-less, still followed on behind the others, on quest for companionship. For all the donkeys' look of sad stoicism, the Skegness beach life was probably a good one, by equine standards, better than most of their kind. And Blue knew tales of pit ponies, in the deep shaft mines of before times, that lived their whole lives underground. Stabled there in the dark like veal calves. Went down on winding gear at a year or so old and never saw the sun again.

Kids were playing in the rivulets left by the retreating tide; kids were playing in the pools. And Blue thought of The Spot. Blue thought of Nick. Blue thought of what happened. And Blue didn't want to think of that, so he spoke aloud, a means he had long-since devised, to block out the thoughts inside.

'You have beautiful hair,' he said, to her, to Sasha, the girl who was beside him; a girl he had not long known.

'It comes from a bottle,' she said

'What good thing doesn't,' said Blue and he swigged from the wine they were sharing and then handed it to her.

Blue had lifted a couple of hard-boiled eggs and two cobs from the kitchens. Bread rolls were *buns* in Blackmoor and Huxley had called them *baps*, but here they were cobs and cobs was good enough. Blue peeled the eggs, while looking out to sea. He took more pleasure in the peeling than he would the eating. Blue was not overly fond of the taste of egg. But he was half in love with the aesthetics. There was a designer's perfection about them: so impeccably packaged that they made him want to believe in a creator God; too immaculate to have arrived by chance; minimal and humble, but so expertly moulded and rounded; so little wastage; pebbles on the outside and then pale and flesh-filled as you ease off the shell. To peel eggs, while looking out to sea, with a stunning-hot girl beside you, Blue concluded, was one of life's authentic sensual pleasures.

Sand got everywhere though. Sand got in the food, in their mouths.

'A bit of grit makes pearls,' Sasha said.

It reminded Blue of his mam, *a bit of rain turns little tatties into big ones*, was one of her sayings. Blue felt like he'd already had enough rain to last a lifetime. Blue took another swig of wine.

Blue was intrigued by Sasha, there was something impenetrable about her, she reflected his gaze. During his seven years in Skegness, Blue had most often sated himself with holiday makers and hen-dos, perhaps to deliberately self-sabotage any chance of forming a real relationship. Though he did dip his net into the nearby rockpools too. Some of the local girls had nicknamed him *Mr Lonely*; he presumed this was because he was a good guy to call when they were lonely. It couldn't be because they thought that he was lonely, because Blue wasn't lonely at all, not one bit. Blue was content with his own company. He didn't need anybody. But they still called him it. And they still called him. It being established that he would sleep with almost anyone, at the drop of a bra-strap, and would retreat into himself just as swiftly afterwards. So they could come and get what they wanted and then stay-over or go home. Either way there would be no emotional mess on the carpet; just the cuttlefish of used condoms and sometimes a frameless mirror with speckled ghost lines on its glass. Normally Blue used it for shaving, propped up on the four-row, junk-shop chest of drawers that was more than adequate to contain all of his possessions. All of his possessions except his van, anyway – bought off a builder – memorial to a past freedom maybe; or just a hobby, a thing to tinker with. Blue had himself become known as something of a plaything: a handy toy with which to scratch an itch and the perfect person with whom to right the scales of justice on a cheating ex. But word had most certainly spread, along the usual female communication channels – among the lending libraries which stored the highs and lows of penises to be commonly encountered in the native population – that Blue was not a guy to waste any time on.

But he cared about them, those women, he wanted to make them happy, if only for a little while; if only for long enough, that was long enough. That was enough.

There was pleasure in those times. There was joy in orgasm, of course, but there was also pleasure in giving pleasure. There was a beauty in the strange uniqueness of every encounter. Not as a tick list or a tally sheet, nor the self-voyeur of the connoisseur, it was simply a gladdening act. And some games are better played with two, Nick taught Blue that. And Charlie taught him to look for beauty. And Blue found that nothing is without worth, if it is enjoyed for its own sake. Everything is art, if you study it as you would a painting or a sculpture. Each clitoris can be licked as if you were a medieval monk, mouthing the sacred lines of scripture as he scribes, with rapture not duty. Sometimes Blue would trace the alphabet with his tongue, from *a* to *z* and then back again in majuscule and repeat until his partner came or could take no more. In all petals there is perfection, not only in the lily.

At twenty-six, Blue had filled out, over the Skegness years, from the younger him, but he was still slim. His jawline was defined and his cheekbones were high, which drew even more attention to his unpaired eyes. And, though they were not of a set, both were curtained with dark lashes, and both were circled with a startling ring of black around the irises. He kept his hair shorn short, which made his twin cowlick horns look like satyr stubs. He was maybe not quite model material, but he was striking; he was something more than boy next door. Though anyone who lived next door to Blue, in that part of Skeg, would probably have more serious things to worry about than whether they fancied their neighbours. Blue's street was populated with lives fissile and flimsy; rubber rafts that could at any moment be flipped by the waves.

They were still there at dusk. But all the wine was gone. Blue suggested they move along. Yates' had a week-night two-for-one.

'Let's go for a swim instead,' Sasha said.

'Isn't it a bit cold?'

'It's not, you know it's not, it's muggy as fuck.'

'I'm not much of a swimmer.'

'I'll make sure you don't drown, I promise.'

They walked down to the water's edge, to the washing machine slosh of the waves. And she slipped from the shoulders of her light dress, which dropped in a single ring on the sand and her bra and knickers fell within it. And she ran with childlike glee into the sea. And Blue, out of reasons not to, untied his faux-leather shoes and pulled off his socks and he took off his black polyester trousers and his white polyester shirt and his red polyester waistcoat, with his black polyester bow-tie in the pocket. He kept on his cotton underpants, but they were half-stripped from him and had to be yanked up after his waist deep dive, which was practiced, much practiced, belied his claim to be no swimmer.

'I think you lie,' she said, circling to him, 'this isn't your first time.'

A string of water and spit still joined them as they pulled apart from the kiss, grit in it too, for making pearls. Blue looked at Sasha's mouth and saw something mollusc-like, but entirely human. There are elements fleshy and liquidous, malleable and moist which make it seem not impossible for us to have sprung from the common ancestor of an oyster.

She drifted on her back to present her dark-nippled little breasts and to watch him watching. Then duck-dived, leaving her rump skyward, coquettishly longer than necessary. She winked as she surfaced again, shaking her head with a wet smile and smoothing back her hair; still blond, even soaked. From a bottle. What good thing isn't?

'That's not your real name,' she said, 'What's your real name?'

'It is, well, it's Bluford, but no one has ever called me that, I'm just Blue.'

'Aren't you though; do you think that I could cheer you up?'

And Blue laughed, despite a lifetime of variations on the theme. And she stroked a strand of hair from one of her breasts, deliberately absent-mindedly.

'So will you do it?' she asked, 'Is it a deal?'

And Blue felt the crossroads that was there, beneath him in the deep, a fork in the salt forest. He trod water, while he faltered – knowing this choice could not be undone, nor returned upon – but desire won: the path wide enough for two.

'Yeah, ok, I mean, I guess so,' he said.

'Deal?'

'Deal.'

Sasha pushed herself downward, using her fingers on his hips to do so, and she rid him of his underwear. She demonstrated just how long she could hold her breath, which was long enough to have Blue breathing heavily.

With giggles and struggles they managed to fuck after a fashion, though it was difficult with nothing to press against and eventually they scrambled out to finish on the sands. Hidden by the piles of the pier next to the piles of their clothes.

And afterward Blue kissed her thanks and dressed again, dusting away the sand as best he could – deserting his drowned pants – and he went back to his staff house to sleep and sober up before his shift started. Before the work of spinning a roulette wheel and gently, politely, separating strangers from their money.

1998 – One month later

The fat man was waiting for Blue when he finished his shift. The man was so fat that other fat people might have liked to stand next to him. But he was so dangerous looking that they probably wouldn't have. He was wearing a black leather coat. All the thugs in Skeg wore black leather coats. It was almost required uniform. Not the sort that rockers and bikers favour, with silver zips and poppers, but almost like military tunics, only made of thick leather, invariably black leather. They were tough and stain proof and they had deep pockets and could conceal the shape of objects tucked in waistbands or belts. So you could see how they would be a practical choice. But more than that, it was kind of like an advert or a piece of advice: I'm the sort of guy who wears a coat like this, now mind your manners, it said. To have such a man waiting for you, was unlikely to be good news.

'Grimes wants to see you,' the fat man said, and motioned with a single bloated finger for Blue to follow him.

The man walked slowly, as if every step was an effort, which, given the width of his legs and the weight they bore, it probably was. Blue could have outrun him easily. And Blue knew that he should run. Blue could sense that this was one of those occasions where to run away would have been the braver act. But he didn't. He allowed himself to be led to a service lift, accessible from outside the casino. Graffitied with hasty marker tags. Surrounded by ducts and air-outflow grills, clumps of heavy duty wiring in Medusa trails. The man produced a small socket-wrench style key and stuck it into a panel, the only way of calling the lift externally.

The lift was small and the fat man occupied so much of it that Blue was close enough to see the stretch-marks in the leather of the man's coat, which he had clearly owned for longer than the entirety of his current belly. He, or someone, had subsequently attached small loops of elastic cord through the button holes, to allow the coat still to fasten, after a fashion, though the edges of leather just but barely met, instead of overlapping. Blue was close enough to hear the man's laboured bulldog breathing. Close enough to smell his sweat. Though Blue was sweating even more.

Blue was ushered into a room on the top floor of the casino, alone, and the fat man closed the door behind him. The noise was no louder than the shutting of a heavy book. Solid, sound proof. The room probably had quite a lot of furniture – cabinets, drawers, shelves, safes, even a sofa – but because the room was large and all the furnishings were around the edges, it still created the impression of being quite empty. The most notable feature was a desk, with a single black leather chair, and beyond it a bank of televisions. Blue didn't think he'd ever seen so many televisions in one room, not unless that room was a Rumbelows. They weren't tuned to regular channels, because each of them played something different. Several seemed to be showing porn. The pictures were flickery – with stripes moving down through them periodically, like breaking surf – but in moving closer Blue became horrifically aware that the actors were familiar. While he had never seen those buttocks from that angle before, he could imagine he knew them. And he definitely recognised the bottle-blond girl upon whom the buttocks humped. And other screens showed other scenes: the same lady, now with a ponytail, slipping from a cocktail dress, before the waist-coated croupier on a bed. And as Blue flicked his eyes between screens, he saw that most of those not showing this amateur smut were of casino scenes. Faces mouthing *deal, deal, deal.* People around gaming tables. Different tables, different nights. Then, one after another, those films paused. Each stopped at an instant of near imperceptible action: the moment a croupier left a losing stack upon the roulette baize, which should have been cleared with the rest; a sleight of hand that let slide a high denomination chip from the side of the dealer's fingers, towards a pretty gambler with a pony tail and a cocktail dress; other times, all within the last month, showing the same partners in crime, in crime.

The click of the lock was the only sound as the door behind Blue opened. Blue knew the man who walked in must be Grimes. He had never seen Grimes before, but who else could it be? Grimes was just like they said: skinny, barely filling his own cheap suit, thinning hair swept sideways over his head with Brylcreem. He could have been a double-glazing salesman, except that Blue viewed him with the foreknowledge of who Grimes was and what he did. He could have been a middle manager, except that there was something feral, weasel, about the way he moved. His voice was almost comically squeaky, but not even a madman would dare to smile about it, not even inside. Grimes looked at Blue like he could see inside.

'You've been watching the videos already, I note,' Grimes said, 'As you know, it's a dismissal offense to fraternise with casino clientele – but such breaches of rules often highlight the kind of person likely to breach other more important rules, if you know what I mean. Which is why we kept an eye on you.'

'You have cameras in the hotel rooms and the staff accommodation?'

'Do we, do we though? Do we have cameras in every room? Or do we have cameras only in the rooms of those already under suspicion? You will never know and if you'll permit me to say so: it's irrelevant. Because that is just not what this is. If you think surveillance and privacy are the matters under discussion, then I'm afraid you are very much mistaken.'

Blue had occasionally supped with bad sorts. Or so he had thought. But when he looked into Grimes' eyes he saw the oblivion dark of a shark; a coldness incomparably beyond anything previously encountered.

Grimes pulled a tri-folded sheet of paper from the pocket of his badly cut suit and handed the page to Blue. It was blank, except for a number typed neatly right in the centre and an address below it.

'In addition to the casino and the slotties and all the property, I also have a small, unsecured personal loan business. That address is my repayment office. The number is what you owe by way of reparation.'

The figure is very large.

'I didn't, I mean, not often … Nowhere near that much … I don't have that kind of money. I don't have any kind of money.'

'I imagine not. Thing is, your girl has fled, done a runner before we could get her. Played you for a proper mug, hasn't she, bet you thought it was true love. I don't think you were the first. I think she's a pro. But either way, you now have to do the repenting for two. I don't expect it all right away. Nonetheless, you have forty days to make some substantial dent in it. You need to show willing, if you know what I mean. In person, in cash. If you haven't shown significant financial repentance by that time – paid to the office at that address – you will be reported to the police and punished by me. For the avoidance of doubt, that means either you are beaten to within an inch of your life and then processed by the courts, or processed by the courts and then – at some later, incarcerated, point – beaten to within an inch of your life. I might add that kicking a person close to death is not an exact science. Errors can occur, if you know what I mean.'

Blue felt like his legs were collapsing. Like his bladder was collapsing. Like the whole world was collapsing.

'You have to see it from my point of view,' Grimes said, 'I can only hold on to all that I have, because no one dares to take it from me. I started out as a nightclub doorman down on the front. Do you know how determined you have to be, to be a bouncer of my size? Do you know how dirty you have to be, how vicious? But I thrived. I own that club now. And I own the casino and a decent share of the arcades and I don't know how many old hotels and guest-houses; I genuinely lose track. No one wanted them; no one wanted to come to Skeggy on holiday anymore, not enough to support all the hotels anyway. So I buy them for a song, wrecked, unused, and I turn them into bed-sits. Renovations done by Ratners, if you know what I mean, but they pay off their mortgages in a couple of years. Housing benefit tenants that terrify regular landlords. But the government pays the rents. They turn up here on the train, they turn up at the bus station. Lives in bags. Broken lives, in shit, splitting, bin-bags. Wanting to start again. They don't start again, they just get stuck here. But if you're an alcoholic or an addict, at least you can be an alcoholic or an addict beside the seaside, know what I mean. And at least you're putting money in my pocket. Doesn't do much for the town, some would say, but it puts money in my pocket. And you know what? I am the town. I am Skegness. I've been broken and scorned and I rise up and I keep going. Only, if people weren't afraid of me, then people would take the piss. My business model is founded on fear, I'm sure you can understand this. My self-respect and the respect I command depend upon it being a well-established fact that no one can cross me and get away with it, know what I mean?'

Grimes clasped Blue on the shoulder with one hand, as if in a fatherly gesture, but more chilling than a blow would have been. Then he pushed a buzzer button on the desk and the door opened again. Three men walked in. The fat man and two others. All of them wore black leather coats. And they all wore driving gloves as well. Tan gloves with knitted backs, like from Halfords.

One of them was carrying a box and he emptied it onto the desk. It was the contents of Blue's locker. The man took Blue's watch, and sunglasses and dropped them into a clear plastic sachet. It had a self-adhesive strip and he carefully peeled off the backing and sealed it shut. He did the same with some other knickknacks: the book Blue was reading, a hat, some coupons torn from free-newspapers, his library card. From Blue's keyring, he took off the keys to the staff house where Blue lived, but handed Blue his van keys.

'You may need your vehicle to get hold of money, or you may want to sell it. Or sleep in it for that matter, since you are not to return to your room under any circumstances,' the man said.

His voice sounded deep as a bass bin by comparison

to Grimes's.

The same man produced a camera and Blue was put against an empty section of wall, where his photo was taken. Multiple shots and angles like mug shots. And they combed out some of his hair and put it in a bag. Then they made him hold a glass and put his lips on it and then pick up a hammer and a knife and dropped them all into plastic bags which they sealed up.

And Blue – sweating like cheap cheese; shaking like a shitting dog – acquiesced to it all without a word or a struggle.

'We do these things so that you are clear, so that you know this will not just go away,' Grimes said, 'Should you successfully evade us, we could simply frame you for some other crime. There are just as often people who need to be punished, as there are those who need to be found, know what I mean. The filth will always track you down in the end, in the unlikely event that we can't find you ourselves.'

'You need to make this right, pal,' one of the men said, his accent was Scottish.

Grimes gave the man a glance, like he'd over stepped his remit in interrupting, and the man clammed.

'Nonetheless,' Grimes continued, 'When you leave here, this may start to feel like a bad dream. You may begin to tell yourself that things like this don't really happen. Not in modern England. You may begin to neglect your responsibilities, if you know what I mean. So I like to leave some kind of solid reminder that I exist. I exist and I can find you.'

At this, or at a signal known to them, two of the men held Blue down on the desk on his back and bunched driving glove fingers forced open his mouth. The third man, the fat man, produced a pair of bird-beak pliers, which Blue could see, even though his head was held rigid. Too rigid even to shake, though he tried. His mouth too full of leather and knit wool to protest or beg, though he tried. The fat man got a grip on one of Blue's molars with the pliers. Blue could taste metal and oil. Even though he was near to choking on his own saliva. Even though his throat was closing up. The fat man had to wrench and twist and eventually brace his considerable weight on Blue's chest to get the tooth out. It came free with a snapping crunch through Blue's jaw and water in his eyes but some meagre relief because the pain marginally lessened, though his mouth was full of blood.

The men let Blue up and Grimes handed him a tissue, which turned near instantly deep red and was then sealed in another bag.

'Violence is not even the worst of it,' Grimes said, handing Blue some more tissues, 'Because there are places you can't return from. There are places where you stay, roaming with the wildness and rocking in the dark. And I can take you there, I promise you. Sending you there is just not any kind of a problem at all. But even I can't bring you back.'

1998

Blue needed a drink, but he wanted to be far from the casino first. So he walked the length of the front. Passed by enough pubs to wreck a navy, but he needed to be farther away. He left Skegness behind in a dwindle of beach shops. Inflatable sharks, inflatable snakes, cricket bats, buckets and spades, whirring wheels on sticks. He walked the concrete promenade, beside the beach; wide as a smile, when the tide goes out; Blue had nothing to smile about. He felt the wind on his stony face, the salt-seasoned wind you only get by the sea. It wasn't cold but he was still shaking. He walked on down to Ingoldmells. Dusk came with him. The lights of the Fantasy Island rides visible over the mining-terrace rows of static caravans. He thought of the time he almost threw himself from the big wheel in Margate. He wondered why he hadn't.

He turned down the street to be hidden in the masses. Normally he could see snapshots of beauty in these crowds. Normally Blue found something in Ingoldmells not just of the beach, but of the forest. Normally he enjoyed a calming solitude, strolling among the trees, even if the trees believed themselves to be people. But presently, the only parts of the forest in evidence were the dark and the discord. Stag groups in Lacoste and tattoos. Stag groups in shell suits. Stag groups in Animal T-shirts and animal costumes. Stag groups in tu-tus. People clutching prizes they didn't particularly want, but wouldn't now relinquish. Hen groups, plastered with sashes and badges and vodka, circling to retrieve recalcitrant shoes, straps that slip, high heels that snap. Constantly a churn of people turning back, like the swirl of tide that fights against itself, the curl of white that spumes alone before re-joining the whole and surging onward.

Blue walked onward too, threading the crowds, past the waltzer that promised a ride *faster than your boyfriend, harder than your husband*. Past the market. Biggest seven-day market in Europe. Clogged with people, flammable with clothing. Selling replica weapons, replica watches, replica jewellery. Selling chest harnesses for bull breeds and foot long hot dogs, Yorkshire pudding wraps, bangers and mash.

Blue walked on, inland, until the crowds began to thin. There was no escaping Grimes anywhere, but Blue felt far enough away to stop; for the fear to ease just enough.

He saw a brash pub he'd never been in before. As Blue approached it, a man was standing outside, under neon. He was trying to light a cigarette, the hand holding the lighter moving in and out as drunk eyes strained to focus. He looked like he was playing an invisible slide trombone.

Blue went in and sat at the bar. He pulled the wad of paper napkin from his mouth and inspected it, the bleeding from his stolen tooth's hole had more or less stopped. The tremble in his hand was visible. He ordered a pint and a whisky. The place was pretty empty. He stared at the television, playing noiselessly. He had some awareness the news was on, but really it was just colour. Just something to look at to avoid looking at his glass or his hand.

The horror of his situation was compounded by the fact that Sasha – with whom he had dared to wonder if a shared existence might actually stand a chance – had been playing him from the start. He was an idiot for trusting someone. But he could shut that hurt away, in the padlocked hangar at the end of the long, lonely road, where he kept the rest. The urgent problem was survival.

The trombone guy from outside came in and took the stool next to Blue. Though it must have been his place originally, because he picked up a glass and, seeing it was empty, put it down with contempt. The guy tapped on the bar like a blackjack player to signal another. The barman free-poured a single malt whisky. It was evident the guy had been there for some while, but he didn't seem like your usual day-drinker. But then he had a diver's watch and deck shoes, and he probably didn't dive or sail either.

The man nodded to the Middle Eastern news story that he presumed Blue was actually watching:

'Stop me drinking alcohol and eating bacon and I'd be angry too.'

'You've been drinking all afternoon and you don't seem to be getting less angry,' the barman said.

'You sure you're in the right line of work? You're supposed to be helping people get drunk, not putting them off.'

Blue and the man sat side by side in silence after this, for the time it took the man to finish his new tipple and tap for another.

'Whisky won't solve your problems,' the barman said, as he served it.

'I don't expect it to solve them, I expect it to anesthetise them.'

The drinker took this as invitation to further share those problems. The barman was presumably already educated.

Blue was informed that the man was a doctor and had just discovered that his wife was having an affair with his best friend:

'A happening so banal that patients tell me the self-same tale every single week; only today, it's happened to me, and so it's a bloody tragedy.'

Blue didn't have much spare sympathy. He wondered if a doctor could tell you how to go about selling a kidney.

'You're a chimera,' the doctor said, 'Did you know that?'

Blue shook his head.

'Your eyes: one brown, one green; it means that you're really two people. You are non-identical twins who fused in the womb. You look to all the world like one person, but you are two.'

Blue downed his whisky and tapped the bar like the doctor, wondered what this new information meant; did it offer light on his life or bad decisions? Perhaps this other him was evil, or just plain dumb? Or maybe that was why he didn't need anyone else: because his twin was always with him?

'But, hey, what do I know, I've only spent my whole life studying. There's a kick back coming now,' the doctor said, like it was the natural continuation of his revelation to Blue, 'People have tired of the enlightenment, they're sick of science and empirical evidence. They want the certainties of ignorance again. They don't want virgin births and resurrection back; they don't want Mohamed flying to Jerusalem on a magic mule, not most of them anyway; but they don't want inoculation either. They don't want doctors and professors claiming to know best; they resent the presumptions of specialism. I see it every day: patients who ask for my advice, despise me because I give them it. It's like we're actively trying to exorcise expertise.

Civilisation should move forwards, but that doesn't mean it has to. You know the high point of culture and learning before the nineteenth century was in pre-Socratic Greece? We went backwards then for two and a half thousand years. We've done it before and we'll damned well do it again. Religion was replaced by knowledge – by fact – and now knowledge is being replaced by opinion. Only opinion isn't an opiate, it's not even a vitamin. It's placebo. It's homey-fucking-opathy.'

As the evening slid on, it became clear that the doctor's aversion to placebo had extended to carrying more active substances; pills he was happy enough to share with Blue. Blue didn't even ask what they were, he just took two from the outstretched palm and swallowed them both with a swig.

Within forty minutes, the reflection of Blue's face at the bottom of his whisky glass looked like it was screaming. But after an hour he felt exquisitely unafraid. What could Grimes really do to him, really? And anyway, maybe his new friend the doctor would lend him the money. Maybe they'd be friends for life. Though Blue hadn't had a friend like that since Nick Nickelson – a friend for life he hadn't seen in half his lifetime.

The TV still cycled silently. Now it was an actor, found dead, in circumstances not considered suspicious.

'You know why they do it,' the doctor said, 'those talented, famous, wealthy suicides? Because they realise that they have all there is. If you have everything and you're still unhappy, then there's nothing left. There's no hope. People say it's darkest just before the dawn. People are idiots. Just before the dawn, it's already getting faintly lighter. It's darkest in the fucking dark.'

The doctor pulled out a cigarette, but left the pack on the bar; then he put a beer mat over his whisky, to stop any evaporating in his absence, and walked outside; presumably to smoke once more beneath the neon, even though there were green glass ashtrays scattered along the length of the bar. But he never came back in. When Blue went out to look for him, he was nowhere around. After an hour had gone by, Blue removed the beer mat and drank the whisky.

The bar began to fill with people. Their faces were blurred and there was a shining at the edges of things. For a while, Blue felt like the bar was in Paris. Though he didn't know how he knew, because he'd never been to Paris. And he started looking for Huxley, scared because he couldn't find him, scared that he was going to be alone again. Then came down just enough to realise that he was alone. Entirely, terrifyingly, alone. And then Blue didn't remember anything, until he was outside in an alley. Lying sprawled among discarded cardboard boxes, staring up at the night sky. And the stars became white stones at the bottom of a pond, at the bottom of The Spot. The type of stones you might see through the gloom and duck-dive to pile on the bank. And he thought of Nick Nickelson. He thought of all that had happened. And all that had happened since. And he cried. He cried tears repressed so many years that the ducts had near closed up. Tears of loss, long since sealed in rock. Seeping out in the black, like coal water.

1998 – Two weeks later

They were probably around the same age as Blue, the couple: twenty something or something, drifting towards being something else. She was short, kind of rounded, plump, in a pleasing way, pale, pillow lipped. The bloke – her boyfriend, her husband whatever, Blue didn't ask – he had dark hair and a bit of a bald spot already coming. One of those that grows only at the back. He'd look like a monk eventually. He was growing a compensatory goatee, but he was a good-looking guy. Both of them had great teeth. Hard to put your finger on why, but they had very middle-class looking teeth. American teeth. Advert teeth. Blue couldn't help imagining them fucking. If they had this apartment they would be fucking in every room for sure. They'd be fucking before they got their bags unpacked. Fucking as soon as they got the keys.

'So, this is the living room,' Blue said, waving his hand expansively, more expansively than the room warranted, though the room was good enough. It had Ikea furniture, all Billy this and Besta that, chrome effect venetian blinds and it had been recently repainted, there was barely a stain in sight. The couple looked about like they were disinterested professional connoisseurs of such living quarters, but shared a glance and a small nod with each other.

Blue showed them the kitchen, tiled and Formica, easy to wipe clean and the bathroom, which had a bidet.

'Would you really use that?' the bloke asked her, as she studied the object.

She blushed, which made her even more beautiful, but sentiment could have no place.

'And so we're back to here,' Blue said, when the short tour was completed, returned to the living room, 'Any questions you want to ask or anything?'

She spoke: 'I wanted to check: there aren't problem neighbours or anything? Just that the place seems cheap; well, it's not cheap, it's at the edge of what we could afford actually, but it's bigger and nicer than all the other flats we've looked at. Most of them are old hotels that look like they've been hurriedly converted; we're not snobs, I promise you, but I really didn't feel like I'd feel safe coming home alone in some of them. But the communal areas are not bad in this block and the street feels fine. So, is there a reason behind the low rent?'

Her partner shot her a look, to signal that this was definitely not a good question. Blue pretended he hadn't seen it.

'No, the neighbours are lovely, when they're there at all. I didn't realise I was behind the market, that's just what I've always charged, since I inherited the place. Perhaps I haven't kept up with inflation. Maybe we'd have to look at the rent down the road, but morally I guess I should let it for the price I advertised in the paper. At least for the first year. Anyway, I need good tenants more than I need the highest rent I can wring out.'

'Well, I think we'd like to take it,' the bloke said, 'We're wasting a ton of time on visits, seems like the landlords with half-decent places just rent to holiday makers.'

'I imagine so,' Blue said, 'Must be why my advert in the paper has had such a big response. I've got a lot of viewings lined up ...'

'So could we sign something then?' the bloke said, almost cutting Blue off, 'It would be nice to make it official, you know, that we've definitely taken it.'

'No problem, I mean, I have paperwork ready to go, just needs the dotted lines filling in. But obviously I'd need a deposit too, if I was going to turn all the other people away. Just the standard: first month up front and a month refundable for damage and security. Then we could call it a done deal, I suppose. If you're sure you don't want to go away and think about it?'

The bloke had already produced a Bradford and Bingley chequebook from a pocket. He was wearing a corduroy jacket with a polo-neck under, like he was a poet or something.

'Oh, sorry, no, I mean, it would have to be cash, just for the deposit. After that I'd prefer a standing order, so I know it's there each month. But for now, I'd need to know it's definite before I could cancel all the other prospective tenants. I'm sure you can understand: you seem like trustworthy people, you honestly do; but the number of rubber cheques I've been given, you wouldn't believe it.'

They were back from the bank only forty minutes later. Blue had the documents ready laid out on the kitchen table.

'Feels a bit weird handing over this much money to a stranger,' the bloke said, as he counted it out.

'You and your trust issues,' she said, giving him a teasing elbow, 'This gentleman – should we call you Jacob?' She asked, looking down at the rental agreement.

'Jake, please, call me Jake,' said Blue.

'Jake has a genuine smile,' she said, 'You can trust a guy

with a smile like that, girls know these things.'

She blushed again, her partner was still counting the money and didn't notice.

'Well it definitely is a nice place, Jake,' he said, 'It would be a shame to miss out on it. And we can move in next week?'

'Any time after Thursday next week. But I guess the week-end will be easiest for us all.'

After the couple had left, Blue leaned against the front door. Pushing against it with his palms, like Atlas holding up the world. But only holding up himself.

'I'm sorry,' he said, to the place they last stood, 'I'm sorry. I am not this person. At least, I didn't want to become this person. But you have each other. I am alone. I have no one to depend on but me. So, I'm sorry for you, but I don't need your forgiveness, because given a choice between you and me, I have no choice but to choose me.'

Then Blue hid the money with the rest of the money. And hid the signed lease with the other signed leases. And waited for the next viewer. He was running three viewings a day, which made things tight, but he had only rented the apartment for a week, so he needed to fit in as many as possible. He had to be methodical with timings and he had to smile genuine smiles and he had to believe himself gelded from redemption.

1998 – Six days later

A cat pinched itself through the first crack, as Blue opened the exterior door. The creature was out so quick that it must have been stood waiting on the opportunity. It was a black cat, with those white socks that some black cats have. But its foot fur was wet, left damp dabs in the doorway.

Cats are fastidious creatures, instinctively swerve from liquids, and of such agility that they but rarely tread a place they would sooner not. So if a cat leaves a line of wet prints, wherever it lately was, there must have been an unavoidable puddle of something.

Blue wasn't long in ignorance: upon entering the one-room office he found a urine lagoon, a piss lake, lapping at the desk legs and bedraggled cabinets. To produce quite so much urine as that, would take a very large bladder indeed. And the owner of such a bladder was both present and absent.

While it was hard to feel pity for one who had pulled out his molar with pliers, Blue didn't feel great hate or victory either, at the sight of the fat man on the floor.

The fat man's fat hand was clutched over his presumably fatty heart, as if to pump start it. His bollard thick legs were bent, curled crooked, like he'd been kneeling before collapsing sideways. Maybe achieving the position had proved the final tiny insult to an overtaxed heart. Blue didn't know where to find the neck pulse, which supposedly separates the living from the dead. And anyway, didn't want to touch skin that he was fairly certain would not have gone such a rancid pallid colour, had its owner not been deceased for a little while. Beyond the body's bulk, the rest of the tale: the reason why the fat man had been kneeling: an open cabinet on the floor: an open safe within it.

Blue paused, his mind ticked, aware that this trail split two ways. Then he thought about how meekly he had let the fat man and the others manhandle him. How he had done nothing while they pulled out his tooth. How he had muttered not a word of protest throughout the pain and indignity of their actions. And that memory drew Blue back to the boy who had tortured him as a child, how he had never fought back then either. Not until he found Nick Nickelson. Blue's cheeks glowed and heated, like a one-bar electric fire in a shithouse staff bedsit. And it was shame – not cupidity, or stupidity, or shock – that flooded him with the sudden hunger to possess the contents of the safe.

Blue had no means of carriage beyond pockets, he looked around the room for something. On the desk was one of those flimsy plastic sacks, used by kebab shops, greasy paper and shreds of red cabbage from the fat man's lunch still atop it. The bag was much too small for all the cash and it would likely tear and definitely show the silhouette of what was inside. There was a pedal bin in the corner though, with a ring of black bin bag visible. Blue pulled out the bag and emptied the contents – mostly other takeaway wrappings – back into the bin. Then, squatting – almost tea-bagging the fat man, to avoid kneeling in the piss – Blue filled the black sack with cash. And he pushed in the envelope from his pocket too, the reason he had come, the sum with which to service his debt to Grimes.

Blue knotted the bag and hasted to escape. Did not look back. Outside perceived himself seen by no one. No one save a cat. A cat licking piss from its paw.

But Blue had barely gone blocks before he hit a runner's wall of fear. A siren, shrieking its canticle, caused him to stop. The siren, on a police car or an ambulance, probably called to a different affair entirely, still hymned the seriousness of this. Singing, as sirens always have, about men drowning. Too late to return. Too scared to go on. Blue crouched in an alley, black bag pushed behind his back in a corner of skip and wall. But stirrings at the alley's end, a ragged addict man of beard and dirt, forced Blue up again and on.

Blue tried to walk his way through the dread. Feeling marked. Seeing every stranger's glance as the knowing eyes of unknown enemy. What towers and ghetto tenements had a view on that office door, Blue knew not. But the streets of a grim side of town anyway swelled with miscreants and ne'er-do-wells. There were surely those who could fathom from the bulges in Blue's bin bag alone that it would be worth any minor hazard involved in taking it from him.

Blue's back was shirt-stuck wet. He was certain his nerves must be visible in his every step. He pictured a growing band of land sharks behind him, swimming in his wake. Waiting on the moment to strike. To force his prize from him at point of knife. Blue tried to catch sight of them in the mirrors of shut down shop windows – glasses darkened by coverings – without looking like he looked.

Limbs hobbled, breathing thin, Blue saw the familiar Royal Mail red of a post office. To step inside at all, would surely offer some safety. And in there he could buy a package box, to disguise the traitorous shape of the wads of notes. And then, a further thought: he could just post this burden away; to be retrieved, safely, in a couple of days. But Blue knew by heart only a few addresses in the world. His childhood home and Huxley's place were both long empty; then there was Nick Nickelson's …

PHASE THE FIFTH

Why is it that a woman can see from a distance what a man cannot see close?

The Return of the Native – Thomas Hardy

1998 – Sunday

Blue instantly regrets picking up the hitcher. From afar, Blue had taken the man to be wearing a brightly coloured pullover. But upon intimate inspection, this was an illusion; created by a corpulent, nude torso, so hairy and so thoroughly tattooed as to leave the impression of wool. Blue's van lists noticeably as the hitcher grips the grab handle and hauls his bulk onto the passenger seat.

'Thanks, pal,' he says, 'Where you headed?'

As he turns to speak, Blue notices that the man has a scar, which runs from the edge of his eye to the bottom of his jaw, in a stark furrow. It doesn't look like a work-related injury, unless the man's line of work is knife-fighting.

'Blackmoor,' Blue says, 'I'm going to Blackmoor.'

The hitcher looks quizzical, which wrinkles his thick-skinned forehead all the way to his shaved dome.

'Blackmoor,' he says, sucking in air through his teeth, 'Are you sure? It's a bit rough for me round there, like.'

The hitcher wanted dropping well before the start of 'The new road in'. Blue is alone once more, along a wide dual carriageway of dark tarmac. This final stretch of the Hansel and Gretel trail of tragedy that has dictated Blue's route. Fairy tales are always about finding the way home. Maybe all stories are.

The road could cope with ten times the amount of traffic

that's actually on it. It might be a motorway, save for the frequent roundabouts, unstrimmed stinging nettles in the centres, nothing planted. The roundabout spur roads sprout off to either side of the carriageway, but then peter out into unbuilt lots. Land long-since bulldozed and cleared, but vacant save for rubble and rubbish. Blue can sense the shape of the planners' dream. He can imagine how each of these wasteland parcels should have become a warehouse or a call centre, an office or a small factory. Maybe even a hotel, in the wildest fantasy. But they remain vacant save for rags of fly-tipped plastic and part buried building waste. Only at the very edge of Blackmoor does the first roundabout spur end at an actual building, a *Kwik Save*, bright white walls and shiny sign lettering, awaiting the coming sun.

Blue is surprised at how easily he finds the Nickelson place, after all these years. The old roads come back to him. Turnings appear in his mind at the moment they roll over the horizon.

Shame strikes Blue as he gets out of the van. He glances at his front bumper, thinking of the dog he once hit. Though that isn't what's triggered the shame: that one wasn't Blue's fault: the dog bolted in front of him, there was nothing he could do. The dog was a pit bull, but a pet, not a weapon. The owner saw it happen and it was clear the dog was hurt pretty bad – its muzzle was inflated, it looked like a monster – so Blue drove them both to the vets. Not from culpability – the dog was unavoidable – but he drove them anyway. The dog was dead by the time they got there. The dog was always dead. Just took a while for them to realise it – the dog maybe last of all – but the dog was always dead.

The old Nickelson place hasn't changed much, since back when Blue was a boy, it was ever this patchwork quilt of repairs. Planks cut in or plain nailed on top. Any homogeneity only a coincidence of weathering. The Nickelson ancestors, upright Methodists who first bought the land and built, would have turned in their graves fast enough to power a mill wheel, at the state of their former home.

Poverty always looked different out at the Nickelson's, on their hand-me-down property; the edge of town plot, big enough that goats and poultry used to pick among the wrecks of old outbuildings and just as static vehicles. Two dogs would invariably charge out to greet you, with fierce barks and wagging tails. Car parts are still scattered among the weeds, but there aren't any animals in evidence, those two dogs must be long since deceased – dead as the one Blue hit that time – and the place looks deserted. The pole prop of a washing line has fallen on the ground and no one has bothered to set it back up. When Blue does so, he sees the grass beneath the forked stave is light deprived, lime pale, the pole must have been lying there some while. Bindweed has grown over the line and flags from the ground as Blue lifts.

Old time miners called it going haywire: when a place was no longer kept in good order, everything just jury-rigged with bailing twine. For the Nickelsons, haywire was almost a family motto. The fruit trees in what passes for an orchard are eclectic and sparse – as if deliberately to avoid producing a sellable surplus – branches now spattered with parasite plants. Beneath them, fruit, wizened and rotted, uncollected. Some puddled in low ground patches, places where last night's thunder storm still lingers. There is a smell of fertile succulence but the land is sloped and bouldered, not a place to be farmed on any scale and soon giving way to moor.

Blue snakes his way towards the front door, through the trees and puddles and limbo for bits of vehicle apparently too valued to be thrown away but never actually needed. Every inch of this place reeks of the past. Blue can near enough see himself as a boy, jumping through the junk with Nick Nickelson. Shooting cans and crows with Nick's jumble sale air rifle. Drinking water from the outside tap. No shirts, no shoes, no problems.

The cage of an old bed base leans next to the entrance. The pane of viewing window is cracked and covered with card from the inside, yellowing and swollen like a bruise. Blue wipes a cobweb from his face with the back of his hand and knocks on the front door. The wood of the steps creaks under his feet.

It's clear there's no one here. The knocking is pointless. But Blue knocks again anyway. A dangle of flypaper, brittle with age, caked with tiny carcasses, sways in air stirred by his arm.

He crouches and peers through the letterbox. On the floor he can see a couple of circulars and an ad-mag, all with dust on them. Nothing recently arrived.

There's the small iron shoe of a pit pony hung next to the door. As decreed: with the curve facing down. Who decided they had to be hung like that? It's just how life is: everything has to be done the hard way. Any time something seems too easy or too natural they'll tell you it's unlucky, or illegal, or that's where the devil lives. And since the Nickelson place is deserted, finding Nick Nickelson will doubtless end up difficult too. Every fairy tale requires resolution by test or quest.

Sunday

'Wait, those eyes, didn't you used to be …' the waitress trails off, as if she has caught herself saying aloud a thing intended as a thought. She settles the bottom of the coffee-pot back down on its counter hotplate.

Blue smiles, or tries to, the smile snags on his teeth.

'I did used to be him,' he says, 'So I suppose I still am him. Though I read that after a given number of years not a single cell of us remains the same; like Theseus' ship, or Trigger's broom ...'

'Still reading then, you've not changed.'

'Or else I have; I think that's what the article was saying: maybe I've altered entirely?'

'No, pet, you really haven't. Well, your accent's changed, you sound like a southerner. But if you've changed aside from that, it's been a canny change. I've tret you to the coffee by the way.'

'Thank you. That's kind. It's Betony isn't it – I've just realised – we were at school?'

'It is. We were.'

'I need to find Nick Nickelson. Is Nick still around? I went up to Nickelson place but it looked like no one had been there in a while.'

Betony turns back from the fat fryer, which spits and stinks. She's slim; in an over-worked way, not a working-out one.

'Only thing I heard, Nick must have come into money lately: bought the whole bar two rounds of drinks one night in the Imperial Hotel, when most generally known to have about the hind-half of naff-all, more likely to brawl over a beer than buy the house one.'

'Yeah, I could imagine that. Do you know where Nick is now?'

'Nope, and if I had any money, they wouldn't see me in Blackmoor again either.'

It's fearsome bright, back out on the street, quite startlingly hot for the North East. Blue pats his head for his sunglasses, finds none, remembers he has none. He feels a faint burn sensation at the edges of his temples where his cowlicks poke up like the Blackmoor headlands at the sea. He can still smell coal smoke on the air, though it's August and he knows the mines are all gone. Blue never even realised that bogies weren't black until he was taken to Margate.

Blue lingers at a corner, unsure of what to do. Feeling edgy and exposed. Already aware that this was a mistake. His breathing seems to come from higher up in his chest, from a shallower part of his lungs which doesn't allow in sufficient oxygen. He wonders if this is what panic attack feels like. And even still, even through that fear, he has to walk the front street.

It is not the place he once knew. They took much else besides when they took the mines. Half the shop fronts are now empty. The half remaining are half price. Everything must go. There is a metallic clank of NHS walking canes on the pavement. Tanning salons and pound shops. Barrys bar – no apostrophe, no apology – burnt out, left standing, as it was when the fire was extinguished. Boards over burst windows. Roof sunken in the centre. Blue's old school, biggest building on the high street, boarded too. Established AD 1887 according to the carving above an entrance, now blocked up. Abandoned. Looks like a church, through adult eyes, grey slate roof, sandstone walls.

'Make a nice community hall that,' an old boy says, seeing Blue looking at it, 'But they do nothing with it. It'll end up getting pulled down.'

The school's higher windows, un-boarded, have all been smashed with rocks or bottles, as if to make a start on the coming demolition.

A small girl passes by, laughing at her own attempt to walk in her father's shadow. Blue knows something of the feeling, if not the mirth. But he enjoys the innocence of her delight. Though he never feels able to fill his father's shoes, he is still his father's son and sometimes he fancies he has his father's eye. An eye for seizing a moment and imprisoning it as if in a photograph; for seeing the beauty in the black, like the dandelions that burst through tarmac cracks.

The Imperial Hotel still looks in reasonable fettle. Green tiled, with a flag pole and a small clock tower. It no longer rents rooms. The second storey is now a 'sports bar', a yellowing banner boasts about satellite TV, the ground floor is a day drinker's pub. To enter is to intrude on a private world, excluded from sunlight. Ex-miners on the dole. Ex-miners on the disability. Old miners on pensions. Old miners are rare. Heads turn. Blue's face feels the burn.

'Not for a spell,' the landlord says, 'Not since the night Nickelson came in here flashing money about. Maybe that drew a tad too much attention. Maybe someone started to lean on Nickelson for a share. Maybe that's what you're doing, for all I know, why are you so keen to hear all this?'

'I'm just an old friend, that's all, we grew up together.'

'Whoa, hold on, you're that boy who …'

'Yeah, I'm that boy.'

'Well,' the landlord swallows, his Adam's apple drops and bobs like a fish-bitten float, 'Well, so, yes, you've been gone a good while. Guess old Blackmoor's changed a fair bit?'

'It'll not have changed for the better, like,' a drinker says.

Blue buys a bottle of dog and takes it to a corner booth, sits with his back to the world, though the pub is not busy. The first slug of brown stings and fizzes at the point in his jaw where the tooth is missing.

He finds a cigarette lighter left on the seat, disposable, but still got gas and makes a flame. Even though Blue doesn't smoke he puts it in his pocket.

Not one to miss out on a toilet that he has a legitimate right to use, whilst van-living, Blue heads to it, once the beermat shows through the bottom of the bottle.

The pub has photos of regulars in one corner, proudly displayed, as if photography is a new and marvellous invention. A curious assortment. None that seem like they could be an age-appropriate Nickelson.

'Hey, you could try at the travellers' camp,' the landlord says, as Blue is about to leave, 'As I recollect, Nickelson's pally with one or two of them. Considering they're not the friendliest of folk.'

Monday

It is said that most people spend their whole lives asleep. And it is invariably said, when said, like that's a bad thing. It's been a while since Blue's slept well. Blue envies, rather than pities, such said-fools as can pass entire lives in slumber.

Blue's van isn't a bad bed chamber though. It was battered, bought from a builder, but on his days off one summer, Blue glued into the pockets and cavities of its metal panels thick quilts of insulation, to keep at bay the worst of heat and cold and noise. Then he attached hardboard, to walls and ceiling, foil-covered on the inside and carpeted without. And across the bare metal ribs of the van floor, scratched and splattered with paint and plaster, he laid more foil lining, then board, then vinyl. His van is not a camper in the truest sense – it has no sink or hob or toilet – but it is functional. Hanging from hooks are two cups, perhaps over-ambitiously. Everything else that Blue still owns fits within a solitary metal trunk, which also serves as the single seat. But the van has a foam, foldout bed. And it is a shield from the world. The metallic grinding slide of the side door closing is a noise that Blue finds comforting. It is the sound that signals separation and solitude. And, if he is lucky, sleep.

The roadside grove that Blue selected as last night's lair lies just outside the bounds of Blackmoor. A piece of waste-ground which would once have been part of a mine. Now filled and flattened. Nothing left of it but a single pit winding wheel – set in concrete on the ground as a memorial – and what was formerly the pedestrian gate. When Blue wakes and exits the van, he pisses onto his own tyre, and stares at that old gate and the ancient cast iron sign above it. It was made when the mine first opened, the miners threading in and out over the narrow-gauge railway tracks would have passed under it every single shift change. The black metal fretwork is unreadably far off, but Blue knows what it says: God Loves Blackmoor. The shape reminds Blue of a picture he saw of *Arbeit macht frei*, the phrase over that concentration camp. And, while it isn't impossible that God loves Blackmoor, if this is merely because He loves everywhere, then the fact would be barely worth remarking upon; while if God does not love everywhere, then Blackmoor seems a peculiar place to have selected for His special affection.

From here, it is close enough to walk to The Spot, and Blue suddenly feels an all-consuming need to go there, to return to the scene of the crime.

The way is familiar, yet strange: a route walked or even run a myriad of times in childhood. It is smaller now, in a physical sense, but also bigger: a sponge swollen with the past.

Blue hikes past sporadic pocks of animal tracks, dogs or foxes mostly, as moor gives way to forest. Just ragged patches of trees at first, becoming gradually connected. Trees occasionally striped with spray-paint war-paint to denote boundaries maybe, or areas slated for forestry work, or just some obscure rogues' cant, like the markings scofflaws, caitiffs and quacksalvers would leave one another.

Irish-green moss shrugs up the trunks of the trees, covering the bases and the northern faces. Clutches of cow parsley and cuckooflower; toadflax, glasswort, hogweed, scurvygrass. Names from Blue's boyhood. Days spent walking with his dad and then Nick Nickelson. Searching for the fabled elephant graveyard of Tarzan's black and white TV repeats. Shows even then looking tired with the advent of colour. Johnny Weissmuller always wrestling the same flaccid crocodile foe and never getting any better at speaking English, despite the years living with Jane and Boy.

A crow caws at Blue's approach to a cleared glade and then flies off. The detritus of logging – broken chunks, smaller branches and loose sticks – have been dragged into piles, to promote regrowth and shelter forest creatures. No one ever went to the bother of burning logs, back when coal was king.

Having brought no water, Blue stoops to drink from a tiny brook that he is certain used to be bigger. Nonetheless, he kneels in green marsh to catch what he can in the scoop of his hands. Wetting his neck. Washing the sweat streaks and dust from his face.

When he reaches The Spot – the natural pond where he and Nick Nickelson used to swim, what they thought of as their private pool – Blue finds it drained. It looks like a bomb crater, cracked and crumbling around the edges. There is only a quaggy slop at its very bottom, brackish with rotted vegetation. The stream that used to keep it filled must have dried or else been diverted, because it should be in full flow. The tree they used to swing from on their *Tarzy*, to fly into the pond's centre, looks in imminent danger of falling. The dirt has eroded from its roots, leaving them exposed and serpentine, something malignant about the way they twist into the depths. The big hangman's bough from which their rope used to be attached – stretching out to steal the empty patch of sunlight over the pond – is cracked and leafless, but looks ready to drag the tree over with the strain of supporting it.

'Time flies and so do I,' Nick Nickelson used to say, without fail, upon every swing of the rope. Probably it came from a TV show or something. At first it was funny, then it became mildly irritating, then it just became a thing, one of Nick's things. One of the things of which Nick Nickelson was composed. And what Blue now realises has long since been a soft internal yearning, is suddenly a burning, a near lustful desire: the need to find Nick.

Tuesday

'You're going to Hell,' someone shouts from a car window at Blue, and then wheel-spins off with a modded-car roar, rear-wheels snaking about on the road, evidence to the inefficacy of a flapping, plastic spoiler.

Blue is left standing in a haze of exhaust fumes and confusion. What was that about? He notices a single shoe beside the road – a smallish trainer – things like that always make Blue think that someone might have been murdered, but not enough to actually investigate.

He had to park further out than he planned, there was no free parking left in town. Mum's gone to Iceland, and so has every fucker else.

Back in Blackmoor, tilting at the windmills of stopped pit winding wheels. Nascent, intimate, alien place. Hunting for Nick and for a myth. Isn't that what childhood is: false memories and fabricated stories? But the thirst for Nick Nickelson is very real. Real enough to combat the urge to leave this place immediately. Which is a pressing urge. Because Blue has never felt the ever-present sense of unbelonging quite so acutely as in this place where he once belonged. Creeping around, eyes to the ground, stranger in a strange town.

Blue passes a man whose face is vaguely recognisable, but he's hard to place. He likely was a miner, because he has tubes up his nose now. Twin tubes that flow down his chest to a wheeled trolley with a diver's tank on it. The trolley and tank both are paint-chipped and dented from long years of service to multiple owners; it must be a strange comfort to drag such a beast about, knowing that it will outlive you to follow another. Blue feels like he's fighting for breath too. He needs to find Nick before he's sucked under the waves.

Blue heads back to the greasy spoon where he met Betony, maybe she's heard something. At least she knows who Nick is, more than can be said for most of the places he's asked at. Though he should try the traveller camp, like the Imperial Hotel landlord said. It doesn't sound like much of a lead, but he should do it. He'll go back and get the van after checking in with Betony.

Blue goes straight to the toilet when he enters the cafe. It's not the Ritz but still feels like luxury next to shitting in ditches. The cafe was nearly empty – just Betony and some old guy with his front door key attached to the bottom loop of one of his braces – so Blue risks giving himself a gentleman's wash in the sink. Dries himself with a wad of paper-towels, his junk feels soapy and sticky when he pulls his trousers back up. He takes off his Tee-shirt and gives his armpits the same treatment. There's water down the front of his trousers now though, so Blue does an odd sideways crab-walk to get to the counter. At least Betony won't think he's pissed himself, though she might think he's soft in the head.

He orders a coffee, he's got enough money for it in change. She serves it with enough of a smile.

She reminds Blue a bit of his first love: Willow: the girl he met when she tried to steal his backpack. Though she was a woman really, older than Blue. And now he thinks back, he's not even sure if he ever did love her, or only loved the time they had, but it was as close to love as he's come.

'You seem jumpy,' Betony says, 'You OK?'

'Just too much coffee,' Blue says, but then anyway asks for another.

'I imagine you'd say if you'd heard anything of Nick Nickelson?' he says.

'I imagine I would. You want that coffee topped off?' she waves a small whisky bottle, below the counter height, but where Blue can see it.

'Isn't it a little early?'

'I'd say it's already too late: if you want to drink all day, then really you need to start in the morning.'

'Well, thank you then.'

She has one too, leaning back against the Fantas in a glass-fronted fridge.

They make some idle chat. Blue staring at the scabs of ketchup on the top of a Heinz bottle, refilled with something cheaper; studiously ignoring the obvious elephant in the room's corner. Betony updates him about kids they were at school with. People long since turned into characters by Blue: they have features that exist only in his mind. He would likely be surprised if he were to meet them, or disappointed, or even irked. Because they would not be how they should be. Though he has to admit that Betony has grown up pretty good. Blue asks if she has kids herself. She nods and points to the name tattooed on her inner arm, but her silence makes it almost like a confession, unlike the eager pride of most parents. Blue figures she's probably divorced, or left in the lurch from the get go. Or maybe she fears a child might put Blue off …

'You have any?' she says.

'I can barely look after me,' Blue says.

'That's the thing with bairns though,' she says, 'You don't have to be ready for them to have them; if you did, they'd be rare as rocking horse shite. You do look like you could do with someone to take care of you though, I'll give you that, like.'

She goes to get the order of a rumpled, older middle-aged couple who've just come in and sat at a booth. She puts her hand on the lady's shoulder while she speaks to them, in a way that would be somehow unimaginable most of the places Blue has lived his later life. Blue wonders if his parents might have become like that – a comfortably old pair drifting onward down the river – had things been different; had that night been different; had Blue acted differently. *Dark crimes merit dark penalties. You'll have heard of a Glasgow smile.* The memories come at him, unbidden. Things he has fought so hard to block and bury. Even the air round here is suffocating with regret, unbreathable – whitedamp, afterdamp, blackdamp, chokedamp – why on earth did he come back? But he knows why he came back: he needs to find Nick.

He finishes his coffee and gets up from his stool. His crotch feels humid but is no longer visibly wet.

Betony bites her lip as she sees him going.

'On Tuesdays …' she says, then it lingers off into the griddle fat air.

'On Tuesdays?' says Blue.

'It's just that you were asking about my boy,' she says, 'On Tuesdays I work late, so he stays at our mam's all night. I mean, when I say I work late, it's not terrible late, just too late for school pickup: we only serve supper at the weekends, I'm generally done by five on a Tuesday. But it gives me a night for myself, you see.'

'Well, that's interesting,' Blue says, 'That is information worth filing.'

'I have a shower too,' she says, perhaps because she feels like she's laid too much of herself out there, 'I prefer it to washing in cafe lavvies ...'

'Well Betony, you are a myriad of fascinating facts. Maybe I'll come by to hear some more of them some time.'

'Maybe tonight?'

'I will ask my secretary how my diary is looking.'

For an instant, Blue feels an overpowering impulse to stay with her, to talk to her, to invite over that red-cheeked elephant; he senses the exhilaration of a weight lifted. But then he swallows it down; just winks and waves and leaves.

The Blackmoor front street is pedestrianised. Yet, although there is so much space – a clear, wide expanse of paving – everyone walks noticeably slowly. Pigeons move faster than the people, strutting about like they own half the town, which they do: the half not covered in anti-pigeon-spikes. Some pigeons even sit down in the middle of the street, there is so little foot-fall to threaten them. The birds stay wide of a dog though – long legged, but Jack Russell colours – hitched outside the co-op. It watches them, almost grinning with the irrepressibly improbable chance that a pigeon will wander within lunge range. Dogs are just clever enough to know hope but not clever enough to worry, Blue thinks, that's why everyone loves dogs: secretly, inwardly, everyone wishes they were a dog.

He sees the entrance to what was the covered market. *If you can't find it at Blackmoor market, you'll not find it anywhere in the world,*

Blue's mam used to say, against all sense and evidence. Blue smiles a melancholic smile. He's happy for that memory of his mam – as she was; before it all went wrong – but she has gone, and so has the covered market: turned into a carpet warehouse.

Beyond it, the high street and shops peter out into terraces in red brick rows. Pegged washing every which where. Miners' cottages. No miners though. Not working anyway. Two old souls, doubtless miners once, raise a distant victory fist salute of still-existence, and then creep to greet each other.

'Y'all right?'

'Canny. Not quite as good as the weather.'

And then Blue sees them. It's just something about the way they walk at first: two men moving down the street as if habituated to carving through crowds; a certain purpose and swiftness to the way they use gaps, different from how the rest of the street ambles. City men, or even, Skeggy men. Blue can't be sure if he recognises them – neither of them is Grimes, they're bigger than that – but they are too far away to know more. He can't see much of their faces anyway because they both wear mirror sunglasses and – despite the heat – they both wear black leather coats ...

Blue ducks into the first open doorway, didn't even see what the sign above it said. Inside, it has the feel of a community centre or something. Smells like cheap catering and dust. He goes in further through another door and then another. Finds himself at a dead end, turns to go back the way he came, but that narrow lane is now blocked by a lady. She is dressed a bit like a policewoman or a traffic warden, but not quite either of those, she's handsome, in a way that's both ethereal and austere.

'You are lost,' she says, it isn't a question.

Tuesday

'You are lost,' she says, it isn't a question.

'Maybe,' Blue says, 'I'm not quite sure where I am, I just kind of came in here.'

'You aren't the first and you won't be the last, people arrive when they're ready. I imagine you need help?'

She is correct of course. But then Blue is trembling like a punch-drunk boxer, it shouldn't take a third eye to see his fear. But he does need help, if help is someplace to hide. That much is true. He sees now that her uniform is Salvation Army. Blue attended a Salvation Army wedding as a small child. Was disappointed when not a shred of weaponry or camouflage was on display. Now he could use some camouflage of his own.

'Is there somewhere I could sit quietly for a while, have a cup of tea maybe?'

'Of course. Everyone is welcome here, whatever they're running from.'

'Is everyone running from something then?'

'Everyone who has not accepted it is running from the grace of God, usually because they're afraid of what He might ask them to do: to give up, or to confront.'

'What did He ask you to do?'

'We should eat, you should eat. You look hungry.'

And Blue is hungry and eager to be somewhere, anywhere, safe, so he nods.

'Thank you,' he says and he nods.

She leads him back and through a door into a room like a primary school hall, floor made of Tetris bricks of wood.

There are trestle tables filled with people eating. Life-ragged. Old folk, broke folk, homeless folk – it's hard to tell – some have come to the Lord maybe, some just for company or a hot meal. Blazer clad sally-army soldiers hold spatulas next to trays of lasagne and a hotplate urn of soup.

'I'm Verity,' she says.

'Blue.'

She is beautiful, or at least she should be. She is tall and has the slight stoop that exceptionally tall people sometimes have, a subconscious venture at assimilation. Blue can become hyper-sensitive to height. Of average height – precisely average height – in times of safety, Blue only takes note of those people remarkably taller or shorter. Only registering those who chose the roads of excess. But with vulnerability comes a tendency to sizing-up, a sudden sensitivity to everyone who is even a little bit bigger. An instinctive, nervy, measure of every interaction and passer-by. Even ladies, it seems, even Salvation Army ladies.

Verity's cheeks are prominent, pretty, but slide quickly down to a mouth set in an expression of certitude. It must be a comfort to be so saved by God. To be quite so saved, it must be hard not to be a tiny bit smug. And Blue is not certain that Verity has successfully steered that course.

Verity leads the way to the lasagne trays, but she herself takes only the smallest bowl and ladles it less than half full of soup. The ladle returned to the urn with some liquid still in it. She doesn't take a roll from the cairn set out for soup eaters. Blue takes a roll, plus a portion of the pasta.

With glances, they select a table to sit at, Blue with his back to the wall, able to survey the room for interlopers. But he tries to look as if he only looks at Verity. Her shoulders are solid, set in a shrug. Her eyes somewhat submerged within her face. When she removes her navy blazer and hangs it from her chair to eat, her blouse beneath is translucent, like she wants the world to see her bra; but she wears a vest, so it can't. Blue hunts for a hint of her quiddity, the thing that makes her her. There is a seductive uniqueness in virtually everyone, if only he can track it down. Sometimes it is as slight as a glint or a sparkle, a corner of smile, or the lines that show where a smile sometimes sits, but it is invariably there. Only Blue can't locate Verity's. There is a blankness, an absence. She is physically attractive, but Blue is not attracted to her. Somehow, he couldn't think to undress her without the fear of finding pins pushed into her legs.

She is clearly taking a reckoning of Blue too, however, and perhaps she is the more astute.

'When I was a girl, we had an Alsatian with piebald eyes like yours. My father called them 'watch tower eyes', said the dog could see angels and demons right alongside the living, said it could see both heaven and earth at the same moment. Can you?'

'I've seen plenty of dirt, if that's the earth. I once stared at the stars, all night long, from the top of a Ferris wheel, trying to decipher if there was a heaven out there. If there was, it seemed too distant for the likes of me.'

'Have you done time?' she asks.

'No. Not the way you mean.'

'Just there's something in you that I've met before: this mishmash of apprehension and bravado: there's a part you've hardened so much that it's left you almost hollow. I've worked in prisons, talked with all types. I saw this thing frequently in there: people who made so much front for themselves that what was behind it disappeared; men who got so used to faking an exterior that they forgot who they really were. I saw it every day in there, but it's strange to see it flying free.'

'The which way I fly is Hell, myself am Hell and in that lowest deep, a lower deep still threatening to devour me opens wide, to which the Hell I suffer seems like Heaven.'

'Paradise Lost?'

Blue nods.

'You're a scapegrace, aren't you? You're hiding from God's forgiveness. Are you afraid He would make you face something that you would rather avoid? You have all the sense for what is there, for what you must do, and yet you refuse it. Maybe your quote is right: you have a bit of Milton's Satan about you. Not the evil, I don't say that, but the pride: you will not ask for grace, for forgiveness, even though a part of you knows it would be freely given. Freely but for the pain of asking, at least. That is the only price: the overcoming of self. It isn't but a penny coin, just that many people have short arms and deep pockets and you: you have the pockets of a poacher. You could hide a partridge in your pocket and that shiny penny is lost in the lining.'

'Maybe I am a poacher, I'm at least a poacher's son.'

'Are you new to Blackmoor?' she says, 'I haven't seen you before.'

'I grew up here. I've been gone a long while. Maybe that was the time I served: in exile.'

'So why are you back?'

'I need to find someone. Do you know Nick Nickelson?'

'I don't, but there are a lot of people who think they're looking for someone, when really they're looking for Jesus.'

And Blue thinks that if Jesus could be content with less, then maybe Jesus could be his friend again. But Jesus wants that copper penny, while Blue is more concerned about bundles of fifties and twenties …

Tuesday

After they've eaten, Verity takes Blue to a back room of the Salvation Army Hall. She bids him sit on a sofa, covered in a throw so all-encompassing it is impossible to know whether its purpose is to protect a good chair or to disguise a threadbare one. There is a portrait of the Queen on the wall, as a young girl; skin smooth and pale and English as that glass and a half of milk that goes into every bar of Cadbury's chocolate. Verity makes tea and hands Blue a cup; she holds her own mug as if her hands are cold, though the room is more than warm enough.

Then they talk. Mostly Verity talks. She talks of things holy in a way that is pragmatic. She tells him of paradise and hell-fire, as if they are the weather. And yet she is skilled, she has a way of penetrating Blue's defences. Because Blue tries to just nod along– to use a croupier's well-practiced feigned interest – but she will not allow it, she forces him to be present in the moment.

'Do you know why you came here?' she asks.

'I just walked in, off the street, I told you.'

'Not inside the hall, but why you came back to Blackmoor. You said you were looking for someone. But I think there's more to it than that. I think you came back because you yearn for something, for redemption maybe? You're like a revenant ghost, which cannot settle to peaceful rest until it has absolution. God knows everything. He knows everything and He talks to me. He wants you to unburden yourself, I can feel it.'

And, for an instant, Blue feels it too. Maybe he does long for redemption. Could God forgive him, when Huxley told him that God was dead?

'Can you take confession, then?' he asks her.

'No, that's a Catholic thing, but I'm a really good listener. You don't need a priest to pardon you. You can absolve yourself, through God's grace, you just need to let it go. Whatever it is that you did. Whatever it is that's strangling you; you need to tell me about it; you need to set it free.'

Blue's mouth opens, but then freezes, his jaw is static, no words arrive.

Verity nods, beckoning, sensing a breakthrough.

But it's too much for Blue. The tension is too much. The atmosphere is too heavy with possibility. Saturated with salvation. Redolent with depth; when Blue knows that it is only safe at the surface. Blue feels the shallows tempting and blanketing, like the sweet bliss of alcohol to an addict: the ailment and the crutch that eases it at once. He lays back to be overpowered by the cool, gentle waves at the shore's edge. Glad to be washed in them. He feels a protective glibness returning, to smash her succubus spell.

'Heterochromia.'

'Sorry?'

'Heterochromia,' Blue relaxes back on the sofa, content to be safely returned to repression, to have defeated her mystical trickery, 'That's what it's called when you have differently coloured eyes. You were telling me that your dog had it. While rare in humans, it's relatively common in dogs. But anyway, speaking of dogs, I knew this boy, when I was just a boy myself, and his family had two dogs. They were one of those families that left the TV playing all day; I mean, if anyone was home, that TV would be on. And I noticed how one of the dogs watched the TV intently, just like a person would, stared right at it, eyes following the action. While the other dog would never give it the tiniest glance. So which dog was cleverer – I ask you – the one with imagination sufficient to believe, or the one who'd figured out it wasn't real?'

Verity's face sinks into a sad smile. The look a person might give to the recently bereaved.

'You're really set on your path, aren't you?' she says, 'Resolutely determined to remain a scapegrace. I can't wake you up, if you're only pretending to be asleep.'

Blue looks at the place on his wrist where a watch isn't, 'I have to go now. I really do need to find someone. But thank you for the food. And thank you for the advice. I'll keep an eye pealed for that penny.'

'No, you won't,' Verity says, 'Because I don't think that penny is lost at all. I think you know exactly where it is.'

Maybe Blue does know where it is. He at least knows its last whereabouts; where it disappeared. He at least knows there is somewhere he has to visit. The desperation to see that place is painful and, although it stinks more of self-harm than of any whiff of redemption, the need to go there is almost as fierce as the need to find Nick.

Blue skirts a circuitous route to stay off the main road. Follows the back of terrace ways that lead out of town, out of sight. The alleys are familiar and yet changed. Wheelie bins now stand by every backyard gate, in place of the metal cans of Blue's boyhood, lids that were used as shields, in snowball fights or while playing at knights. Crusader-cross England flags now block the view into some of the bedrooms, instead of lace curtains. But there is still the cobweb of telegraph wires and washing lines across the sky. Still the grey, grit bins, salt turned to rock in the summer heat. Still white-painted lintels and red bricks blackened with the coal dust of long decades past.

Out of town now, walking away from the coast; Blue does his best to duck from the view of occasional cars, until he hits upon the start of a woodland path that he knows will lead him to his target whilst keeping well away from the road.

The destination is not what Blue expected. The house that he has never been back to – the house that he never leaves – is no more. It has been demolished, bulldozed to a flat, empty plot. Purged like the mines; eradicated from existence. Maybe it had become a haunt for morbid ghouls. Or maybe no one wanted to live there anymore, not after all that happened. Only the big elm tree remains, like a memorial. But its roots are lifting the ground, bursting through and cracking it, as if even the tree is trying to break free and walk away.

Blue is staring into the void that was once his home, when he hears the car curb-bump to a stop behind him. The panic that hits him is at once flashback to the running engine of that night and the pressing, clear and present danger of today. He wheels to see a man already in the act of exiting the vehicle. The man is a leather-coated silverback. Middle-aged, in a muscled way, a scarred shark, weathered survivor of feeding frenzies past. The driver stays in his seat, keeps the engine revving. Blue is already running.

He flees across the empty plot, through a fence that is mercifully no longer there, and into the woods. Blue does not look back, but has a sense of shadows behind. Both of them, he thinks. Blue's run is a stumbling, ducking gait from the steepness and the uneven terrain and the sudden dark of forest and the branches whipping at his face. He falls once, but rolls back onto his feet with the plunging ground.

He hears a man shout from behind, 'Give up, boy, there's nowhere left to go.'

Though they must know that he won't. They must know that he can't. Blue flings himself onward, skidding, half tumbling, down a short drop of shale rock. His hope is youth. His hope is that they are townies and he is in the abandon beyond despair. His hope is that he can take more risks than they will allow themselves. His hope is that he knows these woods. Or once upon a time he did. But he hears them again behind. Telling him he's finished. Not gaining maybe, but not lost.

On Blue hurtles, sometimes near skating on the steeps, riding the heels of his trainers through leaf litter and still damp soil. Using his palms to pinball off trees, to break his speed and then send himself onwards.

Blue has heard no shouting from behind him in a while. They might be tired. They should be tired. Blue is exhausted. They might have lost his tracks in the confusion of forest. He stops a moment, tucked behind a tree. Listens hard. Tries to still his panting. Hears nothing. Not a bird. Not a broken twig. Silence but for the thud of Blue's own heart.

He moves on, still fast but trying to be stealthy now too, over pure pace. If he has lost them, he doesn't want to draw them in again.

Time has its own time, through terror, through forest, through dappled dark. Blue knows he's probably been moving less than an hour, but it feels like two, even three. Every moment is an age, senses so alive: alert to barely visible dangers of terrain, concentrating for any sound of pursuit. He begins to think it impossible that they could still be behind. How could they follow his tracks in this murk, they would surely need a bloodhound to have a chance?

Blue follows a hollow, a creek valley, the stream that once carved it is now just a wet seep, like its course has been changed. It is barely more than marshy, mossy ground but still soaks through his trainers and his jeans, when he sits or stumbles.

Blue shivers, wet from sweat and rivulet. But certain, near certain, that even if his pursuers haven't long since given up, then they are miles behind. He has snaked a devious trail. A childhood passed in these woods was not a childhood wasted, though he has lived ever since wishing it could have been different. Maybe, eventually, he will look back on today, not with fondness, never that, but a certain pride that he came through it. With every tread now, though his lungs and limbs ache at it, Blue dares to believe that he will survive.

He passes a kid's bivouac. Uncovered, just a crossbeam and struts. Looks like the skeleton of some deceased beast. But it marks the start of backyards. Blue knows himself to be nearly back to Blackmoor proper. Which means there must be a decision.

He could leave town now. He should leave town. Jettison this madness and run away. That would be the easy choice. That might be the wise choice. But would that be the weak choice? They were big boots: those that used to stand outside a door now razed from existence. Charlie wouldn't run; Blue knows that.

Betony is mopping the floor, when Blue arrives; wet with sweat; caked in clay; needles and leaves in his hair.

'You come for that shower, pet?' she says.

Tuesday

Betony drives a reddish Yugo, turned redder with rust. Interior of kid's finger marks and sherbet-dip packets, overflowing ashtray.

She parks on the black dirt back-lane of a terrace not far from the town centre. They enter by the back gate. Everyone came in through the back gate in Blue's childhood; everyone but the tally man and the postman. A habitual relic from the days when miners came home filthy in their work clothes; before the pit-head baths.

In Betony's yard, the side-by-side coal bunker and outside toilet, common to all Blackmoor terraces, have been opened up together, to form a little nook with a bench. A plastic pedal-tractor lies on its side.

Blue feels almost envious of the disarray in Betony's house. Blue has never owned enough to be messy. And his possessions have never been mingled with those of another. Betony has Bauhaus towers of Lego among her ornaments and individual bricks scattered like blossom. Small Buzz Lightyear socks flop over the back of a chair. Taped to a yellowing refrigerator, in what would have been the pantry, is a painting of a bright red horse cavorting on a field of Yamaha green. There is no sun, but it isn't needed to show what a sunny day it is, how happy the horse is.

Betony lets Blue sit, and gets a metal ice tray from the fridge, smashes it down on the side of the sink. She pours fat fingers of whisky into two glasses. The ice crackles in the whisky as it warms and splits, makes a Christmassy tinkling as she carries the glasses to Blue on the sofa. She lights a cigarette as soon as he takes his drink. Sucks the coal bright in the low light.

'You going to be stopping long?' she asks.

She's got that baby deer thing, big eyes like Bambi.

'Hard to know. I seem to be at a moment of decision, to tell the truth. But if I can't find Nickelson, I might have to leave fairly sharpish.'

'That would be a shame.'

'Shame's the story of my life, missy.'

'You can only feel shame if you let people shame you. I've packed in caring what people think. Given they never seem to do it much anyhow.'

She tastes of smoke. Blue likes it, the strangeness of it: kissing a smoker. Always has. Not sure it's a thing that could ever become familiar. It's a strange business, when you get right down to it: the beast with two backs: ancient as days; each day newly discovered.

She sweeps her fingertips down either side of the polytunnel forming in his trousers, tracing only the outline, like she's trying to guess what her present is without unwrapping it.

'Maybe I really should have that shower,' Blue says, feeling a sudden awareness of his own scent.

'Let's have one together,' she says, 'I don't think I could wait on you.'

Afterwards, they sit again on the sofa; sated, still damp. Betony leans into Blue's chest as she scrolls the remote control between all five channels. She settles on *Eurotrash*, Jean-Paul Gaultier and that other guy; funny foreigners, poking fun at other funny foreigners. Blue thinks of the time that Huxley took him to Portugal, the only time that Blue has been abroad. The bartender in the hotel spoke four languages and Blue had kissed a girl who was Italian, but spoke English with a German accent and lived in Lisbon. And for all its ridiculing, there is a soft, fond, love of otherness on the Eurotrash programme. Blue thinks that it might not be such a bad thing, to be Eurotrash.

Wednesday

Maybe it's false memory – maybe there is no other kind – but Blue is sure he can remember the smell of the piss, his piss. It smelt salty. Does piss smell salty?

There was piss on his bed and there were screams through the window. *I've seen the photographs*, Nicholas Nickelson said. And he held Charlie tight and they were going to give him a Glasgow Smile. And there was a childish certainty that all of this was Blue's fault. And there was a growing, grownup horror, because no one could do anything to fix it, not unless Blue could, no one but him. And that's what being a grownup means: it means the grownups can no longer save you. And there were moths. Strange thing to have seen, stranger to remember, but there were moths flapping and flinging themselves at the full-beam headlights of the car. None of it was a thing a person could easily forget – however hard they worked at that – but still strange to remember piss and moths.

Blue wakes first, crooking Betony. Not so much spoons as two upturned question marks. He was faintly aware of her poultice warmth even while asleep. It feels like a long time since the succour of another. He thinks of Sasha, they never even said goodbye. Was he nothing but a sucker to her? Still, there is something to be said for subtle exits. He eases up the covers, mentally he's already creeping downstairs. Then he thinks of last night and immediately, he longs to feel the pouch of Betony again. To let the fear disappear for just that while. He read one time of people shipwrecked – floating in a rubber craft, crammed in with not enough to eat or drink – and couples fucked there. They couldn't not. Even in front of others. Even though they couldn't spare the energy or the fluids, they still fucked. Just to own those brief moments when they weren't shipwrecked. Is that all there is: rutting to blot out reality: fucking to temporarily forget how easily your vessel could be split or spilt? Isn't there more? But even as he thinks this, Blue breaths hot at Betony's neck and strokes her thigh, until she wakes to him and opens to him.

'You don't have any sunglasses you could lend me?' Blue asks, as he pulls on his jeans, still warm from the tumble-dryer, 'Maybe a hat as well? That is, please, if you happened to have an old one that would fit me? I'd kind of like to keep a low profile.'

'What are you, some kind of spy?' she says, 'I don't imagine it is worth me asking what's going on?'

'I don't imagine it is.'

She returns with some brown, vaguely unisex, market-tat shades and a mesh-back trucker-cap from Lightwater Valley.

'I didn't have a good time there anyway,' she says.

'With the boy's father?' Blue asks.

She nods, 'I think you need to earn the right to be called a father though, and he's not done so. A tup would have shown more interest in a lamb.'

Blue picks up a clip-framed photo from the sideboard.

'He's a good-looking kid. Takes after his mother.'

'Flattery will get you everywhere. You after something else?'

'Well, to be frank, I could do with a couple of quid for breakfast ...'

'I don't know that I have anything myself. Sonny might lend you something.'

She brings a china pig, pink and smiling. It has a cork plug in its belly, so you can get money out with the pig intact. Betony puts two fingers into it and teases out a five and some coins – shakes it to show there's no more.

'Thank you, I'm very much obliged,' Blue says.

'I miss him you know: my Sonny. It's nice to have a night off, but I still miss him, even for that short time. People need to be needed. People need to be loved,' she stares into Blue's eyes, her lids crinkled, as if she is trying to fathom him, 'Will I see you again?'

'I hope so.'

'*Hope* doesn't sound very hopeful. You want to say goodbye properly then, just in case?'

She writhes as he goes down on her, his fingers pushed in, like in a china pig. His tongue tracing the seam of her. But they fuck slow, looking at one another, kissing, trying to make it not end; though it must end, it all ends. It ends well at least.

Afterwards, she makes him a sandwich for the road, even though she gave him the money for breakfast. He's already taken a bite – Mighty White and Marmite on his tongue – when they kiss adieu once more, well before the door. Blackmoor neighbours are known for wearing out their windows.

Blue blows a kiss and mouths, 'Thank you for having me,' as he slinks out of the backyard, splattered with a child's plastic distractions.

Blue knows that he won't see her again. He will never now return to the cafe, or her house. Some obstinate bit of him will not allow it. A hardened, self-hating part of him will prevent it. And he cannot kill that part of him, because he cannot confront it, not without confronting everything else; he has to keep it all locked away.

Maybe Betony already knows this: she waves a single time, with a half-closed hand, one of the slightest, saddest waves that Blue has ever seen.

Wednesday

Having made his way back to his van – nervy, stealthy, skittish as a rat – Blue feels safer again once in it and moving. He drives the coast road, away from Blackmoor – towards where he was told to find the traveller camp – following the headlands south. Blue's memories blur then jar with the real world. He has to stop and drop from the van at a layby to be sure he isn't imagining things. What once was dark with mine-spoil and jagged with dumped rock, has been conjured into nature reserve. Waves, badger striped with surf, break upon a beach buttered with sand and pale shale. And a path has been laid and maintained across the cliff tops, which used to be crested with continually turning buckets tipping waste. A twin-posted picture board explains what birds might now be encountered: sand martins, oystercatchers, curlews, skylarks, storm petrels, turnstones, whitethroats, great grey shrike. Beside it, another sign explains that the wildlife walk was officially opened by 'His Royal Highness Prince Andrew', thanks to the endeavours of the county council and the local MP. A tiny, gold-starred circle in the lowest right-hand corner of the board forms an asterisk for the afterthought footnote that European Union funds paid for the clean-up operation.

Blue stands, staring out, with the helicopter hum of the sea wind in his ears, watching the slow-motion wheel of seagulls almost static in the sky. He is ripped with dissonance, because what used to be a god-forsaken, man-ruined landscape, is now a place of stark beauty – grassy cols flowing down to shore – but maybe that couldn't have been achieved without the closing of the mines, without the gutting and near snuffing of the town. It doesn't seem a fair trade, for two generations unemployed, and yet the improvement is undeniable.

There is a visible change of colour in the waves, where the seabed drops away; rapidly, the waters off Blackmoor could guzzle anything.

Blue gets back in his van and continues down the coast road, occasional car parks beckon for walkers and twitchers. Then road signs begin to mark the distance to Hartlepool. They hanged a monkey down there. As a child, Blue had found it funny, everyone in Blackmoor did, everyone laughed at the Monkey Hangers. Now the thought of it makes Blue feel sick. Not that they should have been so insular, so unworldly, as to think that a monkey was a French sailor, a French spy, but the act itself: a dense neck and a light body, the monkey wouldn't have been killed by the drop; it must have dangled, being slowly choked. Tiny monkey wrists, bound behind its monkey back. Little monkey legs going kick, kick, kick. Simple monkey brain, wondering, through the terror, what had happened to it: why these people were so baleful, so vengeful. The French men on the ship had loved it, fed it, played with it. Dressed it in uniform, saluted it. And yet these people hated it, hanged it. Choked it to death for being different. Choked it to death for being from beyond their parochial reaches. The image of the monkey suspended, twisting in the wind, intrudes into Blue's mind. Nothing is more dead than a thing hanged.

He finds the traveller camp easily enough. It has obvious appeal:

a flattish field with a sea view and a small stream. A gate has been lifted from its hinges and now rests open, attached by the side formerly chained shut. Blue drives through, but parks near the entrance, reversing round so that his bonnet points towards getaway. The brass Lincoln Imp that is wired to his front grill just grins. The imp is aloof and immune, as always.

The traveller homes are circled in the field's centre, forming a ring as if an Oregon wagon train, making a loose stockade against the possibility of Indian attack. Like a party of pilgrims heading west. Though in truth, they could not head east. Not from here.

Blue walks towards the vans. They are largely campers: self-converted horse transporters and seven-and-a-half-tonners, some buses and Luton box-vans; only a handful of caravans. Many are painted garish or graffitied. Blue studies them, half expecting to see Willow's van – his onetime home – or to see her asymmetrical, cake slice smile. The improbability is near impossible, but given his current strange days of homecomings, it would barely surprise him if she appeared.

The travellers who do appear are upon Blue almost before he is aware. Emerged from among the penumbra of vehicles. Circumjacent but cast apart sufficient that although they are four, Blue can only see one at each gybe of vision. A practiced tactic maybe – to surround interlopers – given that Blue is harmless, entirely pointless. His fingers instinctively rise slightly, into an expression of yield.

They're a curious crew, the encircling band of men: shaven-headed, hatted and dread-locked; shirtless, waist-coated, army-surplussed; dis-unified by a nonconformity that leaves them looking entirely homogeneous. They're all rangy and new-agey – not Romany or Irish travellers – which for some reason is some relief.

The relief is short-lived: 'You're on private property,' one of them opens with; he has a pony mane of bleached hair, running over cropped sides, and narrowed eyes.

Blue shifts his weight, scratches his head behind his borrowed baseball cap, 'Sorry, I ...'

'It's not our property though, so don't worry about it.'

All the men laugh, Blue gets the feeling he's not the first to be greeted this way.

'So what are you after, mate?'

'I need to find someone. I was told you might be able to help.'

'Well, I don't know about that, maybe this person doesn't want to be found. But I suppose there's no harm in asking.'

'I'm looking for Nick Nickelson, an old friend of mine. They said in town that Nick might be with you guys, or you might at least know a whereabouts. We were best friends and it's really urgent. Do you know where Nickelson might be?'

The travellers retreat and gather themselves into a clutch, still some yards away from Blue, and loose enough that they can keep an eye on him, while they carry on a short council.

'You'd better come in and see then,' one says, his arms hang loose; them and too-close-set eyes give him a simian look, but his demeanour is amiable, 'Nick's not with us. But there is a girl who might be able to help you.'

'Are her and Nick ...?' Blue's question fades off, into a shard slash of an emotion so virginal he can barely give it name.

'Nah, I don't think Nick would be her type exactly, and Billy's spoken for anyhow.'

The stream runs through the middle of the camp. The dirt

nearest it has been packed down, or trodden down by use, and strewn with straw and sawdust. The stream doesn't flow fast, but periodically, simple water wheels are set in its course; powering dynamos presumably, or cog setups; one circle of paddles turns a spit above an unlit fire pit.

Sail cloths, strung from thin cables, strain away the brightness of the sun. Chickens murmur as they strut their strange dance, pecking at insects or urchin weeds. Some have clumps of feather over their feet, like the shire horses that used to draw the Coal Fair wagons.

In unused spaces – next to vans, around the edges – there are logs split and stacked, seasoning in the summer warmth, plastic tarps besides them in case of rain.

Visitors are seemingly not unknown, because none of the folk pottering about take much account of the fact that the four travellers have brought Blue in with them. A few brief waves is all. The dogs show more interest than the people. Varied hounds, that look not to have met a pedigree for generations, lope over to sniff at Blue's crotch.

The traveller with the pony mane hair leads through a slot run of alleys between vehicles. Beaten paths through the grass that slalom around tripwire guy ropes of awnings and overflow tents. He takes Blue to a place where a scatter of stackable plastic chairs sit outside a bus. The route marker on the bus front reads 'Out of Service', somewhat redundantly, given that the vehicle has been brush-painted purple and has metal sheets riveted over most of its windows. An attached, wind-out sunshade spreads over the chairs. A bird-feeder dangles from a corner of the sunshade, but the bus is encircled by other vans and trucks – as if it were the hub and the rest fanned out from it, like a bloom of acid from a battery point – it feels improbable that a bird would find its way to the food.

Pony-mane has Blue take a chair and himself knocks on the bus door, waits, enters. Blue looks about at the stelliform alleys down which he could swiftly disappear. But disappear to where exactly? He needs to find Nick.

Eventually Pony-mane returns, with another.

'This is the woman you want,' he says to Blue.

'Billy,' she says; extending a hand no stranger to manual labour, with a soaring swallow tattooed on it.

Billy looks to be in her early thirties, but she has laughter lines on a lean, youthful face, in such a way that she could believably be a decent amount either older or younger. She wears a white T-shirt with a packet of cigarettes rolled up in one sleeve. Her short hair is unruly; held out of her eyes with a thin, red bandanna. She looks like a marginally more feminine Matt Dillon from *Rumble Fish*; her jaw is proud and sharp as the click of a pool cue through the Motorcycle Boy's fingers. Blue thinks of the film, thinks of watching it with Huxley. And Blue feels the ache for that closeness. He thinks of the final, fatal explosion of bullets in the movie, which turns a black and white world to colour, for just one instant. There is a part of Blue that would give it all – the money, safety, life itself – for just that moment of seeing Nick again. Blue wants to bellow this; he wants to drop to his knees and scream at Billy: *Take me to Nick.*

But he just says 'Hi.'

'So you're looking for Nickelson,' Billy says, 'As a rule to live by, of which I've gathered a few, I would never divulge the location of a friend without a very good reason. But Nick told me about you, Blue. I know who you are. I could see how that might be reason enough. I guess no one but you knows for certain what happened that night and why. But, what you did back then … Anyone might have done that in those circumstances. Anyone brave enough, at least. I'm not big on judging people, but where I do, I judge on the intent and not the consequence.'

Wednesday

Many of the travellers sit around the fire, Blue with them, while the brook-powered spit turns a sheep above it. On each rotation, the spit strains on the upturn, before flinging the skinned thing downward in a spastic tangle of legs once gravity assists.

Lamb fat hisses as it drips and hits ember, mixing with the smoke; a sweet pungence, almost incense. The fire is composed of three long logs, pushed inward to the centre as they burn away. A smoulder suited to cooking, but not sufficient to fight the chill of night. Blue is given a blanket to put over his shoulders and lap. Of thick wool, with the look of hospital.

Billy hands Blue a tin cup of home-brew.

'Burns through glass too fast,' she says.

Blue takes a sip, which sears a crack in his lip and the toothless hole in his jaw, but tastes not unpleasant, instantly warms his chest.

'Almost good enough to drink,' he says.

'Would hold four fights to the pint, if they served it in pubs, but we're mellow enough here to handle it. Generally, we don't much bother the wider world and the world doesn't much bother us. Though, saying that, we're being moved on soon. We'll probably just go. Go before the pigs and the diggers even come to clear us out. Life's too short for such battles. When the time comes, when they've got serious about it, we just leave.

And we leave the place clean enough behind us. And shut the gates on the way out … We're thinking of wintering far south, Dorset, maybe Devon, even Cornwall. We'll know when we come to somewhere that would suit us for a while.'

'Sounds kind of idyllic, to where my life is right now. What does a person have to do to join you; I mean, can people join you?'

Billy produces a match, as if deliberately to add pause before answering. She fiddles with it, flipping it along dextrous fingers. She strikes it on a thumbnail and watches the flame die before putting the white end between her teeth.

'Well, we're not into vetting and elections and such, there are no insurmountable obstacles. We just have to feel that you'd fit with the community. You only really have to prove that you're not work-shy and not uncommonly irritating.'

Some of the folk around the fire play backgammon and shithead. A group are throwing knives, closest to the notch, on a wood block. A guitar is plucked and strummed, more in idleness than to entertain. Most of them have a snort of cider or home-brew on the go. Ganja smoke adulterates the wafts of cooking lamb. Each has their own van to disappear into, to be alone, but when they are out in the open, under the sun or the moon, they are together. There are worse ways to live than this.

'Would you feel ready to tell me where to find Nick yet?'

'I'll tell you soon enough, there's no rush. I only know where Nickelson will be on Saturday. So you have tomorrow to earn the information. Your arrival is somewhat fortuitous, there being a little job I could use a hand with, for which a clean-cut clean-skin would be ideal.'

'Clean-skin?'

'I'll explain in good time.'

Blue nods, abruptly less at peace than he had felt only moments before.

'Hey Nuthatch,' Billy shouts to another of the women, 'Will you bring out the girls and make them dance?'

Nuthatch gets up, walks to Billy's bus between oil lamps of cut-off tin-cans which light the ground. Blue gets a further lurch in his stomach, unsure as to what this means, an unavoidable image of kidnap victims or trafficked slave Asians.

Nuthatch returns with a girl in each hand. Drowsy things, stirred from sopor. They share eyes and chins with Nuthatch and each other. Wear pig tails, half pulled free by pillows. The man who was gently strumming at his guitar, picks it up in a more deliberate strain and the girls twirl before the firelight. Lids that had been drooping lift and tiny feet frisk in the dust. Not twins, but sisters near in age, they spin with steps unlearnt save from the other, concentrating and yet in reverie. Blue has never witnessed such clumsy perfection.

Eventually Billy claws both girls over and holds them on her lap. They squeal and giggle.

'My daughters,' Billy says.

They settle into her and soon enough return to sleep, at which point Nuthatch drags them up again to bed proper, before the mutton is even ready, which seems poor recompense.

The cooked creature is taken off to be carved. Tin cups are recharged. The fire, no longer needed for cooking, is stoked high with fresh wood.

And Blue stares at the flames, shivering, seeing within them the half-remembered renders from his nightmares: the blinding sparks of that one night, which annihilated everything.

Thursday

The cockerel crows for its own ends. It no more cares about waking others than an alarm clock does. Nonetheless, there is a sentient impatience to the noise that does not allow Blue to snooze.

Blue's pitch on the traveller's field, was a little on the lilt. And his sleep was anyway uneasy, his mind a hooky-mat of half pulled through thoughts: present troubles and past pains, entangled with what the coming day would bring: the job for which Billy required a 'clean-skin'.

Even ignoring the cock's word on the matter, tiny cracks between the van doors and sills allow in sufficient light for Blue to be sure that, like so much else, morning has broken. Occasional voices pass by outside; too muffled by steel walls packed with insulation for Blue to make out the words; to know if the speakers are making plans or merely passing by. But either way, clearly some of the travellers are already up.

Blue rises too, from his sleeping bag and foldout, foam bed. With his neck and back Quasimodo-crouched beneath the plywood and carpet skinned roof, Blue takes a piss into a two-litre plastic bottle. It is not a job for the unsteady of hand or the faint of heart, but the bottle is wide necked and Blue is well-practiced. He stashes the Trucker's Tizer, out of casual sight and wedged upright, beside the metal trunk, to be disposed of later. It often feels safer to confront a new day with an already empty bladder, but today especially so.

When Blue opens the side door, the steel next to the door handle is cold to the touch, where the edges were too impractical to carpet with the rest. The familiar grinding slide announces Blue's departure from his den and return to the world.

Blue shuts the door again and locks it. His windscreen is misted without and sweated with condensation within. And, in spite of everything, Blue allows himself a small smile. However humble, there is a certain satisfaction to be found from sleeping in a home that one has renovated one's own self.

Blue finds Billy sitting with a tin cup of tea on the steps of her purple bus. Billy has scrubbed up. At least to say that she's wearing a clean T-shirt and jeans and her dark hair is slicked back.

'Do you have a bag?' Billy asks, 'Like a backpack or a big hold all or something?'

'Yeah, I've got a bag.'

Blue drives the two of them into Gateshead. Billy sloped on the bench passenger seat of Blue's van.

'They're on to me you see,' Billy says, 'That's why I need you, for a final run.'

Blue notices a man cutting the grass outside a petrol station, with a ride-on mower, spiralling around in ever decreasing circles.

Billy won't let Blue park in the outside parking, says it's too visible. Makes Blue go in a multi-storey, even though the ramps and spaces are tight for a long-wheel-base van.

The Metrocentre had been promised for years, but it still hadn't opened by the time Blue was taken from Blackmoor, so it means nothing to that part of his childhood. But the Millets rucksack now on his back always reminds Blue of Huxley and as soon as Blue and Billy enter the Metrocentre that pang grows even stronger: because there is an amusement arcade right by the main gate, with the crash of game noises smashing into each other. The two pence shove machines twist the spelk in Blue's soul.

A group of teenage girls are hanging out there, looking like antelopes, legs longer than their frames.

The atmosphere is uncomfortably muggy, green-house hot. The shopping centre has glass ceilings, held up by faux Doric pillars, and the sun is so strong through the roof, the surroundings so white, that it actually feels brighter in the Metrocentre than it did outside. Which makes Blue feel exposed and apprehensive.

All the familiar high street chain names are featured: Tammy Girl, C&A, Virgin Megastores, Woolworths, BHS, Our Price, Dolcis, Morgan, Athena, Debenhams, Past Times …

Billy wants to start with Argos though. She gives Blue a wad of cash but waits outside, keeping a watch on the door, beyond sight of the shop staff.

Blue has never been inside an Argos before, but he figures it out, flicking through the big catalogues, finds what he needs. Writes it on the slip with the little plastic pen. It's like being at the bookies. Blue has been to betting shops a few times. Huxley used to go; at least biannually, to wager on the Booker and Turner prizes. He rarely won – *Too subjective dear boy, too subjective* – but always bet anyway. Blue wants to ram the little pen repeatedly into his palm, he can visualise himself doing it, stabbing until the pen smashes or he mashes his own lonely stigmata. But he doesn't, he just takes his slip to the counter.

Blue's mission is a success. Billy checks the contents of the bulging rucksack afterwards and takes charge of the receipt.

'They'd only let me have nine,' Blue says.

'Nine is fine, nine is good. We'll hit Dixons. Think up another name and another address that you'll remember, they need to have one.'

'Do you mind me asking,' Blue says, 'I mean, I don't get why the made-up names and why you can't just buy them yourself. Isn't buying mobile phones perfectly legal?'

'It's a grey trade and I'm black-listed here now,' Billy says, 'Pay-as-you-go phones are loss leaders: the suppliers compete to flog them as cheap as they can. Probably half what they even cost to make, a fraction of what they sell for abroad. And usually with a bunch of free credit as well. Because the phones are locked to one network and the networks think you'll be buying top-up cards with them for years to come. But I have a contact who can unlock the phones and then ships them to Africa by the container load. I mean, he's not just my guy, there are quite a lot of us working for him. And there are probably a few like him. Probably more of us all the time, because it's a good gig. It won't last forever. I make a near hundred percent mark-up on every phone that goes to Africa – we could clear a couple of grand today – and I sell the network credits off separately in this country on top of that.'

'Africa?' Blue says, 'Isn't Africa poor?'

'Africa is a big fucking place, my friend.'

Vodafone and Carphone Warehouse are in the same indoor square, lit by white streaked windows in the roof. A glass pagoda in the centre of the gallery. Flower petal streets shooting off elsewhere. Blue hits both shops, one after the other, Billy on a bench keeps him covered.

They have already swapped backpacks. Both are now about as full as they can get without badly denting the boxes and Billy says it's better not to do that.

'We'll do Dixons,' she says, 'They'll give you some big plastic carrier bags when you buy in there, then we'll unload into your van.'

There's a Wetherspoons in the Metrocentre – they pass it on the way back to the car park – a front-less false pub, like a film set for a misery drama, artificially gloomy inside, more fake, less wholesome, even than a normal 'Spoons. Yet it seems to attract some of the same clientele: bald-headed men watch Blue and Billy pass by with their bulging backpacks and big Dixons bags of electronic goods. Day-drinking radgies in straining T-shirts, tight over biceps, stretched over bellies, sight the prizes that might be won. The men physically shift their bodies to follow with their eyes, as if their necks have grown so thick that they can no longer turn their heads.

'That's why we parked in the multi-storey,' Billy says, clocking Blue clocking the men, 'It's easier to lose people. You always need to check you're not followed back to the vehicle by some fuck who thinks he can break in when you've gone and nick a free-lunch of phones.'

'What if someone just tries to mug you?' Blue asks.

Billy pauses a moment, looks at Blue, as if anew, then chuckles and rolls an invisible coin along her knuckles.

'Well, then I think they would discover that I am not very muggable …'

They take the lift three floors too high up. Then drop back down again on the stairs. Billy keeps watch, while Blue slings the plastic bags and empties the backpacks into the van. Billy is satisfied that no one saw them, so they head back to the shops again for another run.

Phones4U, Comet, Curry's. Blue buys phones for Harry Angstrom, Rusty James and Lester Ballard, residents of past post codes and random house numbers. The cumulus clouds visible through the Metrocentre's glass roof look unreal, like they're painted on. Both backpacks are bulging and heavy, four hands hold carrier bags. Blue and Billy unload into the van once again.

The Orange shop entrance is beneath a suspended sculpture, metal shards like dangling Damocles daggers, but Blue emerges successfully burdened.

'Last pass,' Billy says, taking charge of the rucksack and the receipt, handing Blue more cash, 'Only a couple left, then we're done.'

Because they are leaving anyway, they are not so careful heading back to the van on the final return. They walk directly to it, not bothering with the evasion tactics of the previous trips. It is a mistake. Three men, who must have tailed them, suddenly close. They're dressed like they're trying not to dress like plain-clothes policemen. An effect which is instantly undone when they flash badges.

'Hold it right there,' one of them says.

Blue pauses, in the action of loading the bags into his van.

'We've been watching you,' another of the officers says.

'We've been shopping,' says Billy.

'Yes, so we hear. You've been creating a lot of suspicion as well. Why do you need so many phones?'

'I'm not sure our consumer habits are any of your business,' Billy says and she pulls from her pocket the stack of receipts, 'Every one of those phones has been paid for, therefore no crime has been committed. I really don't see why this is a matter for the police.'

The officer asks to see the receipts and leafs through them, 'Why are there different names on most of these, different addresses? That smells a lot like fraud to me.'

'They were all bought with cash,' Billy says, 'No credit cards were used, therefore no fraud, we've done nothing wrong. We're both N.F.A. my friend and me – no fixed abode – so we have to make up addresses if we want to buy mobile phones, don't we? We are victims of our circumstances.'

The police ask to see the vehicle documents. Blue has his green paper licence and the V5 folded up together in the glove box. He gets them; his fingers are numb, bumbling with the tasks of unlocking and uncreasing.

One of the officers looks the documents over; taking far longer than the information warrants; eventually he says, 'We would like to search the van now.'

Billy looks at Blue. Blue is sweating. Blue's eyes are wide. Blue tries to shake his head without actually moving it.

'Perhaps you would,' Billy says, 'However, following several encounters with enforcement, I am pretty familiar with the 1984 *Police and Criminal Evidence Act.* Therefore, I know that to search without permission, you must have reasonable grounds to suspect stolen or prohibited articles. Now my companion and I have, I trust, allayed any fears that these items might be stolen. Because we have produced carefully collated receipts for every purchase. And I think we can all agree that mobile phones are not prohibited. So, I'm sorry to say that, although we have nothing to hide, we must on principal decline your request to search the van.'

'You're not the owner of the vehicle, though, madam. Perhaps the owner might speak for himself.'

'What she said,' Blue's legs are trembling, but he shrugs, smiles, tries to look unconcerned, like he's just humouring Billy.

'What's in that bottle?' one policeman points to a two-litre bottle, wedged upright, almost concealed at the back of the van, 'That's a water bottle, but the stuff's coloured. Is that drugs: magic mushroom tea, speed punch, methadone?'

Blue scrambles in to fetch it, already opening it as he comes back out. Stepping over the backpacks and bags, he allows himself to stumble getting down from the van, so that liquid sloshes over the top of the bottle and runs down his hands, drips off his fingers, spills out to splash on the car park concrete, almost on the shoes of the police.

'Piss. It's just piss,' Blue says, grinning like a simpleton.

The policemen step a few paces away in disgust. They hold a brief conversation, largely composed of raised eyebrows and nods.

'Go on then, you two, sod off,' one of them says, 'But don't let us catch you here again. Or we'll figure out something we can arrest you for.'

Back in the traveller camp. On the road to Blackmoor. Billy hands Blue a skinny sheaf of notes.

'Your cut,' she says, 'A bonus for a job well done. As for

the main payment: you'll find Nick at the party on Saturday, guaranteed.'

'What party?'

'The birthday celebrations of one Mr Baggot. A multi-millionaire, who for whatever reason has taken Nick under his wing like some kind of *Great Expectations* thing. I'm close as can be to certain that Nick would never miss Baggot's birthday, whatever else was going on. And I imagine that something else is going on, to bring you here.'

'So where will I find the party? Do you have an address?'

'Just head to the biggest house on the south-facing side of the lake. You couldn't miss it in the mist, must be the same size again as the second biggest property, and come Saturday it will be smothered in so many balloons and flowers, it'll look like Kensington Palace did last year, after Diana died.'

Friday

The nearness to finding Nick is creating a fervency that is almost hallucination. Blue can smell it in the air. Hears whispers of it on the wind. Reflections from the lake paint mirages of the imminent meeting.

But the lake is confusing: Blue is certain it wasn't there when he was a boy. It can't have been, wouldn't he remember that? Yet, lakes don't just appear: the amount of ground that would have to be excavated then transported elsewhere to make a hole that size would be monumental.

It takes Blue a while to circle the lake fully in his van, sweating even with the windows down. It is hot today, high summer for Blackmoor. As far as he can see, at no point can you get down to the water without passing through someone's private property. At no place is there even a public entry, much less a public car park. Grassy swards of gardens, many of them artificially landscaped with natural looking meadow flowers, descend right to the water's edge. The houses are all newbuild, some look barely finished, even the very oldest aren't very old, so the lake would surely have been completely exposed in Blue's childhood. Which makes him sure that it can't have been there at all.

He finds the house where the party will be tomorrow. As easily as Billy said he would: the biggest place on the south-facing bank. Unmissable; even over the high, light-brick walls that surround it. It's built of timber and smoked-stone, as if an old farmhouse, but with windows that run the full height of each floor; Tyneside flats would fit comfortably into its entrance hall. The street outside of its yawning double gates is filled with vans - caterers, bakers, florists - so Blue slots his own van into an available space. Among the huddle, it doesn't look out of place.

Not wanting to risk entry, but needing to scope the property out for possible gate-crash points, Blue walks - with what he hopes is a stride of entitled purpose - across the lawn of the house next door. There are no cars on its drive and no signs of life in its front garden. And from the back he should get a proper view of the party house.

Blue hugs the sandstone side - with faux bricked-up windows - as he slopes his way round. Thinking to make a swift, unseen exit should the rear of the grounds be occupied. But, despite his efforts, he finds himself facing a lady on a recliner. She wears a bikini, bright white, contrasting against skin sun-tanned to sepia. She holds a book, Penguin orange. She is wearing sunglasses, which completely conceal her eyes, and yet Blue knows by the tilt of her head that she is staring at him.

She might be old enough to be Blue's mother, if she got down to it earlyish; probably too old to be thinking about becoming a mother, if she isn't one already. Blue kind of gets the feeling that she isn't one. He's not sure why, but he has that sense: a maternal absence. She's slender, a lady-of-leisure, gently-muscled, gym-thin that Blue knows well from his days at the casino.

'Unless you're bringing some form of salvation from this purgatory, then I'm afraid you're trespassing against me,' she says.

'Come again?'

'This is private property, what are you doing in my garden?'

'Sorry, I'm supposed to be working at the party, I must have got lost.'

'You're not lost,' she lowers her sunglasses with one finger, to look over the top of them, 'What are you doing at the party?'

'I'm a croupier, they're having a fun casino thing. Roulette.'

'You came up with that quickly. Which is not the same as to say that I believe you.'

'Well, I'd better get back to it. Sorry to disturb you.'

'Take a seat. I'm bored near to nausea. No sense in hurrying back to a job of work which is entirely fictitious,' she removes her sunglasses now, as if to give Blue her full attention.

'Wouldn't you worry that I might be an intruder?'

'You are an intruder. Not all intrusions are unwelcome.'

Blue sits down on the recliner she indicated. It is made of slatted teak with tied on cloth cushions, it is clearly expensive but is not terribly comfortable.

'You needn't tell me what you are actually doing, but for God's sake distract me for a moment.'

'Is life on the sun lounger really that bad?'

'In common with most people of substance, I am actively engaged in withering and dying. Every moment not passed running, cycling, swimming, riding, or playing tennis or golf is spent stark naked in insufferable darkness wasting and pining.'

'Pining for what?'

'I don't know, anything. Something to plug the existential hole. Maybe pining for a life less easy. Hardly anyone kills themselves when they're struggling to survive. Suicide primarily inhabits realms of relative comfort.'

'Is that actually true? Maybe money doesn't buy happiness, but I can assure you that poverty makes every single other misfortune infinitely worse.'

'Don't you worry, I know I'm lucky. But you're lucky too, glance in the mirror some time: you could get away with anything with that smile. And I bet you do. Daily. Beautiful people enjoy a tailwind through life. You aren't entitled to lecture me,' she sticks out her tongue, but her eyes are sparkling, she is enjoying the sparring.

'You invited me to do so. You couldn't stand another moment of the eternal torment of endless leisure.'

'You don't know that my leisure is endless. I'm off today, but perhaps my time is largely occupied working as a lawyer, often pro-bono, fighting for innocents that the justice system has failed.'

'Perhaps,' says Blue, 'But I'm betting you're generally to be found out here, reading Samuel Beckett and thus, not unnaturally, questioning the absurd pointlessness of life.'

'Touché. But only until around midday, then I start drinking martinis.'

'Isn't that a bit dangerous, by way of a routine?'

'Oh, I'm sure I'm fast becoming what they would call a high-functioning alcoholic,' she says, 'I'm fine with that. The fact is, there's an easily achieved sense of purpose to each day, if your purpose is mainly to be halfway to getting drunk by halfway through the afternoon. Which does make me think: do you know how to make martinis, darling? I'm quite in the mood for a martini.'

Friday

Blue feels like, when he was wrenched from Blackmoor, brutally orphaned, severed from family, from childhood, from Nick, and then finally from Huxley as well, it was like he was cut from humanity, from all humanity and his own humanity. Though it is impossible for anyone to enter into the mind of another – nobody knows anybody, not really – Blue feels like even parts of his own mind became unreachable, became forbidden ground, no man's land. Though he cannot know what it feels like to be someone other than himself, Blue feels like they are not like him. Which is why there is relief in occasional kindreds. Those who are like him, at least in being not like the others, even if not really like him.

There are dark shadows on the lake, as if a deeper Hades lies beneath, but it is just the shade of clouds. They wade together, Blue and Penny, waste deep in water and martinis. Two islands.

'Where did this lake even come from?' Blue asks, 'I swear it was never here when I was a boy.'

'It was Baggot, whose party we both know you're not working at. The old man came up with quite a scheme, must have been a whisky dream that he managed to write down. When he first heard murmurings that they were planning on building the dual carriageway, he knew they would need monstrous amounts of aggregate and hard-core. So he used what money he had – his redundancy money from the mine probably – and bought a near worthless stretch of land and the rights to quarry it. It was completely coal-less. Not a seam. And the town already on its knees. They all thought he was as loony as Noah building a ship in the desert. But long before anyone else saw it coming, Baggot had it all in place. He charged the government to carve out and cart away a great hollow on the moor for him. And when they were done, he diverted streams to fill it and sold off all the plots around the new lake. The pristine road that paid him to create his lake also made it prime land for weekend getaways. He stocked the lake with fish. Fat, depressed carp that don't care if they get hooked, just so long as it creates some difference in their day. You can hike on the moors and along the coast, swim when it's hot enough, pretend you're part of nature, then return to your luxury spa room. Every last plot sold.'

Penny runs her fingers across the surface of the water and then uses the wet to sweep back her hair.

'Those are fancy earrings,' Blue says.

'They're only emeralds,' she says.

'Only people who own fancy earrings think that emeralds aren't fancy.'

'When your breasts cost ten thousand pounds, nothing else ever seems fancy again.'

The sum seems staggering. Blue almost wants to ask if that was each, or by the brace, but he only tells her that she didn't need to, that she is beautiful. And he isn't lying.

She splashes water at him, by way of answer. In the action, her hand brushes against Blue's bare chest and she lets it remain there just long enough to let him be certain it wasn't by accident.

'After a few more drinks, maybe we'll both think I'm twenty years younger.'

'Most women would be proud to look as good as you do when they were.'

'You should tell my husband that, because he's found himself a newer model.'

'Your husband is a fool.'

'Is he? In the sense of an easily-pleased, masculine shallowness, probably he is. But he's happy, so maybe I'm the fool?'

Penny looks for a moment like her hard-shell will shatter and perhaps consciously to counter that, somewhat mechanically, she shifts the conversation:

'I have a plus-one ticket for the party tomorrow, you know. You're not working there, but you do want to go there, don't you? It's important to you; I could see it in your rather enchanting eyes. Tell me why and maybe I'll take you.'

'I need to find someone. Someone who will be there.'

'Why?'

'I wronged them. Half a lifetime ago. At its base, maybe it's that. But it's complicated by money.'

'What isn't?'

She pulls Blue to her, with a single finger beneath his chin, and kisses him.

They kiss more on her bed. Beneath the creeping light of a Velux. Stripped of lake wet bikini and under-shorts, they are instantly naked. There is no clothing sophistry. She is more creased than he is used to; when she twists, the skin of her side ripples into gills. Her flesh is soft and groups, at knees at neck. Lingers a little as she turns. But she is entirely beguiling. Her store-bought breasts are perhaps too firm – as with movie remakes, Blue senses that he might prefer the originals – but they are intriguing and alluring.

He toys with her, sliding his cock between her legs, opening the line of her, aiming to make her so desperately aroused that she will buckle first and force him inside.

But, just as he thinks he must have won this parlour power-game, she stops completely. She pulls his hand from her breast.

'I've changed my mind,' she says, 'I don't want to anymore. You're a handsome boy, but you're still a boy. And I don't think I want to lose my sense of moral superiority over my letch of a husband. It's nice to know that I could have though. I'll bank some pleasure from that.'

Blue, now lying marooned on his back, is hurt. Through his own familiarity with the sensation, he feels like her words are not even true: he suspects that she really stopped because she had to beat a retreat back inside herself again; she got suddenly scared of the vulnerability that letting go might entail.

'I'll finish you off if you like,' she says, 'I don't want you walking around horny and grumbling.'

And she proceeds to do so, with ridiculous ease. Sitting cross legged beside him on top of the bedclothes. Using both hands, twisting and stroking, she milks him in a way that is simultaneously adroit and utilitarian. Then she cleans him with baby-wipes, from a pack in a bedside drawer. The whole episode leaves Blue feeling empty: denied his comforting role-play of irresistible lover; taken back to being a lonely little kid.

Penny, however, seems invigorated by it all. The re-envelopment of her carapace, the return of control, has her energised.

'Come on, up you get. Since you're naked anyway, let's find

you some new clothes. You looked like you didn't belong to anybody when you arrived.'

She leads Blue to a room entirely dedicated to housing her husband's wardrobe.

'Put on whatever you want for now,' Penny says, 'Then later, after dinner, we'll choose you an outfit for the party. If I'm to have you on my arm, then I intend to turn the neighbourhood ladies green with envy tomorrow, and whisper about it forever.'

'Won't your husband notice his things missing?' Blue asks, even though that seems improbable, given the frankly immoral quantity of clothes in the room.

'As far as I'm concerned, you could take as much as you want and take a bag to put it all in too. With the clothes in our home in Durham and the stuff at the apartment he rents for that schoolgirl in Newcastle, I doubt he has the remotest idea where anything is. Now, what do you want for dinner, lobster?'

Saturday

They eat breakfast at a special bar, apparently named for and solely used for that meal. Swiss muesli with organic yogurt. Milk would have been better: yogurt doesn't penetrate the dryness. Expense is not in of itself improvement. Though her coffee is myrrh on the tongue.

Blue slept in one of Penny's spare bedrooms, in pressed cotton pyjamas. For the first time in weeks he slept right through the night. Though he was extremely, gratefully, aware that he was asleep, which must surely mean that he was not.

Her house being next door, even though the grounds of Baggot's are sizable, she and Blue don't have to step too far: they are almost instantly inside the cordon of security around the party. Which is only to say a handful of big guys in matching blazers, but who are rigorously checking tickets and lists.

Penny wrist drops her invitation card, 'Just me and my plus-one,' she says, demurely looping her arm through Blue's and walking him in, leading from behind.

Blue has his hair waxed with some product she put in it; he wears a suit the grey-blue of mist on a river, tailored from near weightless wool, and shoes polished sufficient to reflect the sky. She wears a black dress, with slits down either side, held together with safety-pins; but in an expensive way, not how the clothes of Blackmoor kids used to be. Blue helped her to tit-tape the top, where it clings, cliff-edge, heckling gravity.

Though it has not long gone midday, girls with trays of champagne stand outside the front door of the house, so that every guest enters drink in hand. The front door is the size of a bank vault's; which it might as well be, given that most things beyond it seem to be gold: as far as the eye can see, gold leaf and gold paint. It must be like living inside a carriage clock. Even the sofas are gold, a kind of shiny gold cloth, soft and smooth as the fur of a puppy. The entrance hall is almost the size of the Metrocentre's one. It has twin staircases rising up on either side, their treads are marble and their banisters are gold-painted wrought-iron, topped with rosewood. The two staircases curve in and join onto the landing on the floor above, at almost exactly the same point, so one of them is entirely redundant. The whole effect is like the palace of some precarious-necked French king.

Blue scans the crowd for anyone who could be Nick. The goal is finally so close now that Blue can feel his blood coursing. People mill and mingle, chatting in small groups. Three men nearby bray, loudly enough that overhearing them is involuntary.

'They don't like us being here, they think we're some kind of middle-class cancer corrupting the town, but this place was dying on its feet before the lake properties were built.'

'Aren't we all middle class now anyway? John Prescott said so, just before the election.'

'Probably, but in Blackmoor that only means someone who eats using cutlery.'

'Says the chap who just demolished the finger buffet …'

They all laugh, Blue assassinates them, using only his eyes.

Penny leads him inward, into another room, skirting

through the manicured mass. Here statuettes of Greece and Rome feature heavily, in nooks and niches and perched upon plinths. Naked women, round hipped, small breasted, bathing or bow hunting. The statues of men are also idealised in the form of an earlier age: muscled, but gently so, from an epoque before steroid and comic book.

A couple argue, for some reason think themselves to be invisible because they stand in a corner. They must have started drinking early, to be ready for battle so soon.

'I barely looked at her,' he says.

'I know that look, and I saw where you were looking.'

'Are we really doing this now?'

'You're a pig,' she says, 'You're just a pig.'

Saturday

There are bookshelves extending across the entire end wall of the room that Blue and Penny are in, but every book has been shrouded in glossy white paper, their covers entirely hidden. The impression is quite striking, one of the more elegant features of Baggot's mansion, but it is impossible to know what the books are, so they must be purely decorative, not even for reference, let alone for reading.

Blue feels an overwhelming urge to run at the bookshelves and clamber up them like an ape, pull out every copy, yank the covers off them and fling the books around the room. Unmask the tomes and his person; reveal himself for Nick. Yet he doesn't. He lets himself be cornered in conversation, backed against a wall by a ring of strangers, trapped by Penny's hand on his arm. He surveys the room as best he can, but pretends to be present in the chat. He knows he should be actively seeking Nick and yet he is allowing himself to be blocked from that, as if this moment is a mirror of the past decade.

The people they are talking to are clearly old Blackmoor, not lake-siders. From being a croupier, Blue has grown unconsciously adept at costing clothes by cloth alone, but the Blackmoor accent is anyway unmistakable.

'Why've you got to be so down on it all. We've the Labour in now, nearly twenty years of Tories, but we've finally seen the back of them. Seen them off for good, I hope. Blair's from

Durham and all, has the Sedgefield seat, though admittedly you'd not know it to hear him talk, like. The Japanese have come, we've got God's own workers here and we're the gateway to Europe, there's canny little can go wrong again.'

'All that could be undone in an afternoon.'

'You're being a workie ticket. The dark days are over, the North East will rise again. Thatcher tried her "managed decline" and she's failed. We're going to revive and be stronger than ever. It'll not be Geordies migrating to Germany, like in *Auf Weidersein, Pet.* It'll be Europeans coming here next. And we'll welcome them with open arms, like they did us. We'll be the rich ones in the coming years, mark my words.'

'Yeah, that'll happen. They'll not let it.'

'Who are "they"?'

'The establishment, the powers that be, the Tories, Westminster, London, they're interchangeable, man, and they'll never let us back on wa feet.'

There is a defeatist, disgruntled pause in the conversation. And Blue seizes it, perhaps it is even a spur, 'I have to use the gents,' he announces, and he slips Penny a wink as he slides himself free of her hand.

'You do whatever you have to do, you strange faun,' she whispers in his ear, 'It's been fun. But if you want my counsel: whoever it is that you're looking for; you don't need them; you are better off alone.'

Blue returns to the ballroom entry hall, coated in gold. Figuring from the high landing he could see every new arrival. The marble stairs are over-sized like in a fairground fun-house, making Blue feel shrunken.

He always thinks he can remember being found sleeping on the bottom step of his parents' house, a small, curled boy, wanting to lie nearer to a dad still up. But because Blue can also distinctly remember being told about the occasion, as an older child, he can no longer be certain that the first memory is not a construct. Yet, just now, he can definitely recall that longing for closeness.

He takes a fresh, slender-stemmed glass of champagne from a waiter's silver tray, as they pass one another on the stairs. All the waiters and waitresses wear striped pullovers, like they are supposed to be sailors, or burglars, or Frenchmen. Blue can somehow tell that they are not local kids, they must have been brought in from outside Blackmoor; no doubt like the labour that built these lakeside houses.

The upper landing provides a clear view of the entrance room below and also – because of windows that run almost the full two stories in height – much of the world outside. There are topiary hedge forms in a line down the drive. Each one is seemingly supposed to resemble something different, which has resulted in many being indecipherably vague in shape.

And in the middle distance, at the end of the avenue of shrubby silhouettes, Blue sees what looks to be a heated discussion. Security guys, in their purple blazers, stand shoulder to shoulder, bodily blocking the driveway gates. Opposite them, three men in black leather coats – lupine, ursine, vulpine – and a slighter, weasel shape, at their head. A blazered figure waves his clipboard in the air. A second talks into a radio. Two more men in blazers join the others and then another. There is an impasse. No one moving. Then the smallest person reaches into his ill-fitting suit-jacket and pulls something out, a slim brick, more probably: a wad. He hands it to the figure with the clipboard. The blazers look at one another a moment or two and then move aside. The leather coats start down the drive.

PHASE THE SIXTH

The end was contained in the beginning.

1984 – George Orwell

1984 - Charlie

Charlie knocked on the door, more rattle than rap, the hinges were so loose. The wood was peeling three colours of paint. Hot to the touch in the sun. The door was half open, but that didn't tell you a whole lot: many Blackmoor folk didn't bother closing their front doors in the summer, if they weren't going out for long, never mind up here by the moors.

She came though, in cut-off jeans like Daisy Duke. Barefoot. Shirt-tied, no bra. Charlie used to worship her like that. She was his church. A faith he failed, like the others.

'Hello, pet,' she said, and opened the door fully, to let him in.

'Wasn't sure you'd be home, saw the car wasn't there. Nick not home?'

'Neither: one at the pub, one at the park; leave you to guess which is where.'

Her smile triggered every kind of pang in Charlie. Her over-bite invited attention. She asked him if he wanted a beer. He asked her when he didn't. She fetched him a can of Nicholas': warm, cheap, just barely a brand, but not the worst you could settle for. Charlie pulled the ring-pull off and then didn't know what to do with it, pressed it onto his little finger.

They sat side by side on the sofa, which had doubtless already seen better days back when it was bought. If it was bought. Charlie took off his camera, which was digging into his back, and put it on a side table, which comprised of one of those giant wooden spools the mines got cable on. It didn't even have a cloth over it, just the paint stencil *TINSLEY WIRE ROPE MADE IN SHEFFIELD*. There was a big TV though, one of those ones much wider than tall, and a fancy *Betamax* video cassette recorder was beside it, quite out of sorts with the rest of the room.

'So what brings you over,' she said, 'Long time since I've seen you outside of school stuff.'

'I don't know, maybe this is going to sound soft in the head. Maybe it's daft to even want to know. Maybe sleeping dogs are best left to their beds, but …'

'Oh, I see.'

'You do?'

She finds a cigarette, clicks a lighter, 'You're up a height because you finally figured out that Nick's yours, huh?'

Charlie looked at Gael, almost as if it was the first time. Though the first time they were just bairns. The first time he probably pulled her ginger pigtails or some shite like that.

'Suppose I knew it was not impossible,' he said, 'Was a strange time, that year of being a hero – I was on the lash close to always – but I could just about keep straight what events happened when. Seems like it's been growing more likely in my mind every year Nick grows though. Apples can fall a distance from the tree, but Nick senior, I'm not sure he's an apple tree at all. More like a clarty great pine.'

'Be fair. Yes, he's about big and ugly enough to stop a clock. But you cut me loose, Charlie, you broke it off. He was there for me. He caught me when I was falling. He's not so bad. We muddle along. And you carry that information with you to the grave, by the way, or that grave will come sooner than you think. If he had any inkling that Nick wasn't his, I swear, he would murder us all that self-same afternoon.'

1998 - Blue

The leather coats start down the drive and Blue instinctively ducks below the landing balustrade, though he doubts they would make him out, high up among the throng.

'You all right, my love?' a lady behind him asks.

'Fine, I'm fine,' says Blue.

But he is not: he doesn't know if these grand marble twins are the only stairs, but it seems not improbable or even unlikely, and given that possibility, he has only moments to descend or risk being trapped.

Descend he does, taking the steps at a clatter, slipping through rude gaps between well-dressed guests. At the bottom, tries to shield himself from the windows, dares not glance, but sure the leather coats must be within yards of arrival.

Blue rushes through an exit door of the entrance hall, the opposite side to that which he went through earlier. He almost knocks a tray of pastries and prawns from the hands of a wasp-striped waitress.

The windows in this new space are hung with curtains of dark scarlet cloth, triple thick, ending in tassels of gold; each one could mark the boudoir of some emperor, but they run every few yards for the whole room length. There are shiny china sculptures of tigers and dragons and other far eastern effects. Momentarily, Blue thinks about taking a samurai sword, from where he sees it on the wall, but it would slow him and cause consternation and how would it even help. Instead he plunges onward, swerving a slalom dance, beyond the edge of social sanity, toward a doorway at the end.

Through it and into a conservatory, or glass-roofed stateroom, greenhouse hot, despite ceiling panes raised wide. Tropical triffid plants overspill their pots. Doors at the extremity are open onto the lakeside garden. Blue murmurs excuse-mes and apologies at the same rate as the pace with which he crabs and tacks his way through the guests toward the beckoning exterior.

Outside, a manicured acre, flat and green as blackjack baize, surrounded by brick and wood palisade. Smoke squirrel-tails its way skyward from a great clay oven where chefs scurry. White clothed tables foreground the lake. Guests are still scattered about, but spread sparser in the space. Blue heads water-ward, at a half jog, hurried but just sub-maniac. There is a boathouse, which surely suggests also: boats.

As he nears, Blue sees a wooden jetty. Low enough to the water that at the end of it a lady in a blue dress dangles her feet into the water; beside her, a rowboat, oars stowed, quivers on ripple waves.

Blue thuds down the planks of the pier, noise bouncing from the drum of lake beneath. The lady turns, she's blond, slight, not far from Blue in age.

'The boat,' Blue says, 'Is it yours? I need to borrow a boat for a bit.'

'It's Baggot's, of course,' she says, as she gestures with a sweeping hand, 'It's all Baggot's. But he's a generous man, he'd not mind.'

She's nearly canny bonny, but with an impish face, stretched at the centre, kind of too pointed, like it's aimed at something in particular, or as if the maker had finger-pulled it outward, as one can with clay. And …

'Nick?' Blue says.

And she stares at him. She stares at his eyes. Her mouth creases into surprise, then smile, then anger, then she laughs.

'Blue?'

1984 - Charlie

They took a walk, more than half to be out of the house before anyone else got home, though that fact went unspoken. Off onto the moor's edge, they went, quickly hidden from view. She swung the half empty whisky bottle like it was a bairn's scran pail. Charlie stopped to take a photo, urged by the way a lone, wind-ravaged tree yearned into the sky, branches like veins.

'You ever wonder how things could have been?' he said to Gael, 'How things could have been different?'

'Only some days,' she said, 'Some days life is unbearable, but other days it is unbearably wonderful. I have a beautiful daughter, it's hard to wish the world other than it is without dishonouring that fact, without being disloyal to my own lovely Nicky.'

'*We* have a beautiful daughter,' Charlie said.

'No, *we* don't. You need to forget that. It did not happen if we do not speak of it.'

'If we could run time backwards, do it all again, would you do it all the same?'

'It doesn't matter if I would or wouldn't, because we can't.'

They sat down on a fallen tree, at a place where moor began to give to woods, and shared further swigs of whisky. Charlie put the bottle down on the soft ground between them, fiddled with his camera.

'You ever notice how folk look worse in old photos?' Charlie said, 'Almost always. I puzzled about it over the years, wondered if they really were, if human kind was growing better looking, or maybe if lack of food and disease and such were responsible for the homeliness of our ancestors. I've come to the opinion that it's just exposure speed. We are not seeing them as they were, but with a touch of blur: their noses are broader, cheeks and chins longer, because they couldn't stay sufficiently still.'

'Lucky them for even getting the chance. No one ever takes my picture. No one has taken my picture in years. Take my picture, Charlie.'

She plucked a stalk of bob-headed grass and put it in her mouth, the end dancing as she pouted, she put both hands upon one knee like a Metro Goldwyn Mayer prima-donna. Charlie laughed and stepped away a few paces. He fingered the viewfinder, pressed the subtle shutter button. Click.

The log of their bench was in a sun trap. Charlie was aware that he was getting hot-necked as he took more shots. She soaked in the shine, stretching out her legs along the fallen tree; then straddled it, as if she rode it.

'They never teach you side-saddle?'

'You know full well they did not.'

She began to untie the knot at the bottom of her shirt.

'Hold on. You sure about this?' Charlie said, though he wanted nothing more than for her to continue.

'You frit, local hero?' she said, 'You more scared of facing naked breasts than mounted police, more scared of my nipples than mine explosions?'

'I played no part in starting those things, they weren't my choice, they were just things that happened to me.'

'Are you wanting me to say that this is no choice of yours

too? Because I won't. If you don't stop me, then you are choosing this; I'll not have you one day say that you didn't.'

She stuck out her tongue and undid the tie of her shirt, let it hang loose. Charlie took a photo, crouched to a better angle and took another. She shrugged the shirt off her shoulders entirely and shook her red hair, flung back her head to stare at the sky. Her freckles dappled out at the sun-hid foothills of her breasts.

'Do you think I could have been a Playboy model?' she said.

'Still could,' Charlie said, 'Still bloody well could.'

'Will you give me copies of the pictures?'

'I suppose. As long as you promise to hide them well, for both our sakes.'

Afterward, they lay there. Sticky with sweat. Coated with plant-shreds and grass-seeds and regret. Aware perhaps that the only thing that could stave off the shame would be to re-enact its cause again and again. To repeat until the crime was normalised. But that was no solution for today.

'It did not happen if we do not speak of it,' Gael said.

Then they parted, before the coming dark.

1998 - Blue

'You're catching crabs.'

'Say what?'

'You're catching crabs,' Nick says, 'With the oars: you're not cutting into the water, you're skimming it. You're cack-handed, man. Give-us the paddles if you're in such a rush; you've clearly never done this before.'

And, strange to say, Blue hasn't. He's barely lived more than a few miles from the sea his whole life, and never once rowed a boat.

They perform an edgy swap, standing up, a pigeon step waltz, wooden dingy rocking, side slapping the lake surface.

Nick hitches her dress up over her knees, to brace her feet into the edges of the hold. Her arms are shaking, but her shoulders hump as she hauls on the oars, the vessel scuds forwards, twice the pace of Blue's efforts.

'That's more like the kid I knew,' says Blue, 'What happened to the tomboy?'

'I changed a lot after what happened. Like I lost that other me alongside the rest of the loss. Maybe I needed to be closer to our mam and being a bit more of a real girl helped with that. Then again, maybe it was just adolescence. But this is my party frock, Blue, I'm still happier in jeans or joggies; mightn't surprise you to learn that I don't generally go about the place gussied up in petticoats. Baggot bought me this, if you must know.'

'He's a generous man.'

'You don't know the half of it.'

They are far from shore now, far from harm, distant enough that figures outside at the function are indistinct.

They beach the boat at the side of the lake closest to Blackmoor. The sunny day is changing fast. Avalanche clouds roll across the sky. Blue and Nick thumb a lift from a sign-painted pick-up, dented like a rented bucket. The driver doesn't even comment on their smart attire, just keeps itching his own beard of neglect. A plastic-bag flag flaps from the end of loosely tied down planks in the back. Except to thank their chauffeur, Blue and Nick don't talk until they get out, near town.

'We need to go someplace safe for tonight,' Blue says, 'Someplace we can get to fast without transport. Someplace that isn't anyplace someone might think we might go. Do you know such a place?'

Nick thinks for a moment.

'I know such a place.'

They get supplies from a corner shop: vodka and cola, Ginsters pies and Walkers crisps. Next to the fridge, newspapers are spread out, tops visible, like hands of playing cards. *The Sun* is not among them. Not in Blackmoor, *The Sun* sells less copies than in Liverpool.

The place Nick knows is a pit-head relic, a concrete building, roofed with corrugated-iron; left standing as a reminder of other times, or missed off the demolition list. Out of town, its private road now overgrown, still passable on foot.

The building's double loading doors and other entrances have all been shackled or boarded shut. Nick leads Blue round the back, and in through a window where a grill has been smashed out, leaving stubs and scars in the render. Her dress wafts into a flower as she drops to the floor.

Inside, hooks hang from the ceiling, cobwebs hang from the hooks. Mould clambers like ivy up the walls. They go into the largest room, erstwhile engine house, sometime pump muscle for a winding wheel. The machinery has all been ripped out for scrap. The floorboards have been pulled up; to be burnt by kids or tramps: there's a homemade brazier in the corner, holes poked in a steel bin. Only a lower layer of ground, still pocked with screw holes, reveals where a section must once have been boarded out. The rest of the floor is rough concrete foundation, pebbles now popping loose. Pipework, insulated in wrapped-plaster like a busted leg, snakes around the top corners of the room. The ceiling is powdery, probably asbestos. Where the roof leaks, cave-pearls and drip-stone have formed. Long dead spiders are coated in white – from the asbestos or whatever it is – bulbous, like they're petrified.

In a mechanic's bay they find some wood still fixed on the wall – silhouettes of hand-tools drawn on – they prize it free and stamp-snap it into rough lumps, get a fire going in the brazier. Already the temperature is dropping, the night will be cold.

They sit by the flames, swapping the provisions and vodka between dirty fingers. Dressed like they've fled their own wedding.

'Why did you come back?' Nick says.

'I came back for you,' Blue says, but he reaches for the bottle and not for her hand.

He wishes they'd bought more booze, what they have already feels like it's not going to suffice. It isn't enough, to reach where he needs to go.

'They took it all from us, didn't they?' he says.

Nick looks around the building. A spectre of itself. Should have been full of activity. Shifts that never stopped.

'They took it all from everyone.'

1998 - Grimes

Why would a person who knew that you put hidden cameras in casinos and hotel rooms and staff accommodation think that you wouldn't have one in your loan payments office? It was a question unfathomable to Grimes. But then, so much of other human minds was. You might just as well ask why it was that they always run for their mums in the end, even when their mums are dead. But then, Grime's relationship with his mother had never been like other men's.

The security staff were all big, buff, blazers straining across puffed chests – a couple with steroid acne – but they were amateurs; just cash-in-hand gym-cunts. Though outnumbered, Grimes and his guys could have broken them without breaking a sweat. But merely because a thing can be done, does not mean it is the best course.

'I assure you there will be no trouble if you let us in,' Grimes said, 'Only if you don't … know what I mean?' he smiled and he looked at the men one by one, slowly, staring into their eyes, 'But perhaps I should give you a more physical promise of good behaviour,' Grimes said, 'Let's just call it a non-refundable deposit.'

And he pulled from his pocket a ply of money, which he handed, uncounted, to the man Grimes knew from body tells was the man the others looked to, whether or not he was officially in charge.

The man said, 'Well, that's good enough for me,' and waived the fold of notes, as if this had been a contest from which he had emerged victorious.

Probably the man knew, certainly Grimes knew, that it was actually an avenue of escape. Grimes had allowed them an out, a way to step down without confessing to each other that they had done so. Though the men each sensed in themselves that they were scared, it made it easier not to have to admit the fact in public.

The party was opulent, though Grimes had been to lusher. He recalled an event with an orgy of beautiful people in the foyer – oiled and writhing like fish in a ship's hold – only by way of entertainment. Grimes had not been terribly entertained by them, but then he was compelled to be there for other reasons. Grimes did not much socialise. Grimes needed nobody. Grimes stood alone. Grimes did not suffer from that desperate need of the weak: to love and be loved. Grimes believed that such holes in human souls are better filled by being feared.

Grimes dispatched his employees to spread out in their hunt for the miscreant; chose a solitary route through the throng. He ignored the askance glances, the side eyes. There is insufficient time in life to educate all who might merit it. It was inconvenience enough to have to leave Skegness. And Grimes did not appreciate being inconvenienced.

Hardly anyone was eating the finger food. Saving themselves for what was to come. Delicacies were stiffening back into the likeness of the dead things they were. Even though, in present day, he could live a life of whim, Grimes was still angered by waste. From habit, he loaded a bowl with larger items at the bottom, so that they could support a pyramid of smaller things, maximising capacity.

'You're tucking in to that buffet, old chap,' a man said, 'Not eaten in a while?'

He chuckled to himself, then stopped abruptly as Grimes turned and stared, silent, expression almost quizzical, eyes dead as Diana. The man dropped his gaze. Then put down his glass. Then left the room.

Grimes knew the man, as he knew all the upper echelons of the assembled people. Thinking themselves protected by wealth and connections, bonds and stock options. Thinking they were immunised against the stench and the dark like they were inoculated from fowl pox. And yet they would only need to walk through certain neighbourhoods to learn that they were not. Which is why they never would walk through certain neighbourhoods. Why they rarely walked at all, save for in such plazas and parks as they were assured contained only harmless herbivores: they instinctively avoided the vertigo of their own vulnerability. Once you have shivered under the shadow of the boot, no amount of cashmere will ever quite warm you up again. Grimes could have taken any person in the room and had them blanched and begging in a short enough while. Merely in conversation, he would have needed enact no violence, just talked. He might have spoken of options and futures. He could have asked about their families. There are ways of turning any given chatter into a pledge of unending terror. Grimes's eyes alone could convey a considered commitment to plunge life into unremitting hell or to end it all together. Grimes's every expression testified to and rendered certain the fact that he would do whatever he said he would do and also such things as went unmentioned. Such threats as were merely implicit in the complicity of knowledge. For simply to comprehend that there exists another world – beyond yet beside the world of laws and courtrooms – is to agree to be bound by its powers. You cannot call the police, once you understand that they cannot help you.

Grimes cupped his bowl in palm and continued his patrol. Raptor eyes sharp for target. He spotted the man Baggot. Who looked as described and was haloed by hangers-on and staff. Aging, over-weight, soft and a sop. But he had made all this from his own vision and gamble, Grimes had to accord him that.

Grimes watched Baggot a while, before continuing on his way. Reading the crowds as he walked among them. He deciphered the silent words of guileless flesh, learned which were lovers and which were rivals. The struggles of buffaloes for mates and dominance are everything to buffaloes. And yet they mean nothing, because there exist lions.

To thrive in Grimes's line of work, a man needs a limitless reservoir of rage. A man needs to have had a childhood that gifted him enough venom to last his entire life. So that, however easy it gets, however many pleasant things he surrounds himself with, he will always have sufficient anger left. It is not everyone who is capable of causing any given stranger pain. Grimes had long since separated himself from society. It was only a short step after that, to hate humanity in its entirety.

Grimes would only need to look down at the line where his trousers met his shoes to have his reservoir of rage refilled. People thought his suits were badly cut, but he couldn't bear not to see that bulge of extra cloth. The same as at his cuffs. Though obviously, in adulthood, there could be no possibility of growth, he couldn't cope without that sense of abundance. Just the idea that there might be a gap – a dirty socked, mockable interval between trouser and shoe – would be enough to make Grimes's knuckles clench white. His housekeeper knew that, in addition to a fridge and two freezers to be kept brim full, toilet roll stocks must be maintained at a level of superfluity close to insanity. Close to insanity. Grimes had spent most of his life lingering on that brink, but he had never felt the need to see a shrink. His issues were simple enough to self-diagnose, without squandering money and peeling apart the scars. In the end, it is always about the beginning: every crack traces back to a point of impact.

1984 - Blue

They came for Charlie in the middle of the night. Blue – just a boy, naked save for underpants – awoke to a tempest of revenge. Fists smashed their anger on the front door. Full beam lights, hurtfully bright, blinded the view through Blue's bedroom window.

'You need to come here now, Charlie,' a silhouette shouted, black and angular.

More figures clustered around it, haloed by headlights, merging into their own and each other's spiked shadows. Choristers of forests and dark fairy tales, beasts from under the bed.

'Don't go,' Blue whispered, half to his dad and half to God.

Neither one must have heard it, because Charlie appeared at the front porch.

'What the Hell's going on?' he said, 'I've not gone back to work.'

'That's what they all say.'

'What are you doing here? You're not even a miner.'

'I've got reasons of my own. This is not just because you're a scab: you're worse than that, I've seen the photographs.'

And the word, that word, *photographs*. And the voice that spoke it was the voice of Nick's dad. And so Blue knew that this was his fault: they'd seen images of his sin at The Spot. But in punishment, the sin had passed to the father, for the shadow men grabbed Charlie, held him by arms and shoulders.

'Dark crimes merit dark penalties,' Nickelson said, and he produced a Stanley knife from the deep pocket of his dungaree pants, held it at Charlie's cheek, 'You'll have heard of a Glasgow Smile?'

And Blue's mam screamed then. Blue had never heard that noise before. Hadn't even known there could be such a noise, though the sound shrieked free like a beast finally released. A screeching uncorked genie, a cave-bound banshee. It cut through the night and the walls and the idling engine. Geraldine shook as she screamed it; she shook and her arms rent at the air. A shadow shape slapped her. And Charlie struggled, tore a hand loose, punched one of them. They grabbed him again, but it was clumsy, and he swung a second time. Another shadow joined the fray and they had him tight, head in a lock, though still he writhed in their grip.

Blue – mesmerised and paralysed – watched the moths, dense as snowflakes, flapping and flinging themselves at the searchlight headlights of the car. Knowing, with growing grownup horror, that no one could do anything to fix this, unless he could, no one but him. And that's what being a grownup means: it means the grownups can no longer save you. Yet his underpants hung so wide, from his skinny child's frame, that they remained almost dry, while the piss poured onto the bed.

'That's enough with the hubbub,' Nickelson said, 'You got to just take what's coming, else it could be even worse,' and he pressed the flat side of the Stanley blade against Charlie's throat, above where his other arm had Charlie in a head lock.

And Blue knew then, Blue knew what he must do. And shame – the shame of the piss, the shame of The Spot – shame gave him the strength to do it.

Blue crept side-foot, Indian-wise, downstairs – past that last step, where it was said he once slept – silent, though over the engine and the screaming and the shouting he could not have been heard had he stomped. His child heart a turvy convulsion, in its sudden man's chest, he went into Charlie's pantry darkroom, light-less save for the foxfire of the safe lamp. The cogged enlarger crooked-bent like a scientist at a microscope. The plastic trays of alchemic liquids. The drying lines and doll-size pegs. Charlie's Nikon, sitting there, film-less, loading door adrift. Newest secrets brewing in the black tub beside it. But what Blue needed was beyond all that. Gone from all objects thus far used.

He moved the stool, with a screeched whimper he knew not whether stemmed from its legs on the lino or his own self. He climbed the stool's trembling height to sweep instantly sticky fingers across the top of the cabinets until they met the key he knew was hidden there. He put the key into its slot, and unlocked that one lock he was not to unlock.

Charlie could close the shotgun with just a slight flick of his wrist, but it took Blue two tries to clench it shut, having pressed a pair of sibling shells into its chambers, brass caps like brave soldiers' buttons. The lever snapped straight, to prove the task accomplished, and Blue used his palm to force back the twin hammers one by one, certain his thumb wouldn't reach them once he gripped the stock. His arms were quivering and the gun was heavy, yet its snout led him outward, as if it had been longing for the occasion.

'You've grown too proud, Charlie,' a voice said, 'If you were still in a terrace, maybes the neighbours would help you.

Out here, there's just you and us.'

'I did it, it was me, you need to leave off our dad,' squeaked Blue, probably inaudibly, as he came to the open front door, barefoot, barely able to stand with shaking.

All eyes had been locked on the still struggling father; they never saw the son, not until Blue stepped over the thresh-hold. Even as Blue began to exit, the gun-muzzle had already aimed itself at Nicholas Nickelson in the yard, still with his Stanley knife held by Charlie's head, still with his big-muscled bicep throated in a choke hold.

Off to Blue's side, edge of vision, Blue saw the man who had been holding Geraldine lunge round at him to grab for the twelve-gauge. But the gun was a living creature, with a mind of its own, with views of its own, about how things should go. As the man tugged at the shotgun, sticky child fingers tightened to hold on. Squeezed to hold on. As the man tugged at the gun, the roar hit Blue's ears, barrel-sparks blinded him, the kick knocked him back. Half out the door, half sprawled, half dressed, half blind, half deaf, Blue saw how his father and the father of another clung together, as if their differences were dismissed, in that moment of being flung upward and swung down. Both mouths still wide with wonder, they hugged like blood-soaked lovers. The lead-shot in such proximity had peppered beyond them too. A shadow man clutched his hand and the paint can he was holding had exploded. Spatters from it had scattered with the force. White paint flowered up the elm tree like mistletoe. White paint sprayed the car bonnet like the first hint of snow. White paint mingled with the rich, Christmas red of blood.

'We were only going to put the fear in him and paint *scab* on the house,' said the man with the can, flinging the remains of it from him as if it were molten, 'We were just scaring with the Glasgow Smile. We never would have done that.'

He addressed this to Blue's mam, as if such an explanation might suffice, to undo any ills of the night.

Geraldine had stopped screaming with the blast of the barrels. Like the shock had shocked her from shock. She stared at the mess of two men, entangled and joined, sudden blood brothers. She stepped the short distance to them, but she didn't go to cradle Charlie. She walked right on past, as if this was a thing of but modest concern to her. She walked right on past, as if the last thread that kept her tethered to the world had been severed. She walked right on past, as if she was going to the market for something; for something to make all this all right.

1998 - Blue

'You killed my dad, Blue, I should hate you. I did hate you at first. Then I missed you and hated you both. Then I just missed you. Then, after a decade or so, I suppose I almost stopped thinking about you at all. Seems strange to say it. Seems strange to think it, that time could move on as much as that, but that's what time does, I suppose, and eventually, it did.'

'Time doesn't only make us older; it makes us other. You stayed here and moved on. I moved on and never left.'

'I would have phoned you – back when we were bairns – I would have phoned you, when you were first taken away. I wanted to phone you. Even though I hated you. But I had no number to call and mam had no phone. And they said it was better we had no contact. I would have written you, but they wouldn't let me. Said it was unhealthy. And I had no address anyway. I hated you. I knew it was an accident. But I still hated you. But I still would've contacted you. If our mam would've let us, I would've. Even if not to speak, even if just to call you and hear your voice and say nothing, just hear you and hate you. But our mam wouldn't let us.'

'How is your mum?'

'She's OK. She's good. She fell in love with Australia from watching *Neighbours* and *Home and Away*, then fell in love with an Australian by correspondence dating. Second-time-rounders.

Beautiful Brits and rich Aussie's, kind of a thing. But he's a canny man, I've met him, I like him. They've asked me to move to theirs, but I've no mind to: they live about a four-hour drive from nowhere much at all. He owns a ranch; mam owns a pack of all-sort rescue dogs that are always getting loose and attacking the cattle. But what they have seems real. Whatever that means.'

Blue wonders what all this means to him.

Lit by the brazier flames, two screws and a yawning hole make a ventilation unit look like a human face. Blue has spent much of the years since losing Huxley seeking solace from the inanimate. It occurs to Blue that his long retreat into the illusory safety of solitude has been a deliberate act. It was a place that he knew would always be there for him, if he needed it. Just as a sober alcoholic still remains an alcoholic, so the loner and loneliness. The damaging bliss is forever within reach. But that doesn't mean it is the right choice.

'He made me watch videos, Blue: my dad. Made me, let me, I don't know … But he oughtn't have. I don't know. I still don't know. What happened at The Spot, what didn't happen at The Spot …' Nick trails off.

Blue wants to say something. He wants to ask her for something maybe. To beg for it even. But he can't find his way even to the sounds that begin such a thing. The noises with which to start the words to say what he needs to say. Things that have not even been confronted internally, cannot now be said out loud. They have no form, neither the means of making one. Such thoughts are trapped away, deep inside, like the rats that lived in the mines: terrified of daylight. Blue puts his suit jacket around Nick's shoulders and puts his arm around the jacket. Eventually, he finds some form of sleep, moulded from vodka and fatigue.

The sunrise – even through winding house windows turned opaque with dirt – is such a fierce scarlet that you'd think the whole world was on fire.

'Red sky in morning, sailor's warning,' says Blue.

'Sometimes, in Blackmoor, I've known it snow in June,' Nick says, 'But summer always comes.'

'I need to get my van,' Blue says, 'I need to get away from all this. Only, maybe they're watching it. I mean, they know I have one. And they worked out I was at the party. So maybe they saw it there? I need to run, but I can't leave without my van.'

'Are you going to keep running forever? Are you always going to be running away? Maybe you wouldn't need to run, if you weren't so alone?'

Blue and Nick go back to the corner shop, called The Corner Shop. The storekeeper – an elderly Asian man, in a furry, funnily Russian-looking hat – nods as they enter, like he's been expecting them. Blue gets a bottle of Dandelion and Burdock pop, a drink he had forgotten existed. They buy a bunch of plastic-wrapped junk by way of brunch. The storekeeper hand-writes the purchases in a ledger book.

Then, apropos of nothing, he says, 'I saw a very very strange thing, when I was a young man, just after Partition. Let me tell you: no hate is more ferocious than a country split in two. There were horrors which I can never speak of. Horrors such that you would not wish to hear of. I was on the road. Fleeing for my life. Living like a refugee, like a very fugitive. Hiding in ditches, if I heard a motorcar or voices. Not passing near to villages, unless at dead of night. And I came on the third day of flight to a field, where a dog was lying down in the shade of a stack of fertiliser sacks. They used a fertiliser made of ground-up fishmeal. It smelled like the cesspits of hell, if it had been out in the sun. And a vulture was circling overhead. I promise to you, it had been following me for days. Vultures had grown very brave. But the vulture must have smelled the reek of the fishmeal, saw the dog, so very still, and took it to be a carcass. There were very many unburied corpses at that time. The bird dropped to the ground and pecked at the dog. Vultures lost their fear, you see, in those days of dark. But the dog jumped up with a bark, woken from sleep and ever so angry. The dog, he bit the vulture's wing. The bird could not fly off, the dog would not let go, so they circled round and round, flinging up dust and ruction.'

There is a long pause. The storekeeper smiles, like his story is satisfactorily concluded.

'What happened then?' asks Blue.

'I do not know, in truth, I heard an engine and had to hide. I had very pressing problems for my own. I could not pass the time watching fighting creatures. Maybe they are still engaged at battle to this day,' the storekeeper winks, 'For me, which one won was not the point, what gave me very much strength – the hope to survive, which I did survive, one day to come to this hard, cold, kind place, finally to buy my shop – was that the dog looked like it was dead and smelt like it was dead, but the dog was not dead.'

'Do you have a phone we could use?' says Nick.

Someone watching from a window of Baggot's mansion would see a curious spectacle. An image almost from an earlier age.

A time of wagon trains or travelling players. A person lurking in one of the many cars, still parallel parked all the way along the street, among the caterer and cleaner vehicles, perhaps a person employed to watch for arrivals, or to keep a close eye on a specific white van, would see a convoy roll past. A caravan of campers, self-converted horse transporters, seven-and-a-half-tonners, buses, box-vans and trailers. Like a self-congesting herd of herbivores, winding through a narrow pass, the strange assemblage fills all sides around itself. It blocks in all the parked cars through its flow. Until it stops. Bumper to bumper, save for one space, in front of a purple-painted bus. A vehicle so large that it might even hide from view, the two figures who descend and climb immediately into a van; which slips into gear and slots into that available spot in the wagon train. And, this momentary sojourn ended, the caravan continues, a trail that blocks the entire street, until its great tail has passed.

Blue doesn't know for sure, if such a person, or people, are watching. Hoping to lay hands on him. But if they are, they can surely do nothing, save for stand confounded. Can do nothing except choke on the exhaust smoke. Can do nothing but curse the dust as Pharaohs trapped behind the Red Sea, behind the exodus, admitting, through teeth gritted, that for once, for today, the slaves have had their way.

The sun sets early, this low on the east coast, it is already starting to dip. Through the greasy, driver's-side van window, facing away from the sea, the sun leaves streaks about itself, crude as a kid's painting. And it lights Nick's ear, like it's inlaid with mother of pearl. Blue watches the road but also the road-sides. This could well be the last he'll ever see of Blackmoor. It's a place as good as any. Possibly it is even home. Or maybe there's no place like home.

The convoy passes signposts that count down the miles to Hartlepool. Blue imagines the monkey, dropping through a trap door. Unforgiven. The monkey kicks, kicks, kicks. For a foot hold that doesn't exist. Hands tied. Eyes blindfolded. Dressed in a little French sailor's suit. The monkey kicks, kicks, kicks. Then that is all.

1998 - Baggot

Happy fucking birthday to me, Baggot thinks, chicken claw fingers clinging to his fitted-sheet, gripping it like he's afraid he might fall off the bed.

'Old age is no place for sissies,' someone said, Baggot's pretty sure it was one of that *Rat Pack* lot, Sammy Davis maybe, or was it Bette Davis? The act of wrinkling his brow in thought sends a shock of pain through Baggot's brain. Old age wouldn't be quite so bad if it weren't for the hangovers. But getting old is better than the alternative. Fewer and fewer of Baggot's marras make it to his birthday these days. Old friends are irreplaceable and uninsurable.

Baggot knows he was never the best loved gadgie in town, but even so, there was a camaraderie among miners never experienced by most men outside of battle. He often feels lonely now. Can't tell who his real friends are. Knows who they're not. But hard to tell who they are ... Working in the mine, for all the shit, it was worth it. Baggot was teamed with a gang of Poles once, in his younger days, before he became a banksman. Best workers he ever met. Would eat just a big hunk of bread with salami and chillies for their bait break. Gave Baggot a love of chillies that he never lost. They play havoc with his piles now, mind.

He swings his legs out of the bed, delicately, one by one. And groans affectionately as his feet hit the underfloor heating.

His bedroom is precisely twenty-three degrees. The heating engineer had said that eighteen or nineteen was the ideal temperature for a bedroom. But the heating engineer had not grown up in a two-up terrace that often had ice on the *inside* of the windows, tell you that. The heating engineer hadn't sifted through snow-covered muck heaps, year of the strike, shovelling waste, trying to find burnable scraps of coal, hands frozen beyond the point of pain, only to become searing agony when they finally warmed up again. The heating engineer hadn't sacrificed his own shed and fences and spare bed and finally his own interior doors, just to keep the fire going. The heating engineer could stick his eighteen degrees where it'd never see the sun. Baggot has his underfloor thermostat set on twenty-three, August and all.

Baggot shuffles his way to the ensuite bathroom, legs together in his black silk pyjamas, trying to hold his old arse cheeks tight. His piles have been playing up for weeks. Alcohol makes them worse. He knows this is going to be a painful, bloody start to a painful bloody day. Still, plenty have it worse don't they. Most have it worse, point of fact. Remember them poor kiddies who died, year of the strike, riddling for coal in colliery spoil, muck stack came down on top of them. And David Jones and Joe Green, killed on the picket lines. You'd not count the suicides. No one counted the suicides. They were probably uncountable. There's a fellow in town, still drinks at the Imperial Hotel, has the names of the official strike dead as a tattoo. *Never forget*, it says under it. But they all have been forgot, haven't they? Whole fucking thing has been forgot, except by them who lived through it.

Baggot gets dressed. A navy-blue serge suit, like the old-time miners used to wear on Sundays. Only Baggot's was made-to-measure by a Chinese who comes to his house special. Says Baggot's suits are 'tailored to conceal the fuller waist,' maybe they do mask his gut a bit, but *conceal* is a bit fucking strong, like. He puts his Ericsson mobile phone into his breast pocket, hard to believe how small they're getting, but still his jacket sags to one side under the weight. No fucker will be phoning Baggot to wish him a happy birthday, they all had their fun yesterday, but the party planner might call to ask something, which always makes Baggot wonder what he pays her for.

He walks down one of the twin marble stairs, with the stilted precision of an overweight, older man, suffering the double indignities of a monstrous hangover and haemorrhoids. He usually tries to alternate which staircase he takes, otherwise why have two staircases which rise to the self-same place? There is no reason, of course; there is no reason, beyond the fact that they look bleeding great. Baggot knows he has belting taste. He once overheard one of his guests – a fashion designer, no less – say he had a house like a footballer. Baggot smiles to himself, you knew you'd made it when you have a house like a footballer.

Baggot hasn't forgot his roots though: still votes for the Labour, for all the good voting does. Could never vote Tory anyroad. No one in the black wall of coalfield country could surely ever vote Conservative again now, not after the strike and the closures. But many never voted again at all. The hurt of rejection and dispossession never healed. The hatred of authority – of the police especially, of the Tories especially – never ended. A scant handful of ex-miners remained engaged, politically militant. But many more never voted again. Never voted for anything ever again. Didn't vote in general elections, nor local elections, and certainly not in European elections. Europe felt too far away from their world.

Though the Europeans themselves were good to the miners, during the strike. French unions paid for miners' kids to have a summer holiday to France. Coach loads of them. First time abroad for most. And the French sent shipment containers of food aid. Sent some snails to Blackmoor one time – Baggot chuckles at the memory – the snails didn't get ate, but the rest did. The French miners even scuttled strike-breaking coal ships docked in Calais, like they were still in the Second World War resistance. Though the Germans helped too. Willy Brandt, who'd been German chancellor, personally sent solidarity money. Italian miners helped an all, and the Swedes. There were no borders in the under country. All for nothing though, at the finish. After Christmas, in the depths of that bitterest winter, more scabs started going back. The bastards picked them off, one by one. The gits got to them. Threats and promises. Dirty play and deep pockets. But they were still scabs, at the finish. Driven in to work with coats over their heads, in armoured police vans, like bleeding paedophiles going to court.

Not many scabbed in Blackmoor. Those who did are not forgotten. Can't get served in the Imperial and are banned from the working men's clubs. Publicly shunned but damned to live in Blackmoor forever; unable to move out or move on. When the mines were all finally closed – just like Scargill had warned they would be – most miners used their redundancy money to pay off their mortgages or buy outright suddenly worthless houses; had to: the DHSS wouldn't give you a penny until your savings were gone. But then you were trapped forever in a town with no jobs. Couldn't sell up and move elsewhere, couldn't find work where you were. That was that. Most of them got parked *on the sick* – on incapacity benefit – wasn't many miners who didn't have a bad back or stiff knees or drill finger anyway and mental health conditions thrived on the carrion of a dead industry. Doctors were sympathetic and the government was complicit; government sodding wanted it didn't they: incapacity kept men off the unemployment statistics. Out-of-work figures would have near doubled with all the miners otherwise. But then you were stuck. And that was that.

Baggot reaches the bottom of the steps, he's almost out of breath. He's going to have to fit one of them Stannah stairlifts one day, that's going to ruin the look of the entrance hall isn't it? People are scurrying about the place, the cleaning teams and the caterers and what have you, taking their trays and trestles away. There are too many of them, all looking too busy, for Baggot to know who he should speak to about fixing him a bacon sandwich. He could always do it himself, he supposes, or maybe there will be some sweet young lass in the kitchen who'll oblige.

It occurs to Baggot that he hadn't seen much of Nick Nickelson at the party. The bonny little thing. Normally she'll have a wee dance with him at some point, just humouring an old man, but it does make him happy. This year, she never even said goodbye.

He knows it's really him in debt to her though. Even if he'd tried to make it up to Nick and her mam, he never really could. Not after what he'd done. Wasn't Baggot's fault, what had happened after, like. Who could have predicted that shit storm? No one could have. All Baggot had done was drop a hint or two to Nick senior, that he might want to keep an eye on his wife. Baggot was maybes not even the only one, Blackmoor was always too small for secrets, especially when tempers were at their evers. All Baggot had done was drop a hint or two. And not pass on that message about Charlie being off the picket line, of course, but that had just slipped his mind, hadn't it? And the man had been so damned full of himself. Anyway, Baggot'd done what he could for them after, Nick and her mam. He'd even just bought their ramshackle old farmhouse, through a shell company, for a lot more than it was worth. Probably double what it was worth. He had at least tried to make amends. To mend the unmendable.

The kitchen has been left spotless, but is entirely empty, feels like a big tile and granite desert, against the activity in the rest of the mansion. Baggot searches the cupboards for a frying pan. He doesn't know how the electric grill works on the giant, digital, cooking range thing, but the hobs are just gas. Fucking gas.

They said the mines were uneconomic, but spent far more per kilowatt hour on gas after they'd closed them all. And on foreign coal, shipped in. Was dearer than dug at home when it was fully costed. And they still had to burn coal at the finish. Were still burning coal to this day, in half the power stations across the nation.

They said the mines were uneconomic, but the strike cost the exchequer eight billion pounds. Not even counting what was paid in redundancies and then benefits to men who would never work again, and to half the next generation, who would never work at all.

They said the mines were uneconomic, but spent sixty-five million a week, over a year, to crush the strike. Fourteen thousand police officers were taken off other duties; not needed for fighting crime, apparently. They thought that was economic. They thought that was a price worth paying, to destroy an industry entirely.

They said the mines were uneconomic, but it was never about the mines, it was about breaking the miner's union, the most powerful union, in order to break them all, once and for all.

The mines were only uneconomic, because the miners stood in the path of changing the economic system entirely.

Baggot puts the frying pan on one of the six gas hobs. Six bloody hobs. Who cooks six things at once, Keith bloody Floyd? Baggot looks in his fridge for bacon, his fridge is near enough the size of a scullery. But the bugger is empty. Scrubbed clean like the rest of the kitchen; absolutely devoid of food, pure white like a fresh fall of snow.

Baggot thinks back to when they built a snowman on the picket line that time. Whole gang of them, grafting like they were still underground, built this towering thing. Must have been eight-foot-high, scarf tied round its neck, lumps of stone for buttons. Would have used coal, back when Baggot was a bairn, but coal was thin on the ground. Police Chief Inspector turned up, didn't he, in a fancy police Range Rover. Riot vans behind him. Was only a small picket, no hint of riot. No sign of any trouble at all. No sign of owt, except a bobby dazzler of a snowman. Police Chief Inspector was a spoiler. Police Chief Inspector revved his Range Rover. Police Chief Inspector drove straight at the snowman, smashed it to smithereens. Police Chief Inspector smashed his forehead and all. Smashed his Range Rover up. Broke his windscreen. Crumpled up the bonnet. Couldn't even drive away, Range Rover was damaged so bad. Because the miners had built the snowman round a fucking concrete bollard. Small victories.

Baggot leaves the kitchen. Proper hungry now. Once your

stomach has started anticipating a bacon sandwich, there's no telling it to be quiet again.

He makes his way to where they'd had the finger buffet thing set up. But it's good as gone already. All the food has been shovelled away into black sacks. Left out too long to be eaten, they must have thought, but it probably would have been all right. Would have been fine. Will go to landfill now. Nearly makes Baggot weep at the squander; not from his own hunger, but to think there'd been mothers driven to digging vegetables from farmer's fields, year of the strike. Stealing spuds and turnips in dead of night, just to keep their kids fed. It's enough to make you bubble.

Baggot makes a mental note to get a couple of pigs. He saw some bonny pigs at a country house hotel he stayed at one time, great big ginger beasts with ginger eyelashes. Would be a fine thing, to have a pair of pigs. Not to eat, like, not to turn to bacon sandwiches, but to save on waste. Though he supposes you needed to be careful, to avoid attracting rats. Baggot hates fucking rats. About the only thing worse than a scab: a rat.

When the miners finally went back – the strike broken, to watch their industry be dismembered by degree – there were no rats. In the absence of crumbs or scraps, or even excrement to eat, the rats had cannibalised. They ate themselves to extinction.

1998 - Blue

They are in a meadowy feed field that Billy knew. A place near a racecourse – near Stratford-upon-Avon – with bolt-cuttable gates.

Blue and Nick sit with tin cups of wine – handles tied with twine – on the back step of Blue's van - doors all open to let the inside cool and air – facing out to a view better than any hotel in town could sell you. *Even a tramp can share in the sunset*, Charlie once said, *They cannot take that away from him. Look for beauty and the world will seem less harsh.*

Swarms of some breed of big beetle have suddenly appeared. Swirling squads of them, in a sky the last pigeon-feather red blues of day. The insects have emerged in their multitude at a single synchronised moment, as defence against predation: that by overwhelming volume, some must survive. Blue knows of similar stories: sand scrambling turtles, giant spidery crabs, trails of buffalo crossing crocodile-infested rivers. In the beetles' wilderness plight of sky, the apex beasts are bats.

So Blue and Nick sit, watching big strange beetles, wafting on a faint wind, hoping not to die unwed. Thinking, at least as much as insects can think, that they hope not to die unwed. And bats, feeding frenzy mad for the bonanza, hunt, determined to leave widows in their wake. The bat-wing flaps are like a slow-frame black and white film, stuttery and erratic, silhouetted against the brink light heavens. Some beetles pebble to the ground, when they sense a bat. Some bats dive bomb and still catch their prey in free-fall. And trees, in the breeze, appear to breathe.

The traveller vans, in a protective, huddled union, feel like home. Blue feels at home. If home can be this movable feast-hall. Is it possible to have spent your life homesick for a place that you never knew existed, which isn't even a place? Is it possible to be rootless, homeless, yet still at home, because of who you are with?

'You were never at home last week; where were you?' Blue says to Nick, 'Was pretty hard to track you down. Looked like no one even lived at yours anymore.'

'I came into some money. Quit my shit job and went to Ibiza. It's mad, man. Could honestly have stayed there forever, but I always go to Baggot's birthday. He's been canny good to me and mam.'

'Came into money?'

'Our mam got an offer on the house from a developer. Way more than she thought it could ever go for. The building must be worth naff all; but it's got land, I suppose. With the lake front stuff, and the clean shore, the new road, maybe land prices are going up in Blackmoor now.'

'She gave you a share?'

'Yeah, a good share. So I quit my shit job and went on holiday. What else would I do? What would you do if someone gave you a chunk of money?'

'Funny you should ask,' Blue says, 'It's something I ask myself.'

He motions Nick to come inside the van. Shuts the doors. Switches on the lights. Gets a ratchet screwdriver from the trunk that serves as storage and seat, starts undoing stainless steel screws from a wall of the van. When the last screw is out, he lifts free a carpeted hardboard panel. Moves aside so Nick can see. Pressed into the indent nest of the metal, in place of the thick quilts of wool that Blue formerly used for noise and heat insulation, are bundles of cash. Most are neatly banded together with strips of paper, like how they come from a bank. Wads of fifties and twenties, sufficient to stuff full a pedal-bin bag.

'That's why those guys are after you?'

'In part, at least. I nearly posted it to you,' Blue says, 'Crazy as that sounds, I came close. I realised just in time that it would have been numbingly dumb. Didn't even know your house was sold. But I thought maybe I owed you. Some kind of compensation. Maybe you don't need it now. But we could live a long time on this. We could live well on this. We could go abroad. We should go abroad. Grimes grows smaller the further he gets from Skegness. And it's our right to live wherever we please, across all of Europe. We could go to Ireland. We could go to Italy. We could go to France. We could see it all. I know how to live on the road.'

'You killed my dad, Blue. Are you not scared that I'll just take the money, now I know it's there: rob you blind and make a moonlight flit, by way of my revenge?'

'I'm sorry. I'm so sorry,' Blue chokes out the words like they're water on a drowning man's lungs, 'I knew I had to find you. But I didn't understand why. I need forgiveness. Need to beg for it at least. I've got no one else. And so much stuff bottled up. I thought I could bury it, but it's been eating my flesh from the inside out. It's devouring me …'

She puts a finger to his lips, 'Shh. Not now. This is the present. There'll be time enough in the future for the past.'

'I've got no family left in the world.'
'You've got me now.'
'Are you family?'
'I could be …'

Acknowledgements

Adrian and Aoife
Amanda Preston
Claire Malcolm
David O'Malley
John 'Jack' Inch and the Durham Mining Museum.
Librarians, staff, volunteers, & security guards of the National Coal Mining Museum.
Simon and Rick, just because old friends are irreplaceable and uninsurable.
Kat Last
Duncan Roy
Leon Bell
Kettle and Larkin
Mum and Dad.

About the Author

Jonathan Trigell is the author of four thematically very different novels: *Boy A*, *Cham*, *Genus*, and *The Tongues of Men or Angels*. Admired for a gritty but literary style, among other prizes, Trigell has won the Waverton Award, the John Llewellyn Rhys Prize and the inaugural World Book Day Prize.

Trigell's novel - *Boy A* - was dramatized by Cuba Pictures and Film4. It was directed by John Crowley (Brooklyn, The Goldfinch) and starred Andrew Garfield and Peter Mullan. The production won four BAFTA Awards and the Jury Prize at the Berlin Film Festival. Trigell's strong family bonds to the North East of England underpin his latest work: *Under Country*.